TAKING *Anna*

J. Lynn Bailey

ISBN-13: 978-1-7341395-1-8

*For my great-great-grandmother, Anna Cain.
Thank you for your passion for the written word.
I caught the bug.*

Prologue

Dillon Creek Echo
Serving Eel River Valley Since 1878

As with any small town one might come across, Dillon Creek, California, will draw its visitors in, luring them into their quaint shops. The people, kind and warm and with their festive ways, will make one want to stay just one more day. And they should.

But beneath the layers of niceties and genuine smiles, those not from Dillon Creek will find the secrets if they stay long enough. There are always secrets. Secrets that protect families. Secrets that live on the outskirts of the minds that keep them.

What happened on that oddly warm summer night in July seven years ago changed a town forever. No driver named. No charges filed. Remnants of the aftermath—two crosses and flowers on a country road on a blind corner—make it impossible for the families of those deceased to drive past.

The truth of it is, there always needs to be a scapegoat. Someone to blame when tragedy strikes, somewhere to put the anger, the feelings, the grief, a place needed to put these things because life on life's terms simply cannot coexist when the misery of the world is far too heavy to bear. It's easier this way—or so we think.

And when there are no answers as to what happened on that awful night, fear is the root of what we say, what we think, what we do. Living in a world that is chaotic and loud and full of sadness, the path of forgiveness is hard to find when all we have are two dead bodies of two young boys.

The truth is, the town didn't divide like the parting seas, but it quietly and slowly separated like a diverting creek with an erosion problem. It ran on both sides of the street—the Atwood side and the Morgan side—and the residents of Dillon Creek, attempting to pick up the pieces of what was left, felt secretly compelled to choose a side based on loyalty, based on family, based on politics. And not a damn person talks about it.

It's hard to imagine life without Conroy Atwood and Tripp Morgan.

I made the choice not to run the news article in the *Dillon Creek Echo* about that night, and I still feel it was the right decision for my town, my people. Other news outlets ran it— *The Times Standard*, *The Humboldt Beacon*—so I didn't need to add fuel to the fire with the residents of Dillon Creek. Their hearts were too broken.

I ran the obituaries instead.

One day, I hope Dillon Creek will stop quietly squandering the questions about who was driving that night, who was to blame. The outcome of knowing is just that— knowing—isn't it? It doesn't bring back Tripp and Conroy, and it only prolongs the healing. But in the case the Atwoods and the Morgans ever find out, I have confidence that they'll have the ability to feel both sides of the coin—even if the coin might be two-headed.

—Ike Isner, Publisher of the *Dillon Creek Echo* Newspaper

I

Welcome to Dillon Creek, California

Dillon Creek Pizza
Last Tuesday of the Month—Noon Sharp
June

"I heard Agnes Coolidge is in the hospital again," Delveen says, taking a bite of her salad, no dressing and littered with pickled red beets. Her lavender-colored hair is a statement, and she knows it. No right-minded seventy-five-year-old woman has purple hair and lipstick to match—not in Dillon Creek anyway, aside from the diva herself. One can see Delveen Constance coming from a mile away.

Pearl says, "Well, I heard that Dale Bradford is at her side while her husband is God knows where."

Delveen pipes in again, "And I heard that Colt Atwood's coming back home from that MBA league." She looks at Clyda, who quietly eats her soup.

"NBA, Delveen." Erla rolls her eyes. Erla's hair is a simple gray but very well kept, not a strand of hair out of place. "Secondly, Dale is Agnes's cousin. Her husband died three months ago. We told you this last week, Pearl." Erla grows impatient.

Pearl takes a sip of her Diet Coke and shrugs. Her round, short, perfectly shaped white curls stick to her head like a helmet. Remnants of her red lipstick stain her front two teeth.

Mabe sets her glass of beer down, the foam outlining her lip. "The Atwood boy is back home?" Her hair is more salt than pepper.

Mabe looks at her old friend Clyda, and still, Clyda remains quiet.

"Shh. Not so loud." Pearl looks around. "I heard it from Pixie Puckett at the beauty shop when I was getting my hair set." Pearl gently cups her thin white curls again. "Don't want to spread any rumors."

Absolutely no one is in Dillon Creek Pizza at noon on Tuesdays, except for The Lunch Guys, which consist of Bo Richards, Lance Belotti, Rue Samuels, Ben Taft, and Archie Tander—five retired dairymen who come in every day at noon for the lunch special, which is unlimited pizza, a salad, and a soft drink for two dollars. They've been coming in together since the mid-1950s, and Dillon Creek Pizza has kept their price since then, not charging the men with inflation. They talk about family and the world and its issues, but mostly, they play dice. The Ladybugs though refuse to pay less, as they feel everyone needs to make a living wage.

The Lunch Guys are grateful, and The Ladybugs are stiff.

On the occasion that The Whiskey Barrel, the only bar in Dillon Creek, is closed, Toby Lemon might wander down to Dillon Creek Pizza at noon on Tuesdays to nurse his habit that no one talks about.

Clyda looks at Pearl. "How would Pixie Puckett know my Colt is coming home?"

Clyda Atwood raised three sons in Dillon Creek and not a single gray hair on her head—due to Pixie Puckett's magical ways. Just a head full of flaming-red hair. But no one talks about that either. Colt Atwood is her grandson.

"Her husband, Tony, saw it on the television just last night. He got hurt or some damn thing," Pearl says.

"And why wouldn't you just ask me, Pearl?" Clyda sets her water glass down.

"Because you never talk about it."

Clyda smiles. Takes a small bite of her pizza.

Mabe takes another sip of beer.

Delveen takes another bite of her salad.

Pearl touches her hair again. "We ought to plan a parade for his homecoming."

Clyda rolls her eyes. "Pearl, the boy is a pro basketball player, not a veteran."

And Erla says, "I call to order the meeting of the Dillon Creek Ladybugs, Club Number 227."

2

The Whole Town's Talking

Anna

"And that's when I told Merna she ought to take more vitamin D. Damn woman is so stubborn." Dorothy sighs. "You think you can talk some sense into her, Dr. Cain?"

I look at Dorothy from the patient table as I attempt to listen to the heartbeat of her dog, Nibbles. "Well, Mrs. Lovell, my job is solely animals. I'd have her talk to the other Dr. Cain."

My father, James, is the local physician in town and has been for the last thirty years.

"Of course. Don't know why I was bothering you with all that." Dorothy shoos the conversation away with her hands.

Nibbles's heartbeat is strong, but his stomach is definitely upset.

"He's been throwing up?"

"Yes. And gas. Oh my good word. This little dog can clear a room in two seconds flat."

Nibbles, a shih tzu, looks up at me from under the tuft of hair that sits at his brow line.

"And loss of appetite?" I ask.

Dorothy nods. "Hasn't eaten in two days."

"Well, I'd say Nibbles has indigestion. Stop at Wilson's Grocery on your way home and grab some canned pumpkin. No additives. No sugar. Just plain old canned pumpkin. Two teaspoons in the morning for two to three days, and if that doesn't solve Nibbles's troubles, give me a call."

"I sure will. Thank you, Dr. Cain."

Dorothy takes Nibbles from the table, and they exit the patient room. I follow them out.

"Tell your mother hello and that we missed her at cribbage last week," Dorothy says as she makes her way to the front counter.

"I will."

Dorothy meets my assistant, Kimber, for payment.

"Laurel's in room two with Strait." Kimber looks up at me from the front counter.

They knew it was coming.

I knew it was coming.

Strait was her eldest son, Conroy's, dog. Strait is a seventeen-year-old black tri Australian shepherd. Named after George Strait. All of the Atwoods' dogs are Australian shepherds, and all five are named after country singers—with the exception of Colt's dog, Tupac.

I open the door to room two and see Laurel and Strait. Her red-plaid flannel top, blue jeans, and black rubber boots—not for mud, but cow shit—is a signature outfit for Laurel. Her short bob is tucked behind her ears.

She could work any woman out of a job. She raised five boys. Helped her husband, Daryl, run the ranch, and still had time to volunteer in our class when Colt and I were at Dillon Creek Elementary. Recently, I heard she'd opened up the Atwood Ranch as a wedding venue.

"Hey," I say and look at Strait lying there on the table, barely breathing.

Her eyes fill with tears. "I told him to hang on."

I quietly shut the door behind me. I walk to the table and touch Laurel's arm.

Laurel doesn't cry. I know she's here because neither she nor Daryl has it in them to put Strait down with a bullet.

It's been seven years since Conroy and Tripp died.

And still, I feel it, the grief, like a pain that flares up for a bit. Rears its ugly head. Then absorbs back into my flesh, only to arise on another day when Conroy and Tripp's memory somehow comes alive again.

I can only imagine what Laurel feels.

Quietly, I push the stethoscope through his long black chest fur and listen at several places.

"He's barely getting around these days, Anna," Laurel whispers.

I nod and look into her baby-blue eyes that shine like crystals, even when she's sad.

"Daryl couldn't do it. Took him out to the barn ... but he couldn't pull the trigger."

Laurel Atwood doesn't allow a single tear to fall, as if she keeps them, controls them.

I listen to Strait's lungs. His breaths are shallow, and I know he's approaching his time real soon. Laurel knows it, too.

I take off my stethoscope and put it around my neck.

There are some times in life that don't deserve words. The brevity of it all, the spent moments, the love shared, the smiles—that's the life our dogs give us. And for just a minute, we think they're human. The truth of it is, our dogs know our hearts just by one simple glance. Strait, I'm convinced, is a human in a dog's body.

I gather the necessary tools in the cupboard so that Strait can cross over the rainbow bridge and run into Conroy's arms again.

I fill the appropriate parts of the needles with the fluid needed and walk back over to Laurel and Strait. "This won't hurt him, Laurel. It's just going to put him to sleep. It might take a few minutes, but he'll be relaxed and calm, okay?"

Laurel doesn't need to be asked if she wants to stay in the room or not. I know she wants to be here with Strait when he takes his last breath.

With the sedation drug in my hand, I gently insert the needle into the muscle of Strait's back leg.

Strait's eyes, one blue and one brown, slowly start to close as Laurel strokes his fur. He doesn't have fight or resistance. He's just tired.

Breathe, Anna, I say to myself as my eyes start to burn, thinking about all the memories Strait has given us.

When he chased a mountain lion up a tree that was stalking a calf.

When Conroy broke his leg and Strait laid at his feet until Conroy could get around again.

When Colt and I wandered off at age seven on the property and Strait wouldn't leave our side until Daryl found us hours later.

And when Conroy died, I think a piece of Strait died, too. I think he's hung on for so long because he knew Laurel and Daryl needed him.

Strait is fully relaxed. I take the clippers and shave off a tiny patch of fur, and then I insert the needle with pentobarbital.

Quickly, Anna. Just like a bandage. The quicker it's ripped off, the better.

Sometimes in life, we have to be the ones to let go. Make the hard decisions.

I slide over a stool to Laurel, so she can sit at eye-level with Strait.

It's more than letting go of Strait; she's also letting go of part of her son again.

"I'm going to give you a few minutes with him, okay?"

Laurel looks up at me. "Can you stay, Annie?"

Annie.

She's the only person who calls me Annie—with the exception of my family, the Atwoods, and Tess.

I pull over another stool and sit with her as she loses a piece of her son and her heart just one more time.

It's been several years since I've been to the Atwood Ranch.

Since Conroy and Tripp died.

Since the night Colt and I made love.

Since Colt and I went our separate ways.

The ranch holds many memories of us and our families in good times and in bad. I think the only way to capture the raw beauty of our area is by air or being among the redwood trees, inside them, between them.

The Eel River Valley is surrounded by mountains of redwood trees. Not surrounded in a way that makes you feel claustrophobic, but in a way that gives you just enough space between the sky and trees that you could escape—if you wanted to.

I did. Once. For college and veterinarian school at the University of California, Davis.

But I was lured back by Joe East. It's really all his fault.

He said, "I'm retiring, Anna. I want you to take over the practice—and not because of your fancy education, but because you're the right person for the job. Your compassion and empathy and bedside manner are three of the most important qualities you must have for this job."

I agreed to come back for a few weeks. Work side by side with Dr. East. That was just over a year ago. I went back to Davis, California, only to collect my things. My dad and mom along with my brother and sister—Adam and Amelia—and of course, Tess, my best friend, came down to help me move home.

But Dillon Creek has always been home.

As my truck snakes through the dairy land, green fields peppered with fence line, I know each piece of land and who owns it.

The Atwood Ranch takes about three minutes to get to by car from town if you don't get stuck behind a tractor or a cattle truck and more than forty minutes if it's the dead of winter and we've had more than ten inches of rain in two days, which is common in Humboldt County.

The Atwood sign sits on two redwood posts just off Grizzly Bluff Road.

The Atwood Ranch

I take a deep breath and take a left. The old 1992 Ford I drive was inherited when I bought the business from Dr. East.

Strait's ashes are in a simple sterling silver urn next to me. Off to the left is the ranch. But the place looks great.

The Atwood residence is a two-story white house with black shutters, circa 1894, but Laurel, along with a team of contractors, restored it when Colt, Tess, and I left our separate ways and went to college.

Three big new Fords are parked in front of the house—belonging to Laurel, Daryl, and Colt's older brother, Calder.

My phone rings. It's my older brother, Adam.

"Yo," I answer.

"Dad said you were at the ranch?"

"Yep." I stare up at the house.

"Tried calling you at the office. Kimber said that you had to put Strait down?"

I roll my eyes. Kimber has many wonderful attributes, but patient confidentiality isn't one. Another problem is, Dillon Creek is a real small town, and talk gets loud. But the thing is, I like Kimber.

And no matter what I say about the whole confidentiality thing, her response is always, "Nobody needs to suffer alone with a broken heart."

And I can't come up with an argument for that because Kimber might be on to something.

I don't say anything to Adam when he asks this. "Yes, Adam. I had to put Strait down. Why are you calling me? When's the last time you picked up a phone?" I ask.

"Look, Mom is planning a surprise birthday party for you. With Colt coming back into town, I … I just wasn't sure …" He stops the sentence there.

Wait. What?

The air that I breathe somehow becomes thinner, almost nonexistent.

I see Laurel come from the barn toward my truck.

"I have to go," I say.

"You okay?" Adam asks in his big-brother voice.

Laurel gets closer. I look at Strait's urn on the passenger seat.

I want to ask him how he knows Colt is coming back into town when he lives twenty minutes away in Eureka, but the words won't come.

"Adam, I need to go."

He sighs on the other end of the line. "Okay. But text me later."

"Yeah," comes out, and I hit End.

I grab Strait's urn and hop out of the truck to meet Laurel.

When I hand her the urn, she smiles. Not a happy smile or a content smile or even a *I think I'll be okay* smile because I'm sure losing Strait has brought up a lot of stuff from Conroy's death and the rift between the Atwoods and the Morgans, which sits on the town like a wool blanket.

"Thank you, Annie. What do I owe you?"

"Nothing."

"I have to pay you something."

I change the topic. "The place looks great, Laurel."

Laurel looks around. "It's gettin' there."

"A wedding venue too, I hear."

Laurel shrugs. "Something to keep my mind busy, I suppose."

They have two big barns—one, I assume, Laurel has turned into something a bit prettier inside for weddings.

"Would you like to see it?" she asks.

"I should get back to the clinic," I say, not because I need to get back, but because I feel my heart starting to crumble under the memories that Colt and I made here.

The Atwoods, the Cains, and the Morgans. Now, we're all distant acquaintances who met and loved a lifetime ago—or so it seems.

I turn back to my truck.

"Anna?" Laurel calls.

I turn back around. "Yeah?" My voice is softer as I attempt to swallow the lump of grief sitting inside my throat.

She takes a few steps toward me, Strait's urn against her middle. She's hesitant. "I need to go through Conroy's things for the rummage sale. With the boys gone, I don't think Daryl can handle it. But it needs to be done. Would you be able to help me?"

Colt's coming home, I want to say. *Can't he help you?*

"I can make it work. Sure."

Because Laurel has always been there for me. She's never asked me for a single thing in my life.

3

Guys in Robes

Anna: Age Ten

"Anna," Colt whispered, his hands shaking.

Pastor Mike delivered the sermon. Something about God and shepherds. I wanted to think he was talking about dogs even though I knew he wasn't.

Dogs are more entertaining than the guys in robes, I thought.

"What?"

My brother, Adam, sat next to me along with my mother, Nora, and father, James. Mom was pregnant with our sister, who came along a lot later than anticipated, but nevertheless, she was "a gift from God," as Mom always said.

I was sitting next to Colt. The Atwood brothers sat in a line from youngest to oldest—Colt, Casey, Cash, Calder, and Conroy—and then, of course, there were their parents, Laurel and Daryl.

The Morgans always sat in front of us, which included Tess and Tripp and their parents, Bruce and Mavis.

Church was the only time our parents made us sit with our families. Other than that, we could mix and mingle around the small town of Dillon Creek all we wanted.

"I love you," Colt said.

It wasn't out of the ordinary for Colt to say this to me. But the fact that his hands were shaking made my stomach turn into a fit of knots.

I tried to make him laugh. "Nah, you love basketball and dogs, Atwood."

Colt shook his head, staring down at his sweaty hands.

Pastor Mike spoke.

And Mr. Wilson's bald head, owner of Wilson's Grocery, sitting one row down and to the left, nodded in agreement with Pastor Mike.

"I love you like I love basketball. Sometimes, Annie, you're all I can think about. Is … is that normal?"

The knots in my belly began to unravel, only to find themselves in new knots.

I searched for the words. "Colt, you think about me all the time because we're always together. Now, shut up and listen to Pastor Mike, or we're both going to get into trouble."

Colt nodded. Licked his lips and stole another look at me—maybe because he needed one last look or maybe because there was something more. But how the heck would I know? I was a ten-year-old girl getting boobs and a period. Which both really sucked.

The truth was, I was "becoming a young woman," as my mother had said two weeks ago.

I nibbled on my nail—had a bad habit of biting them—as I listened to Pastor Mike.

Colt reached over and touched my hand. I looked up at him, and he shook his head, mouthing the word, *Stop*.

I did.

The truth was so much easier to swallow when we said them quietly to ourselves in our heads, when we didn't give it life. Because the truth was, I loved Colt Atwood, too.

On Sundays, our families—the Morgans, Atwoods, and Cains—would gather together. This particular Sunday, we were at the Morgans' in town. Their house was just off Main Street. They owned a six-bedroom Victorian that creaked when the wind blew and moaned when the rain came.

Tess, Colt, and I were in the front yard.

Tess was in the tire swing, staring up at the old maple.

Colt and I were lying in the grass, doing just the same.

I should have been thinking about basketball tryouts, "the good Lord"—as my mom would say—or the impending doom of school starting in just a few weeks, but all I could think about was Colt's words in church.

My mother always said, "Stop thinking about yourself, Anna. Start thinking about what you can do for the good Lord."

I never rolled my eyes at my mom. I had once, and she'd threatened to smack me into Monday. I never did that again because I hated Mondays. My mother wasn't a violent person, and truth be told, I didn't think she could do it, but I didn't want to test the waters. My mom never tolerated disrespect.

"Why are you so quiet, Anna?" Tess asked.

"I don't know," I said.

"I heard Vince Renner has a crush on you," she continued.

I felt Colt's body tense.

"Vince Renner is a bag," Colt said.

That was code word for *douche bag*.

"Oh, he is not. You're just jealous, Colt," Tess teased. "Someone's moving in on your girl."

Colt shook his head. He never argued Tess's statement. Never budged.

Even when Colt was little, he'd had jet-black hair and bright blue eyes. A blue the color of shallow water in some tropical place.

"I'm not his girl," I said and stared up at the old maple, making pictures in my head with the leaves.

Old woman.

Whale.

Cat.

I did my best to distract myself.

"Anyway, the whole town knows that you two will always be together. Even when we're old and gray and almost dead. You'll be like Erla and Don Brockmeyer." She laughed.

I pulled myself away from my images in the leaves and looked over at Colt, but he was already looking at me.

"What?" I whispered.

"Nothing," he said, the back of his head resting on his hands. "If I gave you all the money in the world, would you marry me, Annie?"

What I wanted to say was, *Yeah, probably.* But we were ten years old.

Instead, I said, "No." Because I knew Colt Atwood was destined for bigger things than Dillon Creek, and I wasn't willing to let him just settle for what was in front of him. What was comfortable. "It just wouldn't work, Colt."

4

Seasons Change

Colt

I push into her, gritting my teeth. I feel the muscles in my back contract. Jordan was and is my girlfriend at the same time.

We break up.

We have sex.

We get back together.

We break up.

We have sex.

We get back together.

We're at the in-between stage right now. The part where she orgasms, and then I do, and then we start our relationship over again.

She's on top of me. Her tits in my face. Her mouth open. Eyes closed. Legs spread wide.

I feel myself pulsate inside her, and I know I'm getting close.

But she's got to get off soon, right?

It's difficult to move my right leg because of the boot my foot and ankle are in.

Dr. Wiseman didn't say, no sex. He said, no strenuous activity.

Sex with Jordan isn't strenuous. Addicting maybe. But not strenuous.

I grab her and pull her to me as she moves against me.

Her legs wrapped underneath my thighs, she pants in my ear and then screams my name.

I hold her hips to me and push myself up off the bed with my left leg. Sinking deeper inside her, I lose it.

She falls next to me in bed, against the white sheets.

Both panting, we lie here, untouching, and stare at the ceiling.

My cell phone rings, and I pull it off the nightstand and look at the screen.

It's Pete, my agent.

"Can you, just once, not answer your phone?" Jordan asks. Her long, dark hair against the pillow.

"Hey, man." I sit up and pull myself from the bed. I stand in front of the floor-to-ceiling windows that look over Los Angeles.

"The Golden State Wolves want you bad, man," Pete says. I can hear the excitement in his voice. "So much so that they want to meet this afternoon again."

My four-year contract is up with Los Angeles Heat. I'm a free agent. We have three NBA championships under our belts. I could move on.

My whole NBA career has been with the Heat. They picked me up in the first round, second pick of the draft four years ago, right after college. I'd wanted to leave college before I graduated and sign with the NBA, but my parents had convinced me that I needed a college education to fall back on.

"Besides," my dad had said, "you committed to the Bobcats for four years, so you'd best fulfill your commitment."

So, I had.

"Even with your torn Achilles, my phone has been ringing off the hook with you being a free agent," Pete says. "Let's make them sweat. Go home to Dillon Creek, take the summer off, heal. I'll fly up Rob Lincoln, and he can do your physical therapy up there. Then, we'll talk and we can negotiate? In the meantime, I'll run numbers and get you a max contract."

In layman's terms, max contract is the best contract a player can get in the NBA.

I hear the shower start and turn to see Jordan's naked hourglass figure make its way from the bathroom back to the nightstand for a drink of water.

She doesn't look at me, but she sways her hips, telling me she wants more of what I gave her this morning. When she disappears back into the bathroom, I turn back toward the window as Pete goes on about the recent trading of other players.

We hang up, and I sit down on the bed. My phone rings again. But it's my mom this time.

"Hey, Mom."

"Hey, Colt."

Something isn't right. I can tell because it's in her tone. The way she says my name. "What's wrong?"

She sighs into the phone. "We had to put Strait down yesterday."

I don't say anything.

"Took him to Anna. She took great care of him, of course. Brought his ashes to me today."

Just the mention of Anna's name makes my body do things. My eyelid begins to twitch. My stomach grows into knots. My heartbeat speeds up. My finger taps against the phone.

"Colt? Are you all right?"

Badly, I want to ask how Anna is. I throw on a T-shirt and shorts, feeling weird, talking to my mom while I'm naked.

Strait was seventeen. And maybe part of these involuntary things my body is doing is because Strait was Conroy's dog, and so it brings up feelings I haven't dealt with, feelings that I've pushed to the side.

"How's the Achilles?" she asks.

Mom and Dad came down for the surgery. Didn't leave until they knew I would be well taken care of. It's hard for Dad to leave the ranch. Mostly because of the work, but partly, I think, because when he leaves, it makes him uncomfortable. He likes his work, his family, the small town of Dillon Creek. He hates the city.

"Healing," I say. "I'm sorry about Strait."

"When are you coming home?"

"Tomorrow."

"Tomorrow then." I hear her smile.

I think Mom still enjoys taking care of us, for us to need her.

"Hey, can you bring Dad some of those salted caramels at that one store you took us to?"

"Yeah."

I hear the shower turn off and the doorbell ring. "I'll see you tomorrow, Mom. Love you."

"Love you too, baby."

I hang up and throw the phone down on the bed. I walk/limp through the bedroom, my boot tapping against the hardwood floor.

Tan, my publicist, has already used his key. I didn't need a publicist. But Pete said I did.

Tan and I met our freshman year at the University of North Carolina in the dorms. He quickly became one of my best friends. So, it was fitting for me to ask him to be part of my team. He's one of the only guys I trust.

He's on the phone, holding coffees and a plastic bag.

He looks up at me and rolls his eyes. "*ESPN Now* magazine." He listens into the receiver. "No, he can't do it that day."

Tan goes to the dining room table, sets everything down, and pulls out another phone from his back pocket. "I'll get back to you with dates." Tan listens. "Yeah. Yes. Fantastic.

Talk then." He hits End. "*ESPN Now* magazine is a pain in my ass. That one is for Jordan." He points to the coffee with the black dot on the lid.

Jordan enters the room in just a towel.

"Can you put some clothes on at least?" I ask, annoyed she came out here, wearing only that in front of Tan.

Her eyebrows furrow. "Tan's gay. Why would he care?" Jordan reaches the table, grabs her coffee, and takes a sip.

"I do enjoy a beautiful woman. I just don't feel what straight men feel." Tan shrugs and continues, "You need to be at the plane at ten a.m. tomorrow morning."

"Plane?" Jordan asks.

Tan looks at me. "Did you not tell her?"

I laugh. "We weren't together at the time I decided to go."

"Well, we just fucked for an hour, so I assume I have a right to know now," Jordan says.

One thing Jordan does not do well is hold anything back, no matter who's around.

"I'm going home tomorrow. Tan is coming with me," I say.

Jordan works as an attorney, and her career is demanding, just like mine. We spend more time working than anything else. I think that's why we've made it this long. Our careers have always come first, our relationship second. And the sex is great.

But I haven't been home in a long time. My parents and brothers have always come to my place for holidays, or we've done destination holidays. It's hard to go back for a lot of reasons, but Anna is a big reason. And all the shit that happened with my brother and Tripp when they died. I just didn't want anything to do with Dillon Creek. I always blamed it on my schedule. I was too busy with workouts and practice. Now, I don't have an excuse.

Jordan's never met my parents or my brothers. I can only imagine Jordan meeting Cash, my third-oldest brother. Which might be a total shitshow. The brother who doesn't care what he says or about what people think. He's loud when he drinks, which is more often than not now, according to Mom.

Casey can't stand Cash, and Calder can't stand how Casey and Cash fight, so Calder just loses himself in the ranch. And I stay away. Calder is the only brother who has never left home. Unless you count death as a reason to stay, then Conroy really never left either.

Jordan says she's going to get ready to go to the office and kisses me half on the mouth and half on the cheek. "Call me when you get back," she says.

I look down just in time to see through the top of the towel to her nipples. She's doing this on purpose.

I look at Tan, who's on his phone again. Then, I take her by the hips and lead her back to the bedroom, the black boot in tow. I push the door shut with my good foot, yank off her towel, and lay her down on the bed, and I'm just as ready as she is.

She stares at me dead in the eyes when I push into her.

A grin spreads across her face. "Remember where you get this from, Atwood."

She tightens around me, and I close my eyes. My head begins to spin as I get lost in this feeling. Not on love or anything else, but the feeling Jordan gives me—like euphoria, I guess.

She pulls me down to her, and she whispers in my ear, "I'll see you when you get home." And then she pushes me off, walks to the bathroom, and shuts the door, leaving me hard and uncomfortable.

This isn't the first time she's done this right before I left town. One thing I'm not is a cheater. I think she does this to remind me that she thinks she's in control, that she can live without me, that she has the power to just walk away.

There's only one woman I've walked away from that almost killed me, and it wasn't Jordan.

I grab a towel and leave the bedroom. I go shower in the spare bathroom down the hall.

"That was quick," Tan says, now on his computer.

"Doesn't take long," I say and shut the bathroom door behind me.

It's 9:56 a.m., and we're boarding the private jet that will take us to Dillon Creek.

"Good morning, Mr. Atwood. It's a pleasure to meet you. My name is David, and I'll be your pilot today."

We exchange handshakes.

My father always told me, "Give a firm handshake and look a man in the eyes. And never, ever show anyone you're scared."

"Pleasure, David." I bend to walk through the doorway of the aircraft and sit in a white leather seat, setting my backpack down.

Tan sits down across from me after speaking with David.

"It's a forty-five-minute flight, David said. We're going to land at"—Tan looks at a piece of paper in his hand—"Rohnerville Airport."

I smile. "In Belle's Hollow." I glance out the window at the smog in Los Angeles that looms over the airport, giving off a brownish-yellow hue. I hate the smog in LA.

"Where the hell are you from, Colt?" Tan laughs.

"Behind the redwood curtain."

Tan's eyebrows rise. "Help us, Lord. Do they have vegan options?"

I laugh out loud. "Dillon Creek was built around agriculture, man. Beef is what's for breakfast, lunch, and dinner. I can't believe you agreed to go with me."

"Someone has to make sure you do as you're supposed to." Tan's phone rings. "Hello?" He listens. "Perfect. Thank you." He hangs up. "Rob should be here any minute. He got caught in traffic."

Rob Lincoln, a renowned physical therapist for professional athletes, will be flying with us, Tan informs me.

David greets Rob as he boards the plane. Rob isn't tall and isn't short. He's somewhere in the middle of average. But he's lean—probably from eating kale and healthy shit and everything that goes along with all that shit. Work me to the bone, but I'll eat what I want to eat, which usually isn't so healthy, except during the NBA Finals. I change everything for the finals—from the way I eat, to the way I sleep, to not having sex, to the music I listen to.

"Two weeks out from surgery. How's it feeling?" Rob asks after he shakes our hands and sits in the seat in the aisle over.

"Fine."

"Liar." Rob laughs.

I laugh, too.

Rob and I have worked together on and off since I started in the NBA.

David comes over the loudspeaker as the cabinet lights grow dim. "Please buckle your seat belts and prepare for departure."

5

Small Hearts

Anna

Kimber looks down at her phone. "His plane has landed at Rohnerville." Excitement gathers in her voice. She looks up at me. "I'm sorry."

Kimber is five years younger than I am.

"Sorry for what?" I try to play it off. "Dillon Creek is his home, too."

She bites her lip. "Aren't you the least bit curious as to what he's been doing?" She pauses. "How he looks and stuff?"

I can tell her mind is drifting to places I've seen and touched with my own two hands.

"No." When I say this, Bones—my black tri Australian Shepherd that I got from the Atwoods just about the time I arrived back home—growls. He's just over a year old. I look over the counter, and he's in his bed, looking up at me with his amber-colored eyes. "What? You disagree, Bones?"

He gives a low-pitched bark and rests his head back down on his bed as if to say, *Liar*.

"Me too, Bones. Me too," Kimber says, going back to her phone. She looks up at me again. And then back to her phone.

I roll my eyes and walk back to my office. I hear the clicks of Bones's nails against the tiles as he falls in line behind me. He doesn't usually let me leave his sight, but if I go into a patient room with my computer and my stethoscope, he knows to stay put. Other than that, he's free to roam around the clinic.

Everyone loves Bones. Even Cranky Carl, the Blacksmith Shop owner. When he comes in with his cat, Jinx, Bones greets him with a wiggle of his nub of a tail and lays his ears back, waiting for a quick rub, and I swear Cranky Carl smiles.

His wife, Millie, passed away about five years ago. His daughter got him a cat, Jinx, that I know has brought him a lot of companionship, just as Bones has done for me.

In my office, Bones circles up on his other bed. He yawns, looks up at me, and plops down.

I sit down at my computer and start to work on some patient records.

Plans for my future were different when I was a kid. Although I've always loved animals, I wanted to follow in my father's footsteps. I wanted to be a physician. Had plans to go to medical school.

But when I was twelve, things changed. Adam was gone at a sleepover, and my little sister, Amelia, was in my room with me.

She didn't notice the yelling that night, but I did. It was the first time and only time Mom ever yelled. Used words like infidelity and family and love. It was the first time my mom caught my dad cheating.

At twelve, I understood. I understood what cheating meant. I understood everything. And nobody knew but me. I kept their secret to myself. And I watched as my dad continued to do it.

I swore I'd never be like my father and that's why my plans to be a doctor were tossed like the evening newspaper—without a second thought.

I hear Kimber squeal from the front.

Bones picks up his head, tilts it, and stares at the open door to my office.

"Sorry." I hear her yell back.

I want to ask what happened, but I shouldn't. Since I heard the news that Colt was coming back to town, my stomach has been turned sideways. Nervous I'll run into him at the Wilson's Grocery or Flour and Water—our bakery and coffee shop.

What would I say to him after all these years?

What can I say to him after all these years?

Kimber appears in the doorway of my office.

"You probably don't want to know this, so this is me not telling you that Colt just posted a picture on Instagram of the back seat of Daryl's truck with Tupac with the tagline: *Missed you too, buddy.*"

I try my best not to smile. Tupac is Colt's black tri male, which he got when he turned fifteen.

At the Atwood Ranch, at any given time, you'll see a minimum of five dogs. But during the summers, when Colt was gone to basketball camps in the city down south, I'd come and take Tupac with me. Take him on runs or to the beach. He's always been protective of Colt, on alert at all times, watching, listening, smelling. But when Colt left for college, he couldn't take Tupac with him, and when I left for college, I couldn't make up for Colt's absence because I was gone, too.

So, Tupac stayed at the ranch.

When I came back to town to take over the clinic, Tupac was first on my list, and Laurel made it easy. She brought him to the clinic, so I could visit with him, and when she did, she also brought this little potbellied puppy with bright blue eyes.

"Named him Bones," she said. "He's always digging up the other dogs' bones." She laughed. The name stuck. "Some reason," Laurel said, "I knew he was your dog. I hope you'll take him."

I look up from staring blankly at my computer, and Kimber is gone. I hear a low buzzing sound, and the entire office goes dark.

"That was the other thing," Kimber says in the darkness from out front. "Pacific Gas and Electric issued a lights-out at noon. So much for advance notice."

"Damn it." I stand. "I need to go pick up the generator at Nelson's Feed." I turn to the safe behind my desk, do the combination, and take out my receipt.

Kimber is back in the doorway of my office again. "I'll man headquarters, boss."

Because we're on the same PG&E transmission line as Santa Rosa, where it gets raging hot in the summertime when high winds come through there, PG&E cuts off power to residents to protect against fire. Sometimes, it's just twenty-four hours; other times, it's longer.

"Come on, Bones." But he's already on his feet as Kimber and I make it down the hallway and to the front door. "Call me if there's an emergency."

The clinic is located at the end of Main Street, across the street from Wilson's Grocery, owned by Larry and Bernita Wilson. They've owned the place since my parents were kids. Larry's family owned it for three generations prior. Wilson's Grocery has all the essentials residents need to make a mean pudding cake, bacon and eggs, and beef burritos. Grab toilet paper if need be. Essentially, it has everything but at a higher price. Residents can drive State Route 211 to the 101 to go to Costco in Eureka, but it takes twenty minutes and then twenty minutes to go to Costco in Eureka, but it takes time and a whole lot more patience.

Bones walks up ahead only two feet or so as we make our way down Main Street.

"Good morning, Anna," Juniper, the owner of The Flowerpot, says as she sweeps in front of her store. Stops for a moment, rests her arm on her broomstick, and shades her eyes from the sun.

"Good morning. Do you need anything with your power out?" I ask.

Juniper is in her fifties. Some might describe her as a free spirit, a little on the quirky side. But I'd describe her as thoughtful and introspective.

She pulls a treat for Bones from her pocket, and he sits at her feet, watching the treat.

"No, no. The flowers and I are fine. Have a small generator in back that I bought from Bo Richards a few months back." She gives Bones the treat and pats his head.

"All right then. I'm heading down to Nelson's to get the generator I ordered last week." I wave, and we continue on.

"Morning, Merna," I say as I peek in the door to say hello and take in the scent of fresh dough, coffee, and cinnamon rolls.

Paul and Merna Mantova are the owners of Flour and Water bakery and coffee shop.

"Good morning, Dr. Cain. How are you holdin' up at the clinic?" she asks from the counter.

I'm not a sweets person. I'm more of a savory person, but I will never turn down a homemade cinnamon roll from Flour and Water.

Bones smells it, too.

"Looks like you got everything done before the blackout?" I ask.

"I was up until two in the morning." She laughs. "Paul's hooking up the generator in the back now. At least we'll have coffee for everyone if they want it."

Merna and Paul have lived in Dillon Creek and owned Flour and Water since I was a kid. I don't ever remember them not owning the place.

"You good?" she asks.

"All good," I say.

"All right then. Stop by later if you want some coffee."

"I will. Thanks."

Bones and I begin again, and I hear the truck before I see it.

It's Daryl Atwood's truck, and it's coming down Main Street.

My heart begins to race, and Bones feels it because he sits at my feet and looks up at me, whimpering.

I freeze as the truck drives closer toward me.

You should have sent Kimber down for the generator, I scold myself. *All she needed to do was tell Dusty that it should to be sent to the clinic.*

I ordered it last week, paid for it, but they didn't have it in stock.

Breathe, Anna, I tell myself.

The truck approaches.

Daryl is driving. Laurel is sitting on the passenger side. And I see nothing but a tall figure and his dog sitting in the back seat along with two smaller figures. I know exactly who the tall one is.

Look away, I tell myself. *Make things less awkward. Pretend you don't see them.*

No, no. You can't do that. He'll know, and then it will get really awkward when you run into him.

I look up just in time to catch Colt's eyes on me. His window is down.

I don't look away, and neither does he.

Tupac is next to him.

We stare until we can no longer see each other anymore. The truck keeps going.

After I found Colt trying to console his own heart, I tucked my heart somewhere safe so that it couldn't feel anything. The problem with that is, it does feel, no matter where you put it. And I'm starting to believe that the heart never completely heals from a first love.

"Come on, Bones," I say, and we walk into Nelson's.

"Just got it in. Trevor will deliver it to the clinic, Anna," Dusty says, in the dimly lit store operating on generators.

"Thank you, Dusty." I put my delivery slip in the pocket of my jeans. Push my phone in my back pocket as well.

Dusty leans over the counter to look at Bones. "Hey, Bones. Looks like someone needs a T-R-E-A-T." Dusty looks at me, and I nod.

Bones makes a low groan sound, staring intently at Dusty.

Dusty tosses him a treat, and Bones catches it.

I turn to leave and see Calder Atwood. He takes off his black cowboy hat.

All of the Atwood brothers are comprised of long legs and a long torso, which makes them tall. The brothers seem to have a grin that sets them apart from other men. It's a grin that lets you know their confidence sits deep in their bones and makes you feel as though you're the most important person in the room.

Women and girls alike have always fawned over the Atwood brothers. Even women twice their age and with twice the experience in the bedroom seem to fall at their feet.

But Daryl and Laurel raised the boys right. Though, Cash, the second-oldest brother has been known to get out of hand, but that's not due to his upbringing; it's due to his stubborn nature.

Calder and I haven't come face-to-face since I've been back. We've had waves from across the street. Hellos at gatherings. But no matter how hard I try to escape the Atwoods, I can't.

And now, we're staring at each other.

"Morning, Anna."

Calder's one of the good ones. Never has found the right woman, but I think he will eventually.

"Calder. Everything okay at the ranch without the power?" I say, as if I can do something about it. As if I can help.

"We'll survive. Buying anther generator. Dad's got three going, but Mom's in another wedding season, so we're being cautious."

Bones whines at my feet.

"Okay," I tell him, and Bones wiggles his way over to Calder, who folds his six-foot-five frame down to the floor to give Bones love.

"Handsome boy," Calder says as Bones closes his eyes when he rubs behind his ears.

Neither of us acknowledges the fact that Colt just arrived at the ranch.

Calder sits there for a moment with Bones. I can tell he's thinking, and I'd rather not hear his thoughts.

"Well, we'd better get going. Trevor's going to deliver our generator to the clinic," I say and start to walk out the door of Nelson's as Bones follows.

"Anna?" Calder whispers.

I wince. I don't turn around, but I stop, stare at the door, and listen. "Yeah?"

"You can avoid me all you want, but sooner or later, you're going to have to face him. Dillon Creek is just too damn small for two hearts like yours and Colt's."

I turn my head. Look back at Calder. "I know. But it won't be today."

6

The Stink Eye

Dillon Creek Pizza
Last Tuesday of the Month—Noon Sharp

"Lucy Sandeen was down at Nelson's, looking for a card for her niece next to the Fire and Light section, and overheard Calder talking to Anna," Pearl says, eyes wide with curiosity. "Something about a wedding between the two of them."

Mabe orders another beer.

Delveen sips her Diet Coke. "I heard the whole town stopped and waved when the Atwoods drove through town and that Colt and Anna gave each other *the look*." Delveen awkwardly squints her eyes and slowly moves her head from side to side, her best attempt at *the look*.

Mabe erupts into laughter. "That ain't no look, Delveen; that's the stink eye!" She smacks the table.

Erla looks at Clyda. "It's a wonder that the owner, Junie, doesn't kick us out of here."

"That's no shit," Clyda says.

Pearl looks to Erla and Clyda. "Who's going to kick five old ladies out of a restaurant for laughing too loud?"

The young waitress brings Mabe's beer and leaves the table.

"At any rate, I thought Colt had a girlfriend?" Pearl asks, looking straight at Clyda, but she pays no mind.

"Who the hell did you hear that from?" Delveen asks as she takes a bite of her salad, no dressing and littered with pickled red beets.

"Tony." Pearl shrugs. "I was getting my oil changed at Tipton's, and he mentioned it. Said he saw it on television or some damn thing."

"Well, what's her name?" Delveen asks.

"How should I know?" Pearl says.

"You didn't ask Tony?" Delveen asks.

"About what?" Pearl asks.

Delveen rolls her eyes this time. "Never mind."

Mabe takes another sip of beer.

Clyda shakes her head to what pours from Pearl's and Delveen's mouths—it's usually gossip anyway—nor does she argue with them. She wouldn't waste her breath or her time.

Erla says, "I call to order the meeting of the Dillon Creek Ladybugs, Club Number 227."

7
Eggs and Real Talk

Anna

Tess Morgan takes the spoon from her iced tea and sets it on the paper napkin next to her plate.

We're sitting in the window seat at The Rusty Nail on Main Street. We do this every Saturday morning. Breakfast, just Tess and me.

She's been my best friend since we were infants. A first grade teacher at Dillon Creek Elementary, she's married to her job and tiny little dog, Gypsy. Tess lives on three acres just outside town. When we get a stray in, she's always the one I call to foster the animal, and ninety percent of the time, instead of rehousing the animal, she keeps them because she somehow grows attached.

Her long brown hair rests against her back. Her green eyes might make you feel as though she keeps you just on the cusp of wanted and unwanted. But inside, deep inside her, is the most genuine, loyal person you'll ever meet. Something died in Tess when Tripp died. A spark. Her lights dimmed. If you hadn't known Tess before he died, then you wouldn't notice it now. I do though.

Quietly, families divided. Took sides when the whole tragedy happened.

Mysteries swirled around our town like waves of pooling water.

They drove lifetime friendships apart. Pushed people into corners.

The whole thing was a mess. It's still a mess. It's just that nobody talks about it anymore.

"If you ask me, I think Durant should stay with the Golden State Wolves. To hell with New Jersey," Tess says.

Kevin Durant is Tess's favorite basketball player.

"Torn ACL—that's a tough recovery," I say, taking a bite of my eggs.

I look at my watch. I told Laurel I'd come to her place at ten to help her go through Conroy's things for the rummage sale, only on a whim that Colt wouldn't be back yet. My stomach grows uneasy. My hands become sweaty at the thought of seeing Colt again after all this time.

"What?" Tess asks. "You look nervous."

I sit back in my chair and set my bacon down. "Look, I'm going to help Laurel go through Conroy's things at the ranch today."

Tess chews the last of her toast and wipes her mouth.

It's as if everything in The Rusty Nail restaurant freezes over.

"Anna, Tess, you want to add this to your tabs or pay the bill now?" Merry, one of the owners, asks as she approaches our table.

"Tabs, please," we both say in unison as we stare at each other from across the table.

"Will you please say something?" I put my elbows on the table and lean into them.

Tess sighs. "Your mom is throwing you a surprise birthday party, and she told my mom she invited the Atwoods. Well, you know why she told my mom—so my parents wouldn't shit a brick when they saw the Atwoods there if they showed up."

"Adam already told me."

Tess reaches across the table and touches my arm. "It's been seven years. At some point, I need to figure shit out. Even if I haven't yet, I can't keep you from doing what you need to do."

"I don't need to go to the Atwoods'."

"Yes, you do."

"No, I don't."

"Yes, you do."

"Why are you so stubborn?"

"Why are you so stubborn?" Tess asks, smiling.

"No. It's over, Tess. That was seven years ago. We, me and Colt—it's all over."

Tess slumps back in her chair, crossing her arms. "Bullshit. You never let anything get started."

"Clearly, he's found what he needed."

Tess tips her head back and laughs out loud. "Look, something Colt and I share is grief, okay? This … this I know. We do really sad things when we're not sure how to fix our hearts. That's it. He did a sad thing, and you saw it happen. But somehow, you allowed it to dictate your future." She points across the table at me.

"No, I didn't. I went to college, got myself an education."

"You went to vet school. Graduated top of your class. Who did you date?"

I stop fidgeting. Look at Tess square in the eyes. "I dated."

"You tried to date. But you compared everyone to Colt. And nobody quite measured up, did they?" Tess smiles. "You know I only tell you this because I love you."

We're quiet for a moment as I let Tess's words sink in.

"At some point, Anna, you've got to make a choice. But the way I see it, you and Colt were always meant to be. The stars said it, the sky said it, and I said it. Hell, the whole town has always said it."

I pull my purse up to my shoulder as I stand. I smile. "I love you. But sometimes, your truth is too early for me." I bend and kiss Tess on the cheek.

"See you later," Tess says.

"Bye, Anna," Merry calls from behind the counter.

"Bye, Merry. Thank you."

I open the door to the café, cross the street, and walk to my parents' house, two blocks down from Main. The house I purchased was Cranky Carl's old Victorian when he decided to downgrade. A Victorian built in 1859 on Berding Street. I hired Tom Manzel of Manzel Construction to do the renovations and restore the old house. The living room and dining room are sunken in. The stairs are missing steps. A lot of cosmetic stuff needs to be done and updated, to say the least. But the house itself is structurally sound. So, I'm having Tom almost restructure the old house to pristine condition.

In the meantime, I'm staying with my parents along with my younger sister, Amelia, until she leaves for college this fall.

"Anyone home?" I call out as I shut the door behind me.

"In the office," my dad says, and I hear Bones scramble to his feet to greet me.

I set my purse down on the bench seat. Bones shoves his head between my knees. I give him love, and he melts into my hands.

Dad's office is just off the foyer. The door is slightly ajar.

I peek in. "Hey."

"How's my girl?" He looks up from his newspaper. His socked feet are propped up on his desk.

My father has always had a quiet commanding presence. He waits for the answer that will meet his expectations.

"Good. I'm headed to the Atwoods' to help Laurel go through their things for the rummage sale next weekend."

He continues to read, waiting for me to expand.

"The boys aren't home and Calder has plans, and she could use an extra set of hands."

"I thought Colt came home yesterday?"

"That's my understanding."

He stops reading. Peering up at me through the top of his glasses, all he says is, "Tell Daryl I'll call tomorrow about poker."

"I will." I turn to run upstairs and change my clothes.

"And, Anna?" he says.

"Yes?" I don't turn around to look into his eyes because I know what he's about to say, and I don't want the sting of his words to meet my heart.

"For every action, there is an equal and opposite reaction."

"I know," I whisper.

The only living soul that knows what I saw that day when I went to North Carolina is Tess. But what my father saw was his daughter, his eldest daughter, heartbroken, doing her best to keep the pieces together for the following two years for the sake of her own sanity and her own broken heart.

I think, too, I was trying—*we*, as a community, were trying to recover from the loss of Tripp and Conroy. I was doing my best to help Tess and the Morgans and the Atwoods.

Upstairs in my bedroom, Bones takes his spot on my bed as I change into ripped jeans and a top. I throw my blonde hair back in a ponytail and look at myself in the full-length mirror.

My legs have always made up for my short torso. Long legs that require me to always special-order my jeans online as extra-long. My father has always been lean, and my mother, too, so it's no surprise that Amelia, Adam, and I are all lean. I think we are like this for two reasons. One, Mom allowed us to make our own choices about food, growing up—with guidance, of course. And two, simple genetics.

Colt told me once that my blue eyes had the ability to cut glass and split the seas. He said it wasn't the looks I gave, but the color itself, sharp and fierce. Today, I see it in the mirror, staring back at me.

"Sweetheart?" my mother says, peeking through the door. "Have I told you how good it is to have you home?"

"Every day, Mom." I kiss her on the cheek. "I'm headed to the Atwoods' to help Laurel go through stuff for the rummage sale."

Mom frowns. "Why wouldn't she have asked me?"

She's right. Why wouldn't she have asked my mom first? They're the ones who are best friends.

Instead, I shrug and tell her I'll be home tonight.

I pull up to the ranch and park with Bones in the passenger seat. I get out of the truck, and Bones follows.

Three trucks are parked outside—Daryl's, Laurel's, Calder's.

Brooks, Tupac, Jones, Williams, and Whitley the posse of Australian Shepherds, and all named after music icons: Garth Brooks, Tupac Shakur, George Jones, Hank Williams, Jr., and Keith Whitley, come running toward us to greet us.

Bones plays with his pack, and they dash toward the fence line, barking.

I walk to the back porch. The back porch faces the road. The front porch overlooks the ranch. My stomach twists and turns. My mouth goes dry.

What if he answers the door?

It'll be what it'll be, Anna.

I used to just walk into the Atwood residence because I felt that comfortable, and now, I feel like a stranger.

I knock.

Wait.

I listen to the crows and the dogs barking in the pasture.

My heart starts to race out of my chest.

Finally, Laurel comes to the door.

I take in a deep breath.

"Hey," she says, her eyes twinkling. "Come on in. Are you hungry?"

"No, thanks. Ate with Tess—" But I catch myself. I change my words. "I ate before I came."

Laurel puts on her shoes, pretending not to hear the name I just said. A man comes into the kitchen. A man I've never seen before.

"Hello," he says. "I'm Tan. Colt's publicist." He extends his hand after he sets down two smartphones on the kitchen counter. He's dressed in loafers, trim-cut jeans, and a button-up dress shirt with two buttons undone at the top. His black hair is impeccably combed, not a hair out of place. His skin is like silk, and almost-translucent brown.

"Hi, I'm Anna."

"Oh." He pauses calmly. "You're Anna," he says as if he knows a secret I don't.

"Your hands are so soft," I say as we release from our handshake.

"It's a moisturizer made in LA. I'll give you some. It's amazing. Not that your hands aren't soft—" Tan winces. "I'm bad with making new friends."

"I'm not easily offended, Tan. Don't worry about it," I say.

"I was just telling Tan that the closest thing we have to an Ugert—" Laurel starts.

Tan smiles. "An Uber."

"An Uber." She continues, "Well, the closest thing is a horse. I told him I'd saddle a horse and give him a compass, but he wasn't thrilled." Laurel laughs this time. Genuinely laughs, and all of a sudden, the fear in the pit of my stomach disappears.

"Do you need a ride to town, Tan?" I ask. "I'm going to the clinic afterward. I can give you a ride."

"That would be wonderful, Annie—I mean, Anna."

I freeze. Look at Laurel. Look back to Tan. *How would Tan know that nickname? Why the hell would he call me Annie?*

"Why don't you come help us go through our old family heirlooms, Tan? It'll be fun. Let's see what dirt we can dig up," Laurel says, throwing on a well-loved LA Heat hat.

"Sounds intriguing," he says as he scoops up the phones and puts two in his back pocket.

Before we escape, Colt comes around the corner into the kitchen, and my insides tighten so tight that I wonder if they'll work again after this moment.

"Hey, Annie." His voice is deep, and I bet it touches hell when he speaks. It sounds a million miles away and too close, all at the same time.

I feel him in my bones, just as when we were kids. And my heart begins to ache.

Would things have been different if Conroy and Tripp hadn't died?

The world moves and pauses, and I'm suddenly not in control.

"It's Anna," I say.

And my cunning blue eyes meet his blue.

8

Rose Petals and Bullshit

Colt

My parents set aside some barn space for me to rehab. Rob told Tan what to order, and Tan had it shipped to my parents' house. We set it up last night.

Tupac, my loyal best friend—a black tri Australian shepherd—is lying down next to the stationary bike.

I'm fighting off thoughts of Anna in my head as I push the pedals around in a circle.

"Slow and steady," Rob says, watching my posture and my foot placement, which is still wearing the black boot.

Rob says, "Achilles injuries take a lot of time and patience. Fine tuning." He looks at me. "Put your headphones on. You'll be on this thing for twenty-five minutes."

I slip my headphones on and allow the lyrics of Eminem to carry my drive, my push to return as a stronger basketball player than I was before. After all, I have something to prove. I was on top of my game, playing the best ball I'd ever played.

I was tired when I tore it, but I'd pushed my body in ways that always met my expectations, fans' expectations.

But this was different.

It was game four of the NBA Finals with twenty-seven seconds on the clock. We were tied up. We were playing the Toronto Grizzlies.

All I did was hop.

I didn't dive.

I didn't go up for a rebound.

I simply hopped off my right foot and heard a snap.

I knew what I'd done. My Achilles had been sore in the semifinals, and I never said anything.

When I went down, everything went silent. I grabbed my ankle. I didn't wince in pain. I shouldn't have fucking played. But I'd made the choice to. It was the finals.

All I did was bite my lip and drop my head.

This injury also means that it can change the course of my career.

I've watched Rick Danco, Brady Thomas, and Ladale Conrad try to come back from this injury with devastating results. *Career-ending* is what they call it.

Rob didn't seem to know the statistics when I asked him earlier. Either that or he was putting on a brave face.

I pull off my headphones. "Rob?" I ask.

"Yeah, man?" He's adjusting one of the weights.

"Don't lie to me, okay? I'm used to overcoming odds."

Rob stands, turns toward me, and crosses his arms. "What's up?"

Tupac lifts his head when I stop pedaling the stationary bike, looking up at me. I smile at him. It's good to have him back.

My eyes meet Rob's. "What are the odds that I come back on top and stay there?"

Rob mulls over my words. "Depends on how bad you want it." He shrugs. "The way I see it, Atwood, is you have to be all in. Your rehab comes before anything and everything. You want freedom? It's got to wait. You want to grab ass? It's got to wait. You want love? Fuck that shit. You've got to be all in from all angles. If you're not, then this — this time and rehab—is just rose petals and bullshit."

A slight grin comes over my face as I slip my headphones back over my ears. "Rose petals and bullshit?"

Rob smiles. "Rose petals and bullshit, man."

I allow the lyrics of Eminem to take me to a headspace where the only thing I see is the court, the ball, and me. Just like when Conroy died, I don't allow myself to grieve. I just push on, taking out all my anger, my sadness, my memories out on my opponents and the game of basketball. Out-rebounding, outscoring, outperforming my class of players. That is what the grief does to me and for me.

Rob taps my shoulder and indicates with his hand for me to slow down on the exercise bike, and I pull off one side of my headphones.

"The point is to ease into it. Your Achilles at this point, before the scar tissue is formed, has the ability to re-tear easily. Work your way back up to that, killer."

"What about rose petals and bullshit?" I ask.

Rob laughs. "How about stay fixed, find your pace, and then rose petals and bullshit?" He pauses. "When I said 'all in,' I didn't mean one hundred miles an hour. I meant, mental toughness, stamina, and patience. Now, get to work, Atwood. You've got plenty of it."

Rob and I make our way back inside the house, and I hear Anna's giggle. The giggle is coming from the den.

A warm sensation comes over my entire body. My stomach drops, and the nerves grow inside me.

I grab a water from the refrigerator and throw one to Rob, trying to act as casual as possible.

"I'm going to go shower," he says.

I nod and look into the den where I see my mom, Anna, and Tan going through old boxes from the attic.

Blonde wisps of hair fall around her face. Her worn jeans fit her body in all the right places. As if the jeans were formed for her body alone. Her T-shirt is an old UC Davis shirt hangs loosely. Tells you she doesn't need a man to tell her she looks beautiful. She doesn't need to wear tight clothes or slutty dresses. She's aware of who she is, and she has the confidence to say to anyone who tries to tell her different to fuck off. And that's the way Anna has always been.

Has Anna dated?

Does she have a boyfriend?

According to her Instagram page, there was one guy. But I wouldn't allow myself to invade on her privacy, nor would I put myself through the pain anymore.

The thought of another man making love to her makes my face grow hot.

Tan holds up Conroy's high school football jersey, and I see the look on my mom's face when he does. A look of catastrophic grief and lost time and broken hearts.

She wears the guise only momentarily before she says, "Conroy was such a great football player."

How much does Tan know? How much have they told him?

I've never said a word because I don't want the same damn look that everyone else gave me in town when he died. Sure, people can Google it. Find out all the dirty details about the accident, about how our family fell apart. How my brother Cash's record with the police is longer than a movie script. Nothing too big, just minor offenses, but he can't seem to keep control of his mouth. Or the time I came home from college to find my mother in the fetal position on the floor in Conroy's room, cradling his work jacket like a baby.

Anna sees me standing in the doorway, and I see her take the smallest breath in. Or maybe it's a sigh. I'm not sure which, but it takes my breath away. I nod at her but don't say a word.

"My father was disappointed when I didn't take one of the paths my three brothers did. Doctor, engineer, dentist." Tan holds up a book to my mom.

"Sell pile," she says.

Tan sets it down next to a pile in the middle of the room.

I watch Anna.

Watch her bend at her waist as she goes through a box of clothes.

She knows I'm here.

"I love sports. I always have. I also have a strong sense of organization and planning. When I met Colt our freshman year in the college dorms, we just clicked. I know; we're an unlikely pair. Him being an athlete and me being a gay man from San Francisco. But Colt didn't care about any of that. So, when he signed with the Heat and he asked me to go with him to help out with his lack of organizational skills, I stayed and haven't left." He shrugs.

I know he's telling Anna the story, and knowing Anna, she must have asked.

My mom looks up and sees me standing between the den and the kitchen. "Hey, baby. How was the workout?"

"Slow," I say. I catch Anna's eye again but only for a second.

Tan turns around. "How come you didn't tell me that Anna was a veterinarian?"

I shrug. "Suppose it just never came up."

Tupac wanders into the den and goes straight to Anna, sitting at her feet.

Anna bends down and gives him love in his favorite spot—behind his ears.

A slow trickle of dogs makes their way into the den.

Behind Tupac are Bones, Jones, Brooks, and then Williams, and Whitley. Strait is the only one missing, just like Conroy.

"Anyone home?" my dad calls from the kitchen.

"In the den," I say.

My dad comes up behind me, placing his hand up on my shoulder. "Son. It's really good to have you home." And then he looks at the piles in the den.

My mom says, "You can help if you want."

"No, no. You guys are doing a wonderful job," Dad says. And he walks back into the kitchen where he grabs a copy of the *Dillon Creek Echo* and a cup of coffee. He turns on his small television that sits at his corner and flips on reruns of *MASH*, an old Army comedy that aired from 1972 to 1983.

Calder walks in from the back door of the kitchen. Hangs his cowboy hat on the coatrack next to the door. Calder is the oldest now. Has been for the last seven years. He's taken on the lead like he was meant for the job.

The one thing we don't talk about is Conroy's death.

My father won't allow it.

Calder grabs a glass of water and rests his back against the counter. Takes a sip and looks at me. Grins. "How's the ankle?"

"Still attached."

"That's good." He stares down at the yellow-and-white flooring. "Later, you want to move some cattle? I mean, that's if the city hasn't turned you into a big pussy."

Calder is serious with most people. As much as Cash, the third oldest, tried to ruffle his feathers as we grew up, he just couldn't, no matter how hard he tried. Calder usually wears a sullen expression, but not because of his mood; it's because he's deep in thought. I always thought, if he didn't want to take over the ranch, he definitely would have made a great doctor or engineer. But college was never something he considered. If he didn't want the ranch gig, he'd have had some profession; he'd have had something to do with complex equations or science. Calder has always reminded me of the Marlboro Man—his look, his demeanor. Calm, like Dad's. I think if anyone took on most of Dad's attributes, it's Calder. I'm the tallest of the brothers, but Calder is a close second.

"Can't right now." I look down at the black boot I've been wearing for the past two weeks.

"That's okay, Nancy. You can drive a four-wheeler without using your foot, right?"

Nancy is the code word for *don't be a pussy.*

Rob walks in.

"Got to clear it with the boss." I nod toward Rob.

"What?"

"Four-wheeler. Moving cattle."

"What does that consist of? I'm not a cowboy."

A slow, deep laugh sounds from my dad. Takes a sip of his coffee. Shakes his head.

Calder and I smile.

"Means, rounding up cattle, moving some from one pasture to another. Calder will take the lead, and I'll catch the leftovers with the four-wheeler."

Rob laughs. "Well, that depends. Do you want to continue to play in the NBA and resume on your path as one of the best players to ever play the game? Or do you want rose petals and bullshit?"

I laugh out loud and look over at Dad, watch his tongue move from side to side as he stares at the television show.

He does this when he's thinking—the tongue thing. Mulling over thoughts that have been turning in his head for years, and yet, he still overthinks them. Dad has always known that my heart wasn't set here on the ranch like Calder's—or Conroy's, for that matter. That Casey, Cash, and I wanted something different—and I know that bothers him. The ranch has always been what my dad wanted. Every inch of the land. Every last piece of it has been carefully considered. Which parts to keep, which parts to sell. The cattle. The horses. The bulls. The rainfall when spots on the ranch get flooded. It's his life.

I look at Calder. "Can't, man. Doctor's orders."

9

Seven Minutes in Heaven

Colt: Age Fourteen

"What's French kissing like?" Anna whispered next to me in the barn as we lay down on the hay bales, the rain thundering down against the roof.

My dad had sentenced us to the barn to watch over the calf whose mother died at birth.

A group of us from school played Seven Minutes in Heaven at Cameron Barstow's house.

The truth was, I'd chickened out. I couldn't kiss Lisa Reynolds.

"I don't know. Wet and long," I lied.

I never kissed a girl a day in my life. And my first kiss wasn't destined for Lisa Reynolds. It had always been meant for Anna. I dreamed about it. Felt her body in my sleep—in places I damn well shouldn't. Every morning, I'd have to take a cold shower to wash away my thoughts.

But I'd lied to Anna. The first time ever that I'd lied to her.

"Did you like it?" she asked.

"No."

"Then, why'd you do it?"

I shrugged. "I guess I didn't know that I wouldn't like it."
Another lie.

I had known I wouldn't like it because it wasn't Anna.

"You're confusing, Colt Atwood."

A crack of thunder sounded. But Anna didn't jump. She enjoyed the thunder. She loved the rain. That was something I loved about her—almost nothing scared her.

The calf picked up his head, and then he dropped it back down again.

"Anna?"

"Yeah?"

"What would happen if we kissed?"

The rain stopped as if God himself forbade our lips from touching.

The quiet aftermath of the storm, the drips—the runoff from the barn roof—took place of the near silence.

"You wouldn't be able to handle me, Colt. Besides, we're best friends. Why would you want to go and screw that up?"

But somewhere deep inside my body, I knew Anna was lying to herself. I'd noticed the glances she stole when my shirt was off at the ranch. I'd noticed her at my basketball practices every now and then. I'd noticed her, and she'd noticed me, and nothing between us was innocent anymore, not since I'd gotten hair where it counted and she'd gotten boobs.

It was hard when neither of us wanted to give up our friendship. We both knew that a kiss, sex, whatever would screw it all up, and I thought that was what kept us from doing anything at all.

So, it was just Colt and Anna. Destined not to be together, for fear of losing our friendship.

"How're your parents?" I asked, pulling a piece of straw from underneath me and putting it between my lips.

"Quiet, I guess," she said. "Like nothing happened."

"Does Adam know?"

She shrugged in the darkness. I could make out the outline of her body lying next to me.

"Did you say anything?"

"No." The rain started to trickle again. "My mom seems to have pushed everything under the rug. Makes herself busy with Amelia, so ..." Her voice trailed off as the rain got louder. Disappeared into the sheets that poured against the roof.

I nodded in the darkness, not because I understood, but because I just wanted Anna not to feel alone.

So, we both stared at the roof of the barn and listened to the rain and everything we didn't say, and instead of trusting my instincts, I reached my fingers out for hers, and I put my palm to hers. We lay there until the world around us seemed to disappear.

Conroy was driving Casey and me to the Dillon Creek movie theater for Rerun Saturday. It had two screens, and it was cold as shit in there, depending on the time of year, but they were playing our favorite old movie as a rerun on one of the screens.

"How many times have you guys seen *Tombstone*?" Conroy asked as we made the trip to town.

"Doesn't matter. What matters is, Tess is working the booth, and there's free popcorn on Saturdays," Casey said.

He'd been trying to get with Tess since we were in diapers. Casey said she was too hardheaded, too stubborn, and too beautiful, but he had a hard time letting go of her smile.

"What time's the movie over?" Conroy asked, taking a right off Ocean Street into town.

Conroy was more of a father figure than brother. And he played the part well enough. He was eight years older than me, and Dad was busy with ranch business, so Conroy always took time to show us things. Take us places. Casey and me, that was. Calder and Cash had their own shit. Calder was too busy being up Dad's ass about the ranch. Cash didn't give a shit about anything, except chasing tail and chasing bulls.

If any of our two brothers were alike, it was Casey and me. Casey was quiet and processed everything inside. Like the time Calder and Dad had found Louie out on the back forty. Louie was a rescue dog that had really taken a liking to Casey. We'd had him just shy of three years before a mountain lion got the best of him. When Casey had heard the news when he was twelve or so, he'd sat on the back side of the property until he killed the mountain lion. And never said another word about it.

Conroy pulled up to the theater, and Casey and I jumped out.

"Call me when you need a ride home," Conroy said.

"Yeah," I said as I shut the door.

Casey and I walked to the window where Tess was sitting in the booth, selling tickets.

"Well, if it isn't the Atwood boys, here to see *Tombstone*. That's a huge surprise," Tess said, smiled, popped her gum, and rolled her eyes.

Not only did the Morgans own The Whiskey Barrel, but they also owned the movie house. Being that Tess was only fourteen, her parents only had her work when they were shorthanded.

"Tess Morgan, you know goddamn well we're only here for the free popcorn," Casey teased.

"Five bucks each," she said.

Casey slid his five dollars under the glass, and I slid a ten-dollar bill.

Tess looked at me and smiled. "You know she's working with her dad today, right? That she might not make it."

"Five bucks says she will." I smiled.

"You know, Atwood, you're probably right. I'll take your money anyway," Tess said as she pushed my ticket under the glass. "I'll hold hers for when she gets here. Enjoy, boys."

Casey and I went to the concession stand, and Murphy was behind the counter.

"Large popcorn?" Murphy asked, already putting the butter on it.

Murphy went to high school with us. Smoked a little too much of the green stuff, but always gave us free popcorn.

"Thanks, Murph," Casey said.

"Yeah, man, no problem. Hey, Casey, when are you going to teach me to ride bulls?"

Casey smirked. "When you can pass a drug test, man. I can't put you on a bull with all that shit in your system. You'd be a liability."

"Oh, yeah," Murphy said.

The problem was, we'd had the same conversation last month when *Back to the Future* was playing as a rerun.

When we opened the door, the pre-film played Name the Movie Star, and all that we could see were the tops of the chairs and the tiny pink lights that lit up the path down to the screen.

Per usual, on Rerun Saturdays at two o'clock in the afternoon, we were the only two in the theater.

We sat in our normal seats—ten rows back from the front, eight seats from the right.

The screen went dark, and the movie began.

The door opened, and secretly, I hoped it would be Anna, but it was Tess, and she sat down next to Casey.

The thing with Casey and Tess was, they weren't a thing, but they were. Tess never wanted to make it official, and Casey didn't care. But I thought he did.

Thirty minutes into the movie, the door opened again, but I paid no mind.

"Hey," Anna said. "Sorry I'm late. I'd ask what I missed, but I already know." She laughed and sat down next to me.

I looked down at her and smiled, excited she had come even though I had known she would.

I knew Anna Cain better than anybody. The way she shot the basketball with both hands, the way her lips formed into a thin line when she was mad.

"What?" she asked as she looked up at me.

My heart and stomach didn't do me well in that particular moment in time. Maybe it was the way the light from the theater screen lit up her face or her big, innocent blue eyes that made my heart beat too hard and too fast.

"Nothing, just glad you made it," I said and passed her the popcorn.

"Extra butter?" she whispered.

"Duh."

She looked up at me again. "You always come through, Colt," she said before she shoved a handful of popcorn in her mouth.

The truth was, so did she.

The sun had begun its voyage back behind the mountain of redwood trees as Casey, Tess, Anna, and I made our way down Main Street toward The Rusty Nail.

"Watch this," Casey said.

He touched a few leaves from Cranky Carl's archway outside the Blacksmith Shop.

"Casey, you touch my leaves again, and I'm going to give your ass a whoopin'!" Carl said from inside the shop.

"Sorry, Carl," Casey said.

Casey liked to flick Carl shit, but the feeling was mutual, as Carl also liked to do the same to Casey.

Casey used to shoe Carl's horses when he had them. Worked with Conroy before Conroy got too busy at the ranch.

Because one thing the Atwood boys weren't was assholes. Cash had been known to stir some pots, but he wasn't an asshole.

Besides, Casey filled in for Carl when he needed help at the shop.

The truth wasn't that Carl was cranky; the truth was that Carl was just plain tired.

Tired Carl.

But Cranky Carl had a better ring to it.

"How'd it go at your dad's office today?" I asked Anna as we walked behind Tess and Casey.

She sighed, looking on. "It was fine."

"Liar."

Anna smiled, and then it fell from her face. "She called again."

I listened.

"She pretended to be a sales rep." We walked a little farther before she said, "It's not the fact that my dad is hiding it; it's the fact that my mom won't leave."

I thought on this for a minute. "Maybe your mom feels like she can't."

She bit her lip. "No good husband would ever do that to his wife, Colt."

"What if it's more complicated than you think, Annie?"

This time, she looked at me with fire in her eyes. "I'm pretty sure Pastor Mike said last Sunday that infidelity wasn't part of the Ten Commandments."

"We're also not Catholic, but I see what you're saying. Look, I'm not saying what he's doing is right, Annie. I'm just saying, what if there's more to the story?"

We reached The Rusty Nail, and I knew how Anna got when we were talking about this. I opened the door for her, as Tess and Casey had already walked in. We found them at the window seat.

Merry was taking their drink order.

"Hey, Merry," Anna and I said as we sat down and grabbed menus.

"Two Cherry Cokes?" Merry asked.

"Yes, please," Anna said for both of us.

Truth be told, Cherry Coke wasn't my favorite; Vanilla Coke was. But Anna liked Cherry Coke, and I liked that she liked it, so I always agreed.

"Hey, Colt! Your mom is on the phone for you," Ruby, the other owner of The Rusty Nail, said, holding the receiver of the yellow rotary phone stuck to the wall.

Anna and I exchanged glances.

I looked at Casey.

"Why would Mom be calling?" he said.

I shrugged before heading to the phone.

"Mom? Is everything okay?" I said into the receiver, sitting at the counter of the bar.

"Colt, uh … Mr. Weston Matthews—I guess he's scouting for some of the top basketball players in California. Said he wants to meet with us. Said he's driving up our way now."

"Weston Matthews?" I attempted to pick my jaw up from the counter, but my mind had a hard time understanding how Weston Matthews even knew my name. "He's a retired NBA coach."

IO

Surprise Birthdays and Broken Music

Anna

"Just act surprised, okay, Anna?" Adam sighs as we make our way down to Veterans Hall on foot. "Mom will know if you don't play this up right. She can smell a lie before it comes to life. You know that."

She knows I hate surprises. And why do this on this birthday? Why not a big birthday, like my thirtieth birthday? Why now?

"And there's one more thing," Amelia, my almost-off-to-college, eighteen-year-old sister, says. "Colt will be there."

I stop in my tracks.

"I just didn't want you to be caught off guard, is all, Annie," Amelia says.

She's an entrepreneur, too. She owns an online boutique on Antsy where she makes and sells clothing for animals. Primarily cats and dogs, but when she gets a special request—like a sweater for a llama—she'll do those, too.

I'd say that Adam and Amelia are more alike. I'm the in-between sibling and most like our father. Science and numbers are my love language.

Amelia continues, "Look, the way I see it, you've got to face whatever happened between you and Colt anyway, Annie."

"It'll be fine," Adam says as we reach Veterans Hall.

But there are no cars, and the place looks empty.

Did nobody show? Self-pity maneuvers itself into the tender parts of my heart.

"Come on. I'll get you a drink first thing when we get inside," Adam says, "and I'll grab myself one, too."

"You're a huge help, Adam. Thank you." Sarcasm sinks into my tone.

I pull up my dress so that my breasts aren't hanging out.

Tess talked me into this dress. As part of Operation Surprise Party, it was Tess's job to get me into a cute outfit.

It was Adam and Amelia's job to get me to the location.

My mother is the devil incarnate at the moment because the two things I hate most are dresses and surprises. And she knows this.

"All right, let's get this over with," I say.

With Adam on one side of me and Amelia on the other, her arm looped in mine, we make our way to the door.

Adam opens it.

I wait for it.

The loud yelling of surprise.

I conjure up a face that is both of shock and awe.

But it's dark.

There's no one inside.

Adam says, "Oh, shit." He calls our mom. "Hey, where are you guys?"

Mom asks, "Is Anna standing right there?"

Adam looks at me. "No, no. She ran to the restroom."

"We're at Portuguese Hall. Like I told you."

"No, you said Veterans Hall."

"Adam, there are two halls in Dillon Creek. One we party at and one we don't."

Adam's eyebrows rise. "Okay, we'll be there in a few minutes." He hits End. "My bad. We're going to Portuguese Hall."

Amelia laughs. "Leave it to Adam."

"What's that supposed to mean?" Adam asks as we turn around and head back uptown to Portuguese Hall.

Amelia shrugs, still on my arm. "Adam, you're not a details guy. That's all."

"I run a music venue, Amelia. I can handle details."

"Just not your sister's surprise-party location?"

Ouch. "Low blow, Amelia," I say. "It's not a big deal, Adam."

"I don't know why Mom put you in charge of getting Anna to the venue. She, of all people, should know your faults."

"Amelia." I stop and look at my little sister.

"What's your beef with me tonight?" Adam asks, and the three of us all come to a halt right before Dillon Creek Repertory Theater.

Amelia is being shitty. Not her normal shitty, but extra shitty.

"Wait. I get into trouble because I call Adam out on his lack of details?"

"No, Amelia, we all know Adam isn't strong in the details department, and that's why he has Izzy at The Steeple working for him. But you can't treat him like that."

Middle child—always trying to keep the peace.

"Whatever. I'll just meet you guys there," Amelia says and storms down Main Street toward the hall. Youngest child.

Adam and I stand here.

"Hormones?" he asks as we watch our little sister. "Come on; let's go."

Mom told Adam to give me the excuse that she needed tape. That she was down at the hall, decorating for an event.

"You don't have to do this, you know. I could make an excuse that you got sick. I have your back. You know that, right, Anna?"

"I know. Thank you, Adam."

We arrive at the Portuguese Hall. We're standing outside.

Mom opens the door to the hall. She gets rather impatient with surprises. "Do you have the tape, Adam?"

Adam does not have the tape. Adam is not good with details, but I am.

"Yep. Right here, Mom," I say.

Adam sighs in relief.

"Can you follow me in, honey?" she asks, luring me toward the party that I don't want to be at.

Adam takes my hand and whispers, "Go fucking look surprised as shit, and I'll grab us drinks."

"Right," I say as Adam leads me up the steps toward Mom.

"Happy Birthday!" everyone yells.

I have a mix of both envy and jealousy.

I'd rather be on the other end of this, in the crowd.

I only walked across the stage at high school graduation because my parents made me. But I chose not to participate in either of my college graduations for my undergraduate work and my postgraduate work because it wasn't a graduation requirement, and frankly, it was all bullshit anyway. But the real reason? The spotlight.

Everything in my world goes quiet as I look at all the eyes on me.

The Beckfords.

The Wilsons.

Ebby Ledbetter.

Cranky Carl.

The Pattons.

The Fields.

Dusty Cole.

The Ladybugs.

The Atwoods.

Tess, of course.

The Richardses.

The Belottis.

The Samuelses.

Toby Lemon.

Dale Bradford.

The McBrides.

The Burnses.

Juniper Jones and her boyfriend, Stem—or so he calls himself. They're a little on the earthy side.

The Glens.

The Pucketts.

The Mantovas.

Dan Rigby.

Lyle Lucas and Twila Michaels, who are partners at Lyle and Michaels: Attorneys at Law and also dating.

Ike Isner.

There must be well over a hundred people here.

The Morgans, aside from Tess, are missing though. If there's an event that the Atwoods attend, the Morgans will not be there, and I try not to take this personally.

Adam slips a drink into my hand.

"Thank you," I whisper as my mom takes me by the elbow to say hello to our guests.

Partly, I think Mom does this so she can throw a party, but I know her heart is in the right place. She likes to put her family on display for the town. Parade us around like we're dolls in glass cases, like we don't have demons that sleep in our closets at night.

Like the one Dad hides.

Adam hands me another drink. By this time, I'm feeling better about the whole situation. The party. The fact that Colt didn't come. Daryl and Laurel are talking with Bo and Laney Richards. Calder is talking with Stem, Juniper's boyfriend.

What an unlikely pair, I think to myself as I take another sip of champagne.

"It's good that Colt didn't come," I say to Tess.

We're sitting at a table next to the dance floor where Toby Lemon, the town drunk, is dancing with Mabe Muldoon to "Fly Me to the Moon" by Frank Sinatra. Another sign that Mom indeed had her generation, not mine, in mind when she planned this party.

"You spoke too soon." Tess nods over toward the door.

I look, and there he is. All six feet nine inches of him filling up the doorway as he scans the room.

I drop my head against the table, smelling the bleach from the tablecloth. "I hate my life."

Tess laughs. "No, you don't. You just don't like the fact that Colt is back in town, and eventually, you'll have to figure out where you both went wrong." She takes a bite of a cracker rather obnoxiously.

I pick my head up and eye Colt as he ambles to the bar.

Adam walks up to us and sets down an empty Solo cup. "Here, you're going to need this. Something a little stronger." He takes the flask from his jacket and dumps it into the red cup.

"What is that?" I ask.

"Something I brewed at home."

"That's illegal, Chum," Tess says.

Chum is Tess's nickname for Adam. When we were teenagers, back in high school, he got the flu and threw up in Tess's car, and Tess said, "Dude, that looks like chum that they feed sharks. What the hell did you eat? An entire fish?" And so it stuck.

Adam stops. Stares down at Tess and looks back at me. "Is she for real right now?"

I smile at Adam and Tess and then look to see a swarm of people around Colt.

I swallow everything in the cup.

"Goddamn it, Annie, you're supposed to sip it. Shit. Now, you're going to be hammered, and Mom is going to have my ass because you're drunk."

"Maybe you shouldn't have given her homemade brew," Tess says sarcastically as a plastic smile spreads across her face.

"I'm going to be fin—" And then it hits.

Whoa.

All of a sudden, I feel skinnier.

Taller.

Prettier.

Faster.

Braver.

And it feels really good.

I could march over to Colt Atwood and tell him what I think.

I could also tell him that I dream about him. And most of the times, in my dreams, we aren't making love, but we're having sex. It's hard, full of need, and it's hot.

I could tell him I've fallen in love with him and out of love with him and back in love. But the out of love would just be a lie.

That he's changed. That he's not the same guy he was when we were kids.

I could tell him that Tan is a keeper. A good guy. But he's got to let him go. I can tell Tan does what's comfortable and doesn't take risks, but then again, neither do I.

The home-brewed liquid spreads to my head and my limbs, and everything in my body is at peace right now.

I can do all things.

"Annie?" His voice sends shivers up my spine. "Can we talk?"

Stop with the Annie, I want to say.

We've never discussed what I saw when I showed up at his dorm room that night to surprise him.

I'd made a trip across the United States to see him, to tell him I loved him and that I was willing to take the risk of love because it was the only thing that felt right. Instead though, I walked away, left North Carolina, and never answered his calls again.

"Suit yourself," I say.

Adam takes Tess by the hand. "Another drink?" he says to her.

When Adam and Tess leave, Colt folds his body into a chair across the table from me.

Don't look into his eyes, Anna. But I do. *Regret it later*, I tell myself.

His strong jawline and broad shoulders and big chest reflect years of hard work and dedication to the sport. Something we shared for a long time—the love of basketball. His jet-black hair and his electric-blue eyes search the table.

I've known this boy for as long as I can remember, yet as I sit across the table from him, with the new persona he carries like an old saddle, I can't remember a time when I felt more afraid for us. Afraid that we somehow missed the mark. Afraid that this is good-bye instead of hello. Afraid that he'd settle for less than he is worth. Afraid that my heart will never let Colt Atwood back in again. And not for the things he did, but for what I'd seen my father do.

The heart is a complicated thing. Both desolate and understanding.

Colt peels at the label of his beer. Stops. Stares at me dead in the eyes. I know he's nervous.

The liquid courage oozes through my bloodstream and allows my thoughts to become lighter.

"One dance?" he says. "For old times' sake?"

It's just a dance, Anna, a dance between old friends. "What about your ankle?"

"My ankle will be fine." He unfolds from the chair, standing up to his six-foot-nine frame and filling every inch of it. He holds out his hand. His long, lean fingers were made to wrap around a basketball and also made to rope and ride and tend to cattle.

"What if I can't?" I can barely breathe.

Gently, he leans down and whispers in my ear, "What if you can?"

II

Toby Lemon and Sacramental Wine

"Did you see the way Colt looked at Anna last night?" Pearl asks Delveen as they walk home from First Christian Church, Clyda, Erla, and Mabe in tow.

"A love we'd only wish for those two." Delveen shakes her head.

Mabe pipes in, "I thought we got wine at church?"

Erla looks at her old friend. The one she's watched slip through the years like water through cracks. It happened so quickly and without effort. From the loss of Mabe's husband to the loss of her daughter in more recent years, drinking has seemed to soothe her unrested soul. Erla tries to be patient with her friend, her cousin, but fear keeps her using the softer words, the kinder words. "That's the Catholic church, Mabe. Not the Christian church."

"And besides, I heard the congregation changed from wine to grape juice because Toby Lemon couldn't keep his paws off the carafe they poured from," Delveen says. "After all, they can't kick him out of church. God just wouldn't have it."

In their golden years, one would think that these five women should be settled in their ways, that their lives were unchanging and comfortable, and while that might be true for some, it is far from the truth for Mabe.

"Mabe, I need some assistance with my petunias this afternoon. Come over, would you?" Erla asks.

The group knows that this isn't a question; it's more of a command.

Sundays are especially hard for Mabe. It's a family day and she doesn't have any family left aside from Erla.

"I've got stuff to do today, Erla. Besides, I have my own petunias to deal with."

"Then, I'll go help you."

"I don't need your help."

"Sure you do." Erla can see the annoyance on her cousin's face. It has been some time since Erla visited Mabe in her home, but something inside her tells her that it is time to pay Mabe a visit, so she pushes. "At any rate, I need to grab my pruning shears I left there a while back."

"What pruning shears?" Mabe asks.

"Oh, I don't know what the hell color they were but I let you borrow them after our gardening party."

Delveen and Pearl stop and talk with Juniper at The Flowerpot up ahead.

Clyda is talking to Cranky Carl.

"There've been rumors about those two, you know," Pearl says to Delveen when Juniper goes back into the shop to grab some planting seeds for Pearl. They both try to casually look back at Carl and Clyda.

Absolutely nothing is casual about these two women. While their motives tend to be good in nature, it's their mouths that tend to overshadow their actions.

"I'm going home," Mabe announces and continues down Main Street to her two-story Victorian on Berding Street.

Erla takes a deep breath and says, "I'll be there this afternoon!"

Mabe flips her the bird.

"Mabe?" Erla says as she peeks in Mabe's front door.

From where Erla is standing, there are boxes. Boxes full of stuff everywhere. To the left is the living room, and the only thing she can see among the boxes is one small walkway. To the right is the dining room with more boxes.

They're shipping boxes—unopened, purchased items.

Straight ahead is the staircase to the second floor.

"Mabe?" Erla calls out louder this time, shutting the door behind her.

Mabe appears among the boxes. "I told you, I don't need any of your help. Why must you be so persistent and stubborn?" She places her hands on her hips, Erla's pruning shears in her hand.

"Why didn't you tell me?" Erla asks, almost breathless, overwhelmed, looking around at all the boxes.

"Tell you what?"

"About this?" Erla walks to a box and looks inside. Picks up a packet of planting seeds. This particular box is full of them.

"About the planting seeds?" Mabe looks out the living room window, nervous, and back to Erla, trying to avoid her questions. "I didn't know I had to clear it with the warden before I purchased them."

Erla's eyes narrow. "Mabe Muldoon, you know what I'm talking about."

It could be the fact that Erla and Mabe share the same blood as first cousins and grew up tighter than most. But after Mabe married and Erla married, they started their own families all those years ago, and the two seemed to grow apart. Nothing blatantly happened—nothing of significance anyway.

But when John, Mabe's husband, died, Erla checked with Mabe constantly, enough to where Mabe lashed out at Erla. Told her to stop asking if she was okay.

And then the worst thing happened. Mabe's only daughter, Francine, passed away at just about the same time as Conroy Atwood and Tripp Morgan.

A brain aneurysm is what the autopsy said.

Francine didn't have any children. She lived in Spokane, Washington, with her partner, Sarah.

And Mabe had a hard time coming back from that.

It was Francine's death, yes, but it was also Mabe hadn't spoken to her daughter since she came out, which was at her husband's funeral. Poor timing, of course, but Francine didn't want to go on another second, pretending to be something she wasn't.

But what's more is that after Francine came out, she wrote to her mother weekly, sending postcards from Spokane and Mabe never responded.

Francine also called every Sunday to check on her mother, and all Francine received were short, snippy answers. But nevertheless, she still called.

It was on a Sunday that Francine's number popped up on Mabe's home phone. But it wasn't Francine at all. It was Sarah.

"Mrs. Muldoon?" Sarah spoke softly and articulately. "It's Sarah. I … I have some bad news."

"Mabe?" Erla stomps her foot to get her cousin's attention.

"What? I'm not deaf, you know."

"Well, sometimes, you damn well act like it," Erla says. "What's with the boxes, Mabe?"

The truth is, Mabe doesn't know.

One night, while watching the home-shopping channel, Mabe ordered a ten-piece luggage set for a trip she never planned on taking, and the feeling she got when she received the luggage in the mail helped fill the void in her heart a little.

So, each night, Mabe sits down in front of the television, drinks her two beers or four, and tries to heal her heart a piece at a time.

But the more she does it, the more she needs. Now, she has all these things and all these hours on her hands, and her heart still aches.

"I don't know," Mabe finally says.

It's fear maybe that makes Erla's words stiffer, more rigid, more cunning than usual. "This big, beautiful home, and you can't walk through it. What happened?"

Mabe begins to pick at a loose string on her blouse, her eyebrows rising. "It's none of your concern, Erla."

Erla gasps. "None of my concern? Mabe, you're one of the only relatives I have left, aside from my granddaughter, my daughter, and my husband. You have boxes that fill rooms, and you keep telling me you have no idea what happened."

"Death, I suppose," Mabe finally says. "We get to a point in our lives when we just don't give a shit anymore, Erla. And you wouldn't know anything about that, would you? Now, get out."

Erla tips her chin up ever so slightly. Her lips in a thin line. It's the power play she used with her daughter when she told her she was pregnant at eighteen. It's a play that is both commanding and bold. It's one stare.

"You might be the matriarch in your family, Erla, but here, in the Muldoon house, I'm the queen. Now, get the hell out."

Erla didn't expect Mabe's words, nor did she expect Mabe to act like this.

So brash, so brave.

Erla turns to leave, but right before she opens the front door, she says, "I'll be back tomorrow to help clean up. I'd like iced tea with lemon, please."

12

Dancing in the Dark

Colt

I look at Anna, not in the way I look at most women. I never have been able to do that. Not a piece of meat or a piece of ass. She's something far more than that.

She stands, and I lead her to the dance floor, the black boot making for a slight limp.

Cautiously, I pull her to me and try not to allow her scent to take me back. I can't afford that. I can't afford to go on the trail I went down once she stopped all communication. The truth is, I didn't ask then. I didn't ask why the texts had stopped. Why the phone calls had stopped, the e-mails. It's hard to remember what that time was like, right after Conroy died.

Anna's body goes rigid when I place one hand on her lower back and take her other hand in mine.

Anna did say one thing. She texted it.

We need time apart, the text said.

Instead of processing the grief like I should have, I lost myself in sex and basketball and tried to forget all about my life at home. It was easier that way.

"Is this okay with you?" I whisper in her ear.

"Are you asking my head or my heart?" she replies.

I don't even know what song this is, but it's slow, and I like it this way. "Both."

If anything, I just want to be able to repair the friendship between Anna and me.

Even if I have to put it back together piece by piece.

"Then, my answer is no," she says.

I stop moving and stare down at Anna. I can see the conflict in her eyes, but I don't play on people's emotions, especially not Anna's.

Our hands are still unmoving, our bodies barely an inch away.

"Don't you have a girlfriend, Colt?" she whispers.

Jordan.

"This isn't about sex, Anna, or getting what I want from you. It's about you and me. The you and me I used to know." And then it comes. "What happened? Why'd you just cut me off after Conroy died? I needed you, Annie."

Anna takes a step back, her eyes searching mine. "So, this is about you and your needs?" Anna's hands are on her hips now.

"No. It's about me losing the only relationship in my life that ever made sense."

The music plays over us, filling in all the quiet spots, the spots we don't go, for fear of what we'll say to one another. But that was never the case with Anna and me. As bad as the truth hurt, we said it because that was what best friends did. And the truth for us is that we can't go back to that. We can't undo time or the miles that the time put between us. We have to start over. We're older now; we've changed. But in order to get Anna to do that, I need to know why she just walked away in the first place.

"Was it a grief thing?" I ask as the song comes to a close.

Everything was easier when I didn't have to face Anna. It was easier when I lived in LA. But seeing her again has brought up everything from our past, old feelings staring back at me, new feelings, too.

"I don't want to talk about this here, Colt. It's in the past. I'd rather just move on."

I take a step closer to her, making her look me in the eye. "Then, when?"

Anna doesn't back down. She takes a deep breath. The lack of space between us makes her feel uncomfortable.

"Look, Colt, the past is in the past. Let's just move forward, all right?"

I know she's just saying this to shut me up so that I stop asking.

"Hey, Atwood," Tony Puckett says from a group of men off to the left of the bar. "Come settle the score here, would ya?"

I look from Anna to Tony and back to Anna. "Whatever you want, Anna." I search for the right words. "It was easier to be away from this place."

"I know," Anna says.

"Turns out, the heart doesn't forget."

Conflict fills her eyes; it's written on her face. "And memories suck."

I nod, smiling. "Yeah."

Mom drives home. I'm not drunk, but I definitely feel good, and I'm in the back seat with Calder.

He's looking out the window, but he's not looking; he's thinking.

My phone chirps to signify a text message. I pull it from my pocket.

It's from Jordan, and it's a picture of her and her tits with a message.

Jordan: See what you're missing.

I close the text message and shove my phone back in my pocket. I look over at Calder, who's smiling.

"What?"

His eyebrows rise. "Nothing, man."

"What?" I ask again.

"Any man who can shut that shit down clearly has other priorities."

Dad and Mom are in a conversation about a herd of cattle they'd like to buy.

Conroy was always the one to give the tough talks about life. Calder's kind of taken on that role.

"What's that supposed to mean?"

Calder shrugs, back to staring out the window. "Anna is back, and you're back. You lost her once, dumbass."

"It's not that easy."

"Not that easy?"

A sliver of anger shoots through me. "Oh, so you've finally made your move on Camilla?"

Calder freezes. "It's not that easy."

He uses my line.

It's quiet in the back seat for a minute until Calder asks, "Who—who is Jordan anyway?"

My phone chirps again and then once more in my pocket. I leave it put. "Companion."

Calder shoots me a look. "Brother, it's not. Either you're invested in her or you're not."

"With Jordan, it's easy, I guess. It's not complicated. The sex is great. That's it."

"Do you want to marry her?"

No. "Jordan isn't the marrying type."

"Or the *take her home and meet the family* type," Calder offers. "Nothing like Anna," he says loud enough so that I can hear it. "Who wants a woman with her shit together, a woman you've been best friends with since you could talk?"

"If you fucking remember right, she left me, Cal."

"And did you chase after her?"

"Get off my back. Besides, Camilla doesn't seem to have the Atwood brand on her."

"Her husband died. I'm not a vulture."

"Seven years ago he died." And the grief that I've pushed back since Conroy died tickles the back of my throat.

"Boys," Dad says.

Since I can remember, Dad only uses one tone with us boys when he wants us to stop.

Cal and I don't talk the rest of the way home.

Anna looked beautiful tonight. And it wasn't what she was wearing; it's in the way she has no idea how beautiful she is. It's the way she engages in conversation, how she genuinely cares how you're doing when she asks. It's in the way she smiles and laughs and gives a shit where it needs to be given. But the one thing I've always loved about us is the honesty part. No matter what, we always gave it. But things are so different now. It's as if we dance around each other's feelings. Maybe that's lack of time spent together, but we're changed. Grown up. Seven years is a long time.

Mom pulls up to the house just as my phone chirps again.

Thinking it's Jordan, I roll my eyes and retrieve my phone. But it's a text from Tan. He and Rob decided to stay back at the ranch when we went to the party.

There's a picture of a king snake coiled around itself on the porch.

Tan: Dude, you know how I feel about snakes. HELP! It's HUGE!

I text back.

Me: I got it. Just pulled in.

The motion lights on the garage turn on.
I turn to Calder, Mom, and Dad. "Snake on the porch."
"That damn guy keeps coming back." Dad chuckles.
Ed, the snake, seems to spend the evenings on our porch every summer because it's warm. The porch gets direct sun all day long during the summer months, so in the evenings, when the night air becomes cooler, Ed seems to make his way back to the porch for the warm cement.
The front door opens a sliver.
"Oh, Jesus." I hear Tan say, and we start to laugh.
Ed is a king snake, so we keep him around.
Cal looks at me. "I've been saving the Atwood porch for the past seven years while you were gone. Your turn."
"Has Ed gotten bigger?" I ask as we approach the porch.
"Think he was just a baby when he started coming around."
In one swift move, I reach down and pick him up from the back of his head, pinching, and the front door swings open.
"I thought we were going to die!" Tan says.
I'm holding him up. "It's just a king snake, Tan. They're good to have around the ranch. They kill the rattlesnakes."
Dad laughs at Tan, a slow chuckle. "Before you leave here, boy, we will make an Atwood out of you yet."
Tan is white as a sheet.
"City boy." I laugh and walk down to the end of the fence just off the back of the house and let Ed loose.
He'll be back tomorrow as long as it's warm enough.
Once inside, I wash my hands. Dad is sitting at his spot at the dining room table with his small television and his therapy light.
Cal and Mom and Tan are nowhere to be seen.
"How's the ankle?" Dad asks.

"Sore tonight." I join him at the table.

The Andy Griffith Show plays almost inaudibly.

"You were always a glutton for punishment." He smiles. "Cal was showing me the Graham Cracker."

My arms are folded on the table. "The what?"

"Instant Graham?"

"Instagram?" I ask.

"Yeah, I think that's it." He grabs his phone. Slides his reading glasses on. He finally upgraded to an iPhone. Mom and Cal talked him into it.

"Nice smartphone, Dad."

"The flip phone worked just fine. But your mother said I didn't have a choice. The cell phone company didn't sell flip phones anymore." He searches his iPhone for something. "Here it is. You're C.Atwood14?"

I laugh. "Yeah, that's me, Dad."

"You have twenty-four and a half million followers on Insta—whatever this thing is called." My dad looks up from the top of his glasses at me. "That's a lot of people."

One thing my dad and I have always agreed on is basketball. We don't always see eye-to-eye.

"Yeah."

He scrolls through the page. "Who's Jordan?"

Fuck. "A friend."

"You two seem awfully cozy in this picture." He looks up through the top of his glasses again. "How come we haven't met Jordan yet?"

We're friends with benefits or friends of convenience, and I don't want to tell him that because it doesn't fall in line with his *respect others* rule.

I shrug. But he knows the truth, and I know the truth.

"Saw you talking with Annie tonight. Been a long time since I've seen you look like that. Before Conroy anyway."

Dad doesn't bring up Conroy ever. I think it's too hard for him. Maybe Dad feels like he failed as a father, but he didn't. Conroy made a choice that cost his life. So, I don't take his comment lightly.

"What do you mean?" I ask.

Dad looks up from his phone. Sets it on the table. Pushes his fingers against the wrinkle in Mom's tablecloth. "You look at Annie the way your mom looks at me."

Dad isn't one to be sentimental, nor does he drink, so I can't say it's the booze.

"Whatever happened to you guys, you need to get back to where you started."

"How?"

"I suppose that's only for you to answer. You're the one who stole her heart all those years ago."

"No, I didn't."

"What?"

"I didn't steal Annie's heart."

"Well, if that isn't the biggest line of bull I've ever heard, then I ain't a true cowboy."

"What?"

"Son, she might have told you that she didn't love you, but it's pretty obvious to everyone else."

"But she told me she didn't. I tried."

Dad shrugs. "Sometimes, in life, we let a broken heart dictate our future, too afraid to move forward, too scared of rejection. Suppose it's the way the human in us protects the heart. But in the meantime, you still have that Jordan, too, that you ought to figure out first."

"Yeah." I sit back from the table and cross my arms.

It's the episode of *The Andy Griffith Show* where Barney keeps interrupting Andy and his girlfriend, Mary, from having some alone time.

Dad laughs softly as he watches now. His arms cross the same way mine are. Or maybe it's that my arms are made the same way Dad's are.

My ankle starts to throb, and I know it's time to get it elevated.

"Good night, Dad." I stand and push my chair in.

I take his once-big shoulders into my hands. Shoulders that could protect five sons and a wife are now smaller, frailer shoulders. Shoulders meant to work the fence line and move cattle and deliver calves and rope.

"Night, son. Hit the light on your way to bed?"

I nod as I leave the kitchen and shut off the light.

Dad will sit in the dark and watch *Andy* until he falls asleep at the table. I think it's his way of keeping his mind busy, distracted, so he doesn't have to swim with the grief of losing Conroy.

Guess we all process grief a little differently.

13

Just an Old Friend, Annie

Anna

"There's the birthday girl," my mom, Nora, says, as she sets a plate of pancakes in front of me.

Every morning, without fail, she makes pancakes with nine thousand pounds of syrup and butter. She even cuts them for me. And every morning, I try to gently explain that I can't do pancakes, or my jeans won't fit anymore.

"You need more meat on your bones, sweetheart," Mom says from the stove.

With Bones under the table at my feet, I pour a cup of coffee.

Amelia kisses Mom and me before she dashes out the door. "See you tonight," she says as she shuts the front door.

Adam pads down in his boxers and a T-shirt, clearing away the sleep from his eyes.

He stayed in town last night instead of driving back to his place twenty minutes north. He does this a lot.

"Why don't you just move back to Dillon Creek?" I ask.

Adam sits down next to me as Mom slips a plate of pancakes in front of him.

Mom enjoys having all of her kids under one roof—her roof. I can't blame her for it. Even if she makes pancakes with gobs of butter and tries to force-feed me. She was—is— a great mom.

"Why?" Adam asks with a mouthful of pancakes. Clearly, he still likes the pancakes.

"You're here all the time," I say to him as I sip my coffee. I take a small bite of the mound of pancakes.

"No. It's too stuffy. Too small town. And all the bullshit that goes with it? I'd rather leave it when I leave The Steeple at night."

"But, Adam, you're in the bullshit every day."

"No, I'm not."

"Just like I am. We might not be *in it*, in it, but we're still here for it."

"Whatever." He takes another bite of pancakes and a long swig of coffee.

"Go upstairs and get ready for church," Mom says, putting the spatula in the dishwasher.

"Sorry, Mom. I have some paperwork to catch up on at the clinic," I say, taking another sip of coffee, standing. "Then, I've got to run over to my place and check on the renovation."

"Oh," Mom says. It's her subtle guilt trip. The subtle way she has of making you feel like a pile of shit.

Adam and I exchange glances.

We went to church every single Sunday without fail as kids. I think it tainted us for the future. Church was always a dreaded obligation, especially if we'd gotten in trouble that week. Although I still believe and still pray, I don't feel like I need to go to church every Sunday to practice his will or the power of prayer to exercise my faith.

I kiss Mom on the cheek. "Love you. Thank you for the pancakes."

Bones pads behind me.

After the clinic, Bones and I walk over to my place where Tom is almost done with the renovations. He's outside on the phone. Stud—not to be confused with an attractive male, but rather an anchor board in a wall—Tom's dog, is lying on my front porch.

Stud and Bones take off together around the house.

"Hey, Anna," Tom says.

I've always thought Tom to be attractive. Salt-and-pepper hair. Physically fit to meet the demands of the job. Bronze skin from years of work outside. Recently divorced, he got the dog in the settlement. His ex-wife wasn't from here and couldn't handle our way of life. She was a city girl and needed the luxuries that only Macy's and Nordstrom could provide.

"Hey, Tom. How's it going?" I ask, shielding my eyes from the sun, staring up at my two-story house.

"Almost done. A few more days, and you're set to move back in."

"Really?"

"Yeah." He looks up at the house, wiping paint off his hand with a handkerchief.

Stud and Bones come barreling around the corner, barking at each other.

"Mom and Dad's place is nice, but my own place sounds so much better."

Tom walks to his toolbox and closes it up. "I'll be back here Monday morning, but I think, probably Thursday, you can start to move everything back in."

"I can go inside and look around?" I ask.

"Sure. Just don't touch the walls in the kitchen. Fresh paint."

"Thank you, Tom, for everything."

"This was a fun project to work on."

"Well, I'm glad you feel that way."

Tom picks up his toolbox. "Stud, let's go!"

Tom had an older border collie that recently passed away named Nail. Go figure.

Stud goes back around the corner for another lap, Bones at his side.

"Bones, come," I say.

Bones stops what he's doing and sits at my feet while Stud follows his nose around the house once more.

Tom shakes his head. "I'm convinced you're some sort of dog whisperer or something."

Tom shrugs and calls Stud again, but Stud is on a scent.

I'm hesitant at first because every person is different with their own dogs, their training. "Call him with a lighter or more excited tone." Cautiously, I continue to speak, only because I don't want to step on Tom's toes, "Dogs don't want to come if they think they're in trouble. If you reflect light and air into your tone, no matter the circumstances, nine times out of ten, they'll come. They want to come to a happy owner. Right?"

Tom looks at me and then to Stud.

He tries it.

Stud picks his head up, looks at Tom, and trots over to him.

Tom laughs. "Dog whisperer." He shakes his head and waves as Stud loads up in Tom's work truck.

I wave until the truck disappears and then look down at Bones. "Shall we go inside our new house?"

Bones looks up at me with his amber-colored eyes, as if willing himself to understand my words.

"Come on." I tap my leg as we go inside.

The last time I saw the interior of this place, Tom had it ripped down to studs, and now, it looks like a home out of *Better Homes and Gardens.*

When friends come to my home, I want them to feel as though they'd stepped back in time, but I also want it to feel new, not old.

Bones and I walk in through the side door, which opens off the deck to the kitchen.

The countertops are made with a light–colored granite slab, and the kitchen sink is white porcelain. A gray backsplash runs the course of the kitchen while the light fixtures have a farmhouse feel.

The light-gray paint that Tom suggested looks fantastic, I think to myself as I run my hand along the granite.

Dark hardwood floor with thick slats run throughout the house.

I told Tom I wanted the living room, kitchen, and dining room to be open, and somehow, he's made it all work.

One thing though that I've always envisioned with a home as big as this one is having a family to share it with. A husband, a few children.

Bones eases down onto the floor with a comfortable growl. I get down next to him in the furniture-less living room, lying down on the hardwood, placing my hands behind my head.

I reach into the pocket of my heart where Colt's memories are stored. The ones full of tenderness and young love and a hope that took me to North Carolina in the first place ... on the day I found Colt with another woman.

This is a place I try not to visit too often because the memories have somehow turned themselves into fragments of pain that sit and wait for me. But sometimes, I allow myself the luxury of indulgence in my own sorrows.

"You can't look back, Anna," my dad always used to say. "There is nothing you can do to change it."

I came to the conclusion that my father was a seriously flawed man and that I never wanted to follow in his footsteps. I had at one point. I'd wanted to be a medical doctor. But ages twelve and fourteen and sixteen, I loathed him.

When I worked with him at the doctor's office as his understudy, I started to see texts appear on his phone from a person named Sam.

Sam: I can't wait to see you.

Sam: What kind of wine do you like?

When I asked him about it, he said, "Oh, that's just an old friend, Annie."

Bones, at my side, whimpers in splendor, taking a nap right at my hip. He whimpers again, and I slowly stroke his fur.

Dad ingrained in us that lying was never the acceptable option. Ever. So, when I brought my findings to Adam because Amelia was just a toddler at the time, he brushed them off, too.

"Do you know a Sam?" I asked Adam.

He shook his head. "Don't be so nosy, Anna. Dad and Mom are fine."

It was true—or so it seemed. Sure, they lived almost separate lives. Mom was active in everything in Dillon Creek—from the play productions at Dillon Creek Repertory Theater to the Parent Teacher Organization to Dillon Creek Chamber of Commerce. Mom was busy, and Dad was busy with his practice. He was well known as an intelligent doctor, but more as a great listener. His patients always came first—even sometimes before his family. He loved his work, and we loved him. Of course he loved us, but when his pager or his phone went off, he would, too.

"Hello?" a voice echoes through the door just off the kitchen, making me jump.

Bones scrambles to his feet and barks once, but we quickly realize who it is, so he falls in a heap at my side again.

"In the living room. On the floor."

Tess shuts the door behind her. "Ran into Tom at Dillon Creek Pizza and he said you were here. So, I brought wine and pizza and salad, so we can commemorate this moment."

I sit up and smile and sit cross-legged. "I don't have plates or cups or napkins."

"Well, lucky for us, I brought everything. We can eat straight out of the box and drink out of the bottle." Tess sits down across from me.

I open the pizza box, and it's our favorite—Hot Cowgirl, which includes sausage and jalapeños.

While she opens the wine with a corkscrew from her keychain, I put a slice for Tess on the box in front of her, and I take a slice for myself.

"This place looks amazing." Tess looks around us. "Tom did an outstanding job."

"Do you know he's single?" I say, my eyebrows dancing up and down. "School teacher, general contractor—they kind of go hand in hand, right?"

Tess makes a face and chews her pizza.

"So good," I say with a mouthful of food.

It's quiet.

"So, have you heard from Colt?"

I stop chewing. "No. Why?"

Tess stops chewing. "I don't know. Why not?"

"First of all, he's got a girlfriend. Second of all, just because we're both in town at the same time doesn't mean we're just supposed to fall in love and get married and make babies, Tess, if that's what you're thinking." I take another bite of pizza, attempting to distract myself.

Bones is awake now, waiting for a morsel of anything to drop from our pizza.

Tess stops and laughs out loud. Takes a sip of wine from the bottle and stares back at me. "That's not what I was insinuating at all. I just asked if you'd talked." She goes to take another bite but stops. "Is that what you want to happen?"

I throw a piece of sausage at her. My face turns bright pink; I can feel the warmth. Finally, I say, "The timing has never been right for us."

Tess shakes her head. "No, the timing was right a lot of times; you were just scared."

I mull on this for a moment and look out the front window. Dusk is preparing its descent, settling in trees, the streets.

"How's Nathaniel?" I ask.

Nathaniel is the guy Tess met online. They have yet to meet in person. I think Tess is stalling because she has had a few failed online attempts, and her biggest attempt is trying to get over Casey Atwood.

Casey is riding bulls for the PBR—Professional Bull Riders. When he left right after Conroy died, he didn't so much as give her a second glance or a wave.

"He wants to meet." She rolls her eyes.

"What's so wrong with that, Tess?" I take a sip of wine from the bottle and set it back down between us.

She shrugs. Chews her pizza and stares back at me.

"Meet him in Santa Rosa. I'll go with you if you want, and I'll stay back at the hotel. Just so you're not alone."

"I don't know."

"What's your pro and con list?"

"Pro list. He's tall. He has a job that doesn't require travel. He wears glasses. He's smart, and his grammar is excellent. And he works out."

"I'm confused. Why are you waiting? There's no history between you two. You're single. He's single. He's not from Dillon."

"What if he's not up to my expectations? What if I spend the whole time comparing him to Casey?"

"But you aren't even giving yourself a chance to do that, Tess."

Tess pauses mid-bite. Cocks her head to the right. "Con list. He participates in online dating."

"So do you."

"He lives in Santa Rosa."

"A con? Really?"

"You're right. Moving that to the pro side. His sense of humor is a little quirky."

"And that's a problem? Have you talked with him?"

"Well, no. Just through messages."

"Um, so you haven't spoken to him, so really, there's no true assessment of his sense of humor if you haven't had a conversation with the guy."

"Fine."

"Call him."

Tess takes the bottle to her mouth and gulps down two swallows, staring back at me. Then, she sets the bottle down and wipes her mouth with the napkin. "Let's make a deal. I call Nathaniel, and you attempt to give Colt a chance."

I laugh. "No."

"What are you so scared of with him, Anna? What is it with him? You can give me advice all day long, but when it comes to Colt and you, it's like you're not having it."

"Tess, I need to move on. I know people in this town have a hard time understanding that we're not meant to be. And I get it; I always believed it. But we're just two people going in two different directions."

"And, yet, when you look at him, the whole world disappears around you."

"Does not." I gawk.

"Does to. Ask Adam."

I finish my piece of pizza and think on her words. I throw Bones a piece of sausage, and he catches it in his mouth.

"You're the center of Bones's life. And you're the center of Colt's life. Come on; it's always been that way. You know that."

"We haven't really spoken in years, Tess."

"And whose fault is that?"

"Shut up. Eat your pizza."

My phone rings. It's Laurel's number.

"Hey, Laurel."

"Hi, Anna." It's not Laurel; it's Colt.

"Tupac's limping pretty bad. He won't let anyone come near him. And ... and I'm not sure what to do."

"Why'd you call from your mom's phone?"

"Because I was afraid you wouldn't answer if I called from mine."

This one stings all the way up my spine. *Is he right?*

"You haven't taken any of my calls since you were supposed to take the trip out to see me. Remember?"

His words meet my heart. He's right.

"Meet me down at the clinic as quickly as you can."

"Thank you."

And he hangs up.

Colt is carrying Tupac.

Bones goes running up to Colt, concerned for the welfare of his best friend. He whines at Colt's feet.

"Come on; let's take a look." I lead him into an exam room.

Colt gently sets his dog down on the steel table. Tupac whines when he does.

"It's okay, boy. Let's see what's going on with you." I feel my voice settle in his bones.

His body is still tight with pain, but I know he trusts me and knows my voice.

"Left leg or shoulder—I'm not sure." Colt places his hands on his hips.

Barely, I touch Tupac's shoulder, and he growls.

I look up at Colt. "I'm going to have to sedate him. I need to get some X-rays."

Bones is in the corner of the exam room, sitting at attention, his ears perked, his eyes wide.

"It's okay, buddy."

I walk to the counter and grab a sedation needle and the tranquilizer from the glass cabinet.

"Come over here and put your face next to his, okay? Let him know he's safe and that you're here."

Colt does what I asked, and as he's doing it, I ease the needle in.

"Good boy, Tupac."

Tupac slowly closes his eyes.

I turn on The Fray and begin Tupac's quick procedure by cutting up the area just above the shoulder.

Thank God I only took one sip of wine, I think to myself.

I feel Colt's eyes watching me.

Through my mask, I say, "You're staring at me."

"I'm not sure what else to look at, Annie. You're operating on my dog to repair the dislocated shoulder."

"Where are you going next year?" I ask, trying to detour his mind from what I'm doing to Tupac right now. "Will you stay with LA?"

He smiles, and I try not to. "So, you have been listening to the news."

I shrug. "Sometimes. Occasionally."

I'm lying.

When he was drafted from North Carolina, I was glued to the television set. And when he signed with LA, I wanted to send him a congratulatory text. But I couldn't. That night kept flashing in my eyes.

"Honestly, Annie, I have no idea. But I'm worried about this injury, my Achilles." He smiles. "You're the only person I've told that to."

Achilles tendon tears can be career-ending. Top-notch athletes don't always bounce back.

"I'm using a band of skin to secure the shoulder joint to the humerus bone." I try to draw him out of the fear.

I didn't have to ask Colt if he wanted to elect to do the surgery because of Tupac's advanced age. He wanted it done, and so did I. Not that my opinion matters, but I think it does to Colt.

Bones walks over to Colt and sits at his feet.

"Traitor," I say to Bones and smile in my mask.

I know Bones isn't a traitor, but I know he senses worry from Colt, and he's trying to make him feel better.

I knew Bones would fall in love with Colt.

Just like I had all those years ago.

I close up Tupac with stitches.

I take off my gloves and my mask. "He'll be groggy when he wakes up." I look up at the clock, and it's almost nine p.m. "I'll keep him overnight for observation." I throw my gloves in the trash. "Go home and get some rest."

Colt slips his hands in his pockets. "I'm staying, too."

"Suit yourself."

14

Kicked in the Ribs

Anna: Age Sixteen

"**A**re you hurt?" Colt asked me as my body felt my breath come back.

I couldn't muster up any words since the searing pain in my ribs began. I gasped.

I could see the fear in Colt's eyes, so I reached up and touched his arm. "My ribs. Hurt. Like a son of a bitch."

Carefully, Colt lifted my shirt, and in that moment, even through the excruciating pain, I hoped my stomach looked all right—and not because of where Tank, the horse, had kicked me, but because of my jeans being too tight, which made red marks across my stomach.

But Colt didn't care. He was more concerned about where Tank had kicked me.

Colt pulled out his phone. "I'm calling your dad."

"No," I said and winced in pain when I went to reach for it. "He's got patients to see today. A horse kicked me, Colt. I'm not dying. Just help me up."

Colt reached his hand under my back. The hot pain spread, and the ache deepened as he moved me up to a sitting position.

I cried out.

"I'm sorry, Anna."

"Keep going," I said.

"Should I go get the four-wheeler?"

"No. I've got this."

The visceral ache deepened, and I bit my lip so hard to keep from screaming that it began to bleed. I could taste copper.

Every moment took my breath away. The sharp agony became a stabbing pain, and that was when I thought I should go get checked out.

It was then that Conroy rode up on Little Mermaid, his horse, and all I could see was the silhouette of a tall cowboy, like the Marlboro Man, except handsomer and not as old.

"What happened?" He looked at Colt.

"Tank nailed her right in the stomach."

The pain came back, and I fell into Colt and squeezed the fabric of his shirt. His arm slid around me, and I heard a murmur of voices, the pain shooting from my head to my toes.

Colt's scent—Irish Spring and clean laundry—helped me focus on something different, and it eased the pain.

Conroy approached us with horse wrap, and Colt lifted my shirt.

I didn't care. I just wanted the pain to stop. And there were times it faded, relented to a dull ache, but it didn't last long.

I leaned into Colt as Conroy wrapped my middle with the horse wrap, and both brothers walked me back to the Atwood house.

"You scared the living shit outta me today, Annie." Colt sat down next to my bed in my room.

The painkillers had taken effect, loosening some of my inhibitions.

Colt looked handsome. He'd always been handsome. His long, lean legs and how they eased into Wranglers. His scent and the stubble that he was beginning to get if he didn't shave for a day or so. His sun-kissed face. Colt had Laurel's eyes but Daryl's facial structure.

His button-up shirt exposed his broad chest only a little, and when he took off his cowboy hat and set it on my bedpost, a scorching awareness made its way like pooling water through my body.

Mrs. Hattie, who taught sex education in the sixth grade, would have said it was hormones, but Colt Atwood was in my heart in ways that most other people had never reached. I wasn't sure what Mrs. Hattie would have said about that, but I was almost certain she'd had the same sensation when she was caught with Mr. Livingston in the janitor's closet. So, maybe it was a mix of hormones and love—and painkillers.

I put my hand on his arm. Colt had always had nice arms—defined, bigger than most guys his age due to gym workouts in the winter and ranch work in the spring and baling hay in the summer.

My thumb gently slid over his arm, and I saw the fear in his eyes almost disappear.

"Thank you for today." My voice was gravelly from the miracle drugs.

"What did the X-rays say?" He made a bold move and took my fingers into his.

My stomach grew with butterflies, and my body filled with fire.

"Two broken ribs. Dad said I need to rest."

But my brain wasn't focused on what I'd said. It was the fact that my hand was in Colt's.

He stared at me, and I stared at him.

Without inhibitions—*thank you, painkillers*—I moved my hand to his chest.

Is his heart beating like mine right now? I asked myself.

When my fingertips reached his heart, I could feel his beats matched mine, and that moment was the first of many moments that I knew if Colt Atwood was anywhere, I wanted to be right by his side.

"I don't know how you have this control over me, Anna," he whispered as his other hand took mine.

I wanted him to kiss me.

I'd wanted him to kiss me since the time I realized that boys were a thing.

Like the first time my mom had tried to have *the birds and the bees* talk, which failed miserably.

"God made a man and a woman fit together."

"How?" I asked.

But when she said penis and vagina, I crumbled into a ball of embarrassment.

I wondered why she'd opened with that line. Out of all the lines in *the birds and the bees* talk that parents gave their children, why'd she start with that one?

I hadn't bought it anyway. Because I'd believed, even from a young age, that all couples didn't always fit together like that and that the heart wanted what the heart wanted.

"Come here," I whispered to Colt, unable to lean in, unable to move my core.

Slowly, he moved forward, closer to my body, need in his eyes. I questioned if the need I saw in his eyes was a reflection of my need for him.

Closer he moved.

Closer.

Closer.

So close, I felt his breath against my lips, and my body wanted to explode.

But at the last minute, he moved his head and lightly kissed me on the cheek instead.

It was the kind of kiss that was slow and meaningful, and I felt it in my bones.

"You might think you want me to kiss you for the first time, Anna, but I can't. Not when I know you've taken pain medication. I want our first kiss to be something special, like when Lane kissed Kellie."

8 Seconds had always been Colt's favorite movie.

I understood. I was a bit embarrassed, but I understood.

Colt took his hand and placed it half on my cheek and half on my neck as he looked in my eyes. He was the only one who ever really understood me, aside from Adam, my older brother. Although Adam, too, was going through a phase that Dad didn't agree with.

The pot phase.

But I saw the conflict that danced in Colt's eyes. I knew he wanted to kiss me more than he wanted to breathe. I also knew he'd always put my heart first. That was why we made better friends than we did boyfriend and girlfriend. I knew I couldn't lose him if something were to happen between us. If one of us were to walk away or make a bad choice.

I looked down to Colt's hand, which was now on my thigh. A thin sheet separated our skin.

What I wanted to tell Colt was that I loved him, too, that I needed him, and that scared the living hell out of me. So, instead of saying that, I asked him about his conversation with Weston Matthews, the retired NBA coach who had invited Colt to be part of the Kobe Bryant Basketball Camp and who'd become a quick friend of the Atwood family. Somehow, he'd seen Colt playing down in Los Angeles with his travel basketball squad team.

And as far as Colt and I were concerned, Weston was the best coach to ever coach the game of basketball—aside from the legendary John Wooden, of course.

Before Colt answered me, he looked back toward my bedroom door. Then, he stood, walked to the door, and closed it so that only a sliver of light shone in from the hallway.

He walked back and sat down.

"He thinks I can play with University of North Carolina, Annie." Colt played with his hands, leaned back in his chair, and then looked up at me. "Say something."

I wanted to cry—not because North Carolina was all the way on the other side of the United States, but because this was Colt's dream, and he was making it happen. They'd be happy tears.

"He said that I need to make sure I score at least a thirteen hundred because of my grade point average, but he said, with the skill set I have, he thinks I can go on to the NBA, Annie."

My smile could not be contained. Colt had worked so hard to get to where he was. Countless hours spent on the court, traveling down to Sacramento, San Francisco, and Los Angeles to compete with the best of the best.

"You deserve all of this, Colt."

He was quiet.

"What did your parents say?" I asked.

"You know my dad. He leaned on the bar as Weston told us, moved his tongue from side to side, and said, 'What's this bill going to cost me, Wes?' They talked about numbers, living expenses, dorm rooms, and financial aid, but Weston thinks I can go on a full ride."

"Shut the front door."

Colt slowly shook his head. "Crazy, right?"

"No, it's not. Not at all, Colt."

"Do your brothers know?"

Colt nodded. "All of them, except for Cash. Who the hell knows where he was?"

Cash had always been the misfit. He could fight a bull like nobody's business—so well in fact that he was ranked top in the nation. He'd held top bullfighter in the state of California last year, and he was on track to go professional with it. But a lot of times, he was just reckless.

All of a sudden, my eyes grew heavy. Tired.

"Get some rest, okay?" Colt said.

"I'm really proud of you," I whispered as my head started to give way with sleep.

Colt stood, leaned over, and kissed my forehead. "Need anything before I go?"

"No, I'm good."

"Sorry about Tank," he said.

"Wasn't his fault."

He smiled down at me. "Always sticking up for the animals. Good night, Annie."

"Good night, Colt."

And with that, he shut the light off to my room as he walked out the door.

15

Church Talk

"Mabe didn't make it to church again. She feeling all right?" Pearl asks the group of Bugs sitting at a window seat of The Rusty Nail.

Delveen takes a bite of her salad, this time made with an abundance of cucumbers that she asked for.

"She's all right," Erla says, staring out the window, taking a sip of her black coffee and half a packet of Splenda.

"Should we take her a card or dinner or something, Erla? Maybe pay her a visit," Delveen says.

"No." Erla looks back to the group.

Clyda pipes in, "I really like what Pastor Mike had to say about breathing in the Lord and giving all my troubles to him. Sometimes, I forget to turn all that shit over."

Clyda has no problem using *shit* and the Lord's name in one sentence.

Her take on God and the Bible is quite unconventional, but he works in her life, and that's what's important, Erla thinks to herself.

She also makes a mental note to thank her friend for diverting the subject.

Pearl and Delveen are great when it comes to planning events, raising money, and whatnot, but when it comes to secrets, the whole town's talking after Pearl and Delveen find out.

"Didn't Colt and Anna look so beautiful, dancing together at the party last weekend?" Clyda says.

"Didn't they though?" Pearl says, setting down her water glass.

Delveen says, "Why those two never got married is just a travesty, if you ask me."

"To be young and in love again." Pearl smiles.

"Sorry I'm late." Mabe carefully grabs a chair from the empty table next to them. She slides the chair between Erla and Pearl.

"We were worried about you." Delveen pushes her salad aside and sets her elbows on the table. "Feeling okay?"

"If I wasn't, I sure as hell wouldn't tell you," Mabe says.

Mabe has never been able to sugarcoat anything. Not even a shitshow that's gone really wrong.

Delveen shrugs.

"I'll take a beer, Merry," Mabe says when Merry walks over to get Mabe's order.

"Sure thing."

Erla noticed Mabe's drinking issue when she lost her daughter. But Erla shrugged it off as grief. Mabe didn't necessarily go out in public and drink, but she sure shopped at Wilson's Grocery to fulfill the hole in her heart.

Nevertheless, it doesn't stop Merry from pouring an O'Doul's for Mabe into a pilsner.

Merry walks back to the table. "Here you are, Mabe."

"Thank you, Merry."

"Would you like anything to eat?" Merry asks Mabe.

"What's the soup today?"

"Tomato basil."

"Perfect. I'll take a cup of that." Mabe takes a sip of her fake beer and pays no mind to the difference.

"As I was saying, Clyda, Colt ought to court Anna," Delveen says.

Clyda sets down her coffee. Thinks on this. "God gave Anna and Colt great minds to do their own thinking. And your opinion doesn't count, Delveen."

"No, remember, he has a girlfriend," Delveen says without consideration as to what Clyda just said, which is no surprise to the group.

"Well, I'd say that other woman ought to throw the white flag," Pearl says and then takes a sip of her coffee.

"Erla, what do you think?" Delveen asks, but Erla is looking at Mabe.

"What?" Erla asks.

"What did you think of Colt and Anna?"

"Wonderful. But he's got a girlfriend," Erla says.

"Yes, we've already clarified this, but when two souls are destined to be together, I'd say the good Lord makes it happen." Pearl checks the time on her watch. "Oh, I need to run. My program is coming on in six minutes."

"Don't you have a DVR?" Merry asks, setting down Mabe's soup along with the tab.

"A what?" Pearl says, throwing down some cash.

Merry smiles and rests her hand on the back of Mabe's chair. "A DVR. A digital video recorder."

"A what?" Pearl is clearly confused.

"Never mind." Merry smiles. "You ladies have a wonderful day."

Delveen and Clyda stand after putting their cash in.

They all exchange good-byes.

This leaves Erla and Mabe at the table alone.

The tension is felt.

"Why didn't you answer the door when I came over last week to help you?" Erla asks.

Mabe puts down her soupspoon, wipes her mouth with her napkin, and takes a sip of beer. "I told you, I didn't need your help."

"Mabe, what are you going to do? You have boxes everywhere."

"I got myself into this mess; I'll get myself out."

Erla places her fist against her mouth, willing herself to use kind words. "Mabe Muldoon, you are a stubborn old woman."

"Well, I guess that makes two of us." Mabe takes another slurp of soup.

Erla gets her tail feathers in a bunch, scoots herself away from the table, and stands. "If I didn't know better, Mabe, I'd say you want to die an old, haggard gypsy woman who doesn't give a lick about anyone else."

"I suppose you'd be right."

"Good riddance," Erla says in a huff.

And with that, Erla Brockmeyer storms out of The Rusty Nail but immediately realizes she forgot to pay for her portion of the meal. With a stomp of her foot, she looks up at the good heavens and asks God, *Why?* She's not expecting an answer, of course. She turns on her heel and marches back into The Rusty Nail to the table where Mabe is finishing her soup.

Erla throws down a twenty.

Mabe glances down at it and then up at her cousin. "I could have covered it."

A calmness comes over Erla; maybe it's God or the Holy Spirit—who the hell knows? She says quietly, "No, just spend your money on more crap, Mabe. More crap to fill your living room, your hallways, your rooms." She touches her cousin's shoulder and walks out of The Rusty Nail.

Flowers have always helped Erla, and planting them has always been her therapy. She stops by The Flowerpot, and Juniper Jones is out front.

"Beautiful morning, Erla, isn't it?"

Juniper's free spirit takes some of the tension from Erla's shoulders. "Good morning, Juniper. Indeed it is."

Juniper's glasses sit on the bridge of her nose—not reading glasses, but round, thick glasses that have been a fixture on her face since she was just a girl. Her mother, Lavender, was placed in a home for which we—those who are over the age of sixty-five—do not mention. But it's a place where men and women our age go to die because we just can't think like we used to. Lavender owned The Flowerpot before Juniper took over the shop about five years ago, and she's done a fantastic job. In fact, Juniper has added a debit card system, whereas Lavender only accepted cash and local checks.

"Listen, the Johnny Jump Ups have come in, but I haven't had time to put them out yet. Would you like a package, Erla?"

Erla doesn't squeal too often. In fact, as of late, it's been hard for her to get excited about anything. With Don, her husband, being so forgetful lately, and her cousin Mabe becoming a loon, it's difficult for Erla to focus on much of anything these days. But Johnny Jump Ups do excite her. It excites her so much that she almost does squeal.

"I'd love a package, Juniper."

Juniper holds a finger up, soil underneath her fingernail, as always. Erla is almost certain that Juniper's hands have been stained with soil since she was just a girl. "Just one minute. I'll run to the back to get you some. But don't tell Pearl yet, all right? You know how she gets about her flowers."

Erla nods and smiles. "Your secret is safe with me."

Juniper returns from the back of the shop as Erla is looking through some of the refrigerated flower arrangements.

Erla grabs some cash from her wallet. "How much do I owe you?"

"Ninety-seven cents."

Erla stops. Looks up at Juniper from in front of the counter. "That's it?"

"It's the early-bird special and your lucky day." Juniper smiles, and her eyes disappear behind the glasses. Her cheeks, her skin are the color of a peach.

"You're sure?" Erla asks.

"I'm sure." Juniper nods. "Just take a picture of it when it blooms and send it my way. You have a way with flowers, Erla."

Erla does pride herself on her flowers. She smiles. "I sure will." Erla turns to leave. "Good-bye, Juniper. Thank you. Give your mother my best."

"Will do."

Erla stops by the post office to check her mail before she goes home. In the PO box, she finds a letter from her granddaughter, Scarlet, and gleams with joy.

"Don?" Erla calls from the back door when she arrives home.

A sudden wake of fear enters her bones as her word is met with silence.

"Don?" she calls again, setting down the mail and the Johnny Jump Ups on the dining room table.

Erla walks into the kitchen.

The back door shuts.

"Don?"

Her husband of fifty-four years looks up from his hands. "Oh, hello, dear. I was wondering where you'd gone."

Anxiousness begins to fester in the pit of Erla's stomach. You see, they just had the conversation right after church that she was going to lunch with the girls and that she'd meet Don at home at noon sharp.

Erla looks at her watch. "It's noon, Don. Remember we had this conversation at church before you drove the car home? That I'd meet you at home?"

"Oh, yes. That's right." Don sets the tree trimmer down on the kitchen counter.

Erla knows he didn't recall. But Don says things just to keep his wife from worrying.

"How was church?"

The color drains from Erla's face. She can feel it, and the fear he just tried to subside begins to boil in her stomach.

"It was fine." She doesn't correct him or remind him that he was there, sitting next to her, but she does say, "You made plans to help Bo at the dairy on Tuesday?"

"I did?"

"Mmhmm." Erla busies herself with washing two small forks in the sink.

"I'll give him a call."

For fifty-four years, Don Brockmeyer has been a wonderful husband, father, and grandfather. A retired engineer, from Brockmeyer Engineering and sold the firm in Eureka ten years ago. But he still helps out old friends when they have questions, and that's what Bo asked about at church this morning. A structure question about one of his milking barns.

One of the things that drew Erla to Don was his quick wit and his smarts. Erla's mother, Gloria, advised her daughter not to marry the Brockmeyer boy, but she did it anyway at the age of eighteen. It caused a rift between her mother and her, but the heart wants what the heart wants.

It wasn't until Gloria was on her deathbed that she finally acknowledged that Erla was right and that she'd made the right decision in marrying the Brockmeyer boy.

Unfortunately, there was a loss of ten years where Erla and her mother had barely spoken, but she always kept in close contact with her father until his passing.

Don kisses his wife on the head. A tall man, he's always been able to wrap her up in his arms and make her feel safe. And this day is no different.

"I don't know what I'd do without you, Erla."

"Well," Erla jokes, "for one, you wouldn't eat vegetables of any sort." She looks up into her husband's piercing blue eyes.

Erla feels Don's arm start to twitch, and she knows it's time to let go. A symptom of Parkinson's.

"Come on, young man. I'll make you some lunch."

Erla kisses her husband on the cheek, and he lets go.

"Did you talk to Mabe?" he asks.

"No, not really."

And her fear is swept away, and hope comes knocking. She loves when he remembers.

When Erla got home last week, she was in quite the headspace, and so she told Don what had happened with Mabe. This conversation must have made a big impact on him for him to retain.

"She came to lunch late, and all the girls were there, so it was just not the time to have the conversation."

"You went to lunch today?" Don asks.

Her chest begins to ache, and hope walks out the door. Erla looks away, so Don doesn't see the tears that are beginning to form in her eyes.

"What kind of sandwich would you like?" Erla asks as she grabs the bread.

Erla was a stay-at-home mother to their daughter, Devon, and those were the best years of her life. But Devon was the type of girl who needed adventure. Dillon Creek was just too small for their audacious little girl, and Erla and Don both knew there would come a day when Devon would gather her things and leave. So, when their daughter was accepted to a university in New York, she left and never looked back.

Of course, Devon used to come back to visit on holidays, and Scarlet—their sweet, beautiful granddaughter—would come and stay the summers with her and Don. But it's been quite some time since they've seen Scarlet, and this reminds Erla of the letter they received in the mail today.

"There's a letter from Scarlet on the dining room table."

Don's eyes light up as he walks into the dining room, grabs the mail, and brings it to the kitchen counter as Erla makes his lunch.

Erla and Don don't get much mail nowadays. Even their junk mail has grown slim, and Erla is quite all right with that.

Don grabs the letter opener and opens the envelope from Scarlet.

When Scarlet was little, she'd send Erla and Don homemade cards that would make Don tear up. He's saved every single one, and he keeps them in his roll-top desk in his office.

Dear Grandpa and Grandma,

It's been a long time since I've spent time with you two. I know how much you enjoy letters. I've missed you dearly, and every time I sit down to try to plan a trip back to Dillon Creek, I'm interrupted by an e-mail or a text. But those are all excuses.

So, I'm not quite sure how to start this letter, but I'll try my best.

Hank and I have decided to divorce. We're just on two separate paths, career-wise, and we both think it's for the best.

Mom took a fall the other day, which landed her in the emergency room. Just some bumps and bruises, but she's doing okay. I don't want you to worry about her. I know she's being difficult, but please know that she loves you very much. You did the best you could with her, and I know that because you were amazing with me. She landed another gig in South Africa to take some photos for National Geographic, and I'm thinking I might have to go with her, just in case, you know.

So, in the event that something were to happen to us, all of my information is in a safety deposit box at First Bank in Manhattan, New York. You'll have all the information you'll need.

How's Millie? Give her a big hug for me.

Love you both.

Love,

Scarlet

Don looks up from the letter, worry and concern coloring his face.

They haven't spoken to their daughter in four years. Not by their own decision. Erla and Don have placed several calls, letters, cards, notes to her, but they've never been returned.

The communication just stopped after her last trip home to Dillon Creek.

"I'm going to call Scarlet," Don says quietly, leaving the letter on the counter as he walks away to get the phone.

16

Still Dancing

Colt

Of course I'll suit myself.

Anna tosses me a blanket. "I have two couches in my office."

Tupac is in a kennel and resting comfortably.

"Thank you, Annie," I say. "For everything."

Anna grabs some sort of monitoring device and pushes a few buttons. "This will alert me if Tupac is in pain or if something is wrong."

I lean down against the kennel. "I'll see you in the morning, buddy."

But Bones won't leave his side.

"He's a good dog, Annie."

"He's an Atwood Aussie; of course he's a good dog." She pauses. "He likes you."

Bones looks up at me and then to Anna.

She bends down and gives him a kiss on his forehead. "Keep watch on your buddy, okay?" I hear her whisper into his ear.

As we exit the recovery room, she turns off the light, leaving a small lamp on in the corner of the room.

Her office is the last door on the right.

"I'll take the love seat; you take the big one," she says.

"Are you sure?" I ask.

"No, I'll take the big couch, and you can try to fit on the love seat. Let's mix things up a bit." Anna gives me a look. "Of course I'm sure. Unless you can squeeze all six feet nine inches of you onto that tiny, little couch—which I'd love to see you try—you can have the big couch."

Anna hits the lights, and it turns dark, aside from the desk lamp. I sit down on the big couch. I hear her sit down on the love seat and situate herself. I take off my boot. I should sleep with the damn thing on, but it got old after a while.

She takes a deep breath. It's as if I can feel it.

"Remember when we were kids and you made me hold a king snake that you'd found in the barn?"

I smile. "Yeah."

"Thank you."

"Why?"

"It made me realize that I'm far more capable than I realize."

"Is there something you think you can't do?" I trace her silhouette in the dark.

"Yeah."

"What's that?"

"You."

I hear the word. One simple word. It wouldn't matter if Jordan had said this to me or a woman I'd just had sex with. But it's coming from Anna. The only woman I am capable of loving or being in love with.

Instead of asking why, I ask, "What happened?"

She knows what I'm talking about.

A long silence follows.

But I'm patient—not because I have to be, but because I need to be.

"Does it matter now?" she asks into the stillness. "It's been seven years, Colt."

"It does matter, Annie. When you say that it's me that you're incapable of, then you owe an explanation." I feel my heart begin to race against my chest, making it impossible for me to focus on anything but her words.

"I went back to North Carolina, Colt. Right after Conroy died, like I'd promised. I was on my way to you. But when I got there, everything changed."

I sit up. Stare back at her in the darkness as she lies there and tells me the story.

"I went to your dorm room. And I thought it was odd that you hadn't answered my texts. I blamed it on the grief. I convinced myself that all you needed was me, and once I was there, everything would be okay."

During that time, right after Conroy's death, the following year and a half to two years, was really hazy. I did things I'm not proud of, that my dad wouldn't be proud of. But I did things on impulse, trying to fix the holes in my body where the wind blew through, mainly from losing my brother.

"I'd been there to visit when you moved into the dorms, so I knew where your room was. The door was unlocked. I was so excited to see you, Colt," she whispers. "I was ready to tell you that I was in love with you and that I knew we were supposed to be together. After all those years, I knew you were the one." She looks at the monitor—not because she has to, but because of the pain she's reliving right now in telling me this story.

"I opened the door, and your back was to me. But you … you were leaning into the wall. Your muscles contracted, and it made my cheeks warm. My entire body warm. And then I realized what I was watching, only when I heard a woman call out from underneath you."

The vomit builds from my stomach at the thought of Annie watching me with another woman. The words don't come to me.

"We weren't together, Colt. Don't worry; you don't owe me anything."

But still, the words don't come. My stomach turns, and I can't breathe. I can't deny any of this. I vaguely remember it, but I don't even remember who the woman was.

This memory is what Anna has been holding on to for the past seven years?

"Anna …" I manage and then swallow, praying the vomit doesn't see the light of day.

But she doesn't say anything for a moment.

Then, she says, "I was finally ready to tell you all the things I'd been thinking about. How I wanted to make love to you again. How it felt to be completely in love with you, Colt Atwood. I wanted to know what you felt like from the inside again. What your mouth felt like against my breasts. All of it."

Jesus Christ. My head spins as I try to come to grips with everything. I swallow hard. "Anna … Anna, if I had known you were coming all that way … I would never—"

"That's just it, Colt. If you had known I was coming, then what? You wouldn't have done that? We weren't together. Don't you see? I never, ever want you to hold back from what you want versus what you feel is right."

"Anna." My fingers start to tingle, and my stomach turns into a million fucking knots.

I want to go to her, touch her. Take back those memories that I gave to her. So, I stand and carefully walk without my boot to the love seat and sit down next to her.

I don't care what it takes. I want her back.

I put my hand on her thigh and pull it to me. Then, I tug her body on top of mine, and she sucks in a sharp breath.

This isn't right. I know it. And yet … I can't stop. But there are no words I can say in this moment to take away what she's feeling. Anna said she wanted to know what I felt like again.

She doesn't resist me either, and it's dark, so I can't see the trepidation in her eyes or the fear or the love, and I'm glad. So, I put her mouth to mine, and push my hands to her cheeks, staking my claim, exploring her with my tongue. I hear a whimper. But she doesn't pull away. My hands move from the back of her neck to her bra, and I unclasp it with a simple flick.

I pull it off from under her T-shirt after removing one strap from her shoulder at a time, and I toss it to the floor.

She breaks our kiss, panting. Looking down at me, she pulls off her shirt, and I stare at her perfect, topless body in front of me.

I've dreamed about this day since that night. Her full breasts, her nipples hard, waiting for my mouth, the mouth she asked for. I take her hips in my hands and try my best not to squeeze too tight. I move her where she's sitting directly on top of me, feeling all of me.

Before I kiss her breasts, I run my hands over them, gently at first but harder the second time. I want to know if they feel the same or different. We made love the night before we left for college, the same night Conroy and Tripp were killed.

Leaning forward slightly, I put my mouth around her nipple, take it between my teeth, and tug lightly.

My hands are shaking; she's the only woman who could ever do this to me. She's familiar and somehow changed and so beautiful as I watch her watching me.

This time, Anna reaches down and pulls off my shirt.

I've been trained to be a machine. To work hard and never settle for less than the best.

"Settle for iconic," is what Coach Matthews said.

And so I strive for it but with my body and on the court.

I pull away from her and sit back and watch her, my hands running the length of her chest and stomach. I realize in this moment that this won't go any further. It can't. I won't fucking let it. We won't make love on a couch in her office. The next time we make love, we'll be surrounded by time and space and enough endurance to be intimate for hours.

"What?" she whispers in the darkness.

"Nothing." I take her hips in my hands and hold her to me, feeling her bare chest against mine.

Everything about Anna feels so right to the core of my existence.

It felt right after Conroy died.

It felt right the morning after.

It's never felt quite right with anyone else.

"Can I tell you a secret, Colt? Something I've never told anyone?" she whispers.

"Tell me."

"As I watched you have sex with that other woman, I couldn't help but wish you were pushing into me. I couldn't help but want to be the girl causing the muscles in your back to move with precision and rhythm as you moaned into her hair."

I close my eyes and tighten my grip around her. Anna's heart is the only one I've ever cared for enough to never break. To protect it so that it never got broken.

But it has. Several times over. By her dad. By the death of Conroy and Tripp. By me.

Heartbreak is a consequence of life. If I've learned anything from Conroy's death, it's that.

"I never want to be the other woman, Colt. I promised myself that when my dad started stepping outside of his marriage. I hated him for it for a long time. I hated the other person he had an affair with. I won't be the other woman." Anna pushes off me, sits up over me, and covers her breasts with her hands.

"Don't," I say and move her hands away from her chest. "Don't ever cover yourself up from me, Anna. Please." I know there's desperation in my voice. We both hear it.

She's talking about Jordan. I'm sure Anna's read the headlines or she knows that we were—are—together.

"You will never be the other woman in my life. You are the only woman for my life."

"Does she know that?"

"She will."

Anna leans forward and kisses my mouth. It's gentle and light and full of need, all in the same breath. She stands up and puts her bra on, her shirt, and I stare at her the entire time.

"I can't make a single excuse for what you saw that night, Anna, and if I could take one memory back from you, it would be that one."

"Colt, I want you to go home and get some sleep. I can take care of Tupac. Don't worry; he's in good hands with me. Besides, Bones won't leave him. He's got the best watchdog on his side." She's trying to fill this moment with words, trying to distract herself, us, from what we need to say. "What about your workout in the morning?"

"How do you know about those?"

Anna gives me a *duh* look. "Do you live in a hole?" She laughs.

I love Anna's laugh. I've missed it, and I didn't realize how much until this moment when it rang in my ears.

I smile and watch her.

"Do you keep your social media accounts, or does Tan?"

"All Tan. Sometimes me, but mostly Tan." I pause and watch her tie her hair up in a ponytail. "You follow me?"

She looks at me.

"I think I would know if Anna Cain were following me."

"ACDC14."

"Fourteen—your old basketball number." I take out my phone and scroll through my followers on Instagram. "What's the ACDC? A shout out to the band?" I smile at her.

"Anna Cain, Dillon Creek."

"Ohhh." I spot ACDC14.

Her page is private, but I request to follow.

"Colt, go. Take care of yourself." Anna points to the door.

I stand, slipping my phone into my pocket. "On one condition."

She places her hands on her hips, and I slide my shirt back on. I walk to her and slip my hands through her arms.

"Remember our song?" I whisper into her hair. I feel her smile against my arm.

"Yes."

I start to sing the words to "Just Tonight."

"Those seem to be the words that have always gotten us into trouble," she says as she takes her hand and places it around my neck. "Then, you'll go home?"

"Yes."

I sing most of the lyrics and hum the words I don't know. Anna feels so good. Even with our past, our somehow complicated friendship has become something easier, better, lighter.

I bury my head in her hair, leaning down and getting lost. It almost blurs my vision. "You still use the same shampoo?"

Anna doesn't say anything.

We're still dancing, and there are no words, no melody, no music, just the sound of two hearts asking for a second chance.

Sweat drips from my hair and down my face. Rob's in my face about being at the top of my game. And when I want to quit, he won't let me.

"You asked me what it takes, son!" Rob yells. "This is what it takes. Blood. Sweat. Tears."

The one-legged toe raises will be the death of me.

"Does it burn?"

"No," I lie, my voice shaking because I'm tired, but I keep pushing.

"Liar. Okay, we're done for the day."

I wipe my forehead with a towel.

"Tomorrow morning," Rob says.

"You good for the day?" I ask.

Rob, I've discovered, has no problem finding things to do here in Humboldt County. He's also the type of guy who scales mountains by himself and takes survival courses for fun. He's here for physical therapy, and then he's gone again. But I have noticed if Mom makes her homemade biscuits for dinner, Rob is always home early.

"Are you kidding? If I could train all my clients up here, I would. I hate LA. So, yeah, man, I'm totally good. This is God's country." He takes a drink of water. "Tomorrow morning, six a.m."

17
It's Complicated

Anna

It's morning. Colt came back for Tupac. Left like he promised last night.

Bones is sitting and staring at the front door of the clinic. The door they just walked out of.

"Come on, bud," I say. "He'll be fine. Don't worry."

Bones whines softly as he looks back at me.

"Come here." I bend at my waist, and Bones comes to me. Buries his nose between my legs. Maybe it isn't Tupac he's worried about. Maybe it's Colt and me. I give him a good scratch behind the ears, and he groans. "What are you so worried about?" I whisper.

He pulls his head up, stares at me, and cocks it to the right, as if willing himself to understand what I'm saying to him. I'm convinced that Bones was once a wise, old man and has come back as a dog.

Flashbacks of last night push through my mind, and I try to force them out. Guilt starts to seep in like honey through rotting wood.

He has a girlfriend, Anna. How could you have been so careless, so stupid, so selfish?

My face grows warm at the thought of Colt and what we did last night. My insides grow weary, tired.

I walk back to the counter, and that's when I see the cash.

Colt left several one-hundred-dollar bills on the counter.

I'd told him not to worry about it.

I shake my head. I should text him and tell him he shouldn't have. No, I shouldn't. That will just ensue a conversation that I don't want to have, that we shouldn't have. And I told him what I'd seen seven years ago.

You twit. I close my eyes and shake my head. *I was caught up in the moment*, I tell myself or my conscience—I'm not sure which.

"Morning," Kimber says with two coffees in hand. "Thought you could use this." She waggles her eyebrows as if she knows something I don't.

My whole body sighs. "Yes, thank you."

She hands one to me.

"So"—she pushes her purse in the cubby to the left under the counter—"how was last night?"

I take a sip of Merna's coffee from Flour and Water. She makes the best coffee. I'm not sure what she puts in it, but it's caramel and medium roast, which is my favorite.

"Last night? It was fine. Why?"

But then it hits me.

Nothing, absolutely nothing, happens in Dillon Creek without at least one person knowing, and Colt's truck parked outside the clinic until late makes for good gossip.

"Nothing."

Kimber sees the cash on the desk. "What's this?"

"Tupac had a dislocated shoulder. Had him at the clinic for observation after a quick surgery. The owner insisted on staying for awhile."

Kimber sits down in the chair behind the desk.

"The owner? That's what you're calling him?"

"Colt," I clarify. Confused and exhausted, I take another sip of coffee.

"How about NBA superstar or McHottie or The Legend?"

I try not to smile as my face warms again.

Bones greets Kimber with a paw on her leg.

"Well, good morning to you, good sir."

Kimber is also active in our live theater in town—Dillon Creek Repertory Theater. Sometimes, she'll walk about the office and recite lines from William Shakespeare and F. Scott Fitzgerald and Jane Austen. I don't know why she chooses those authors, and I've never asked.

She gives Bones a good rub behind the ears.

"Did you sleep last night?" Kimber asks as Bones retreats to his bed in the lobby. She pulls her chair to the desk and puts the cash in the cash bag.

"Somewhat." *No, not really.*

Kimber looks at the schedule. "Slow day, so if you need to go home and get some rest, do it."

I should. I know I should, but in vet school, we learned to go without sleep and to work under stressful environments because that could be our reality. I don't see that too much in Dillon Creek, but they prepare you for everything. The truth is, I don't want to go home and deal with the guilt. I don't want to look at the situation, or myself. I'd rather push it down and move forward, and the only way I know how to do this is by work.

I push away from the counter and go to the back to wash my hands.

As I turn off the hot water, I hear the jingle of the front doorbell. I hear a deep voice, a familiar voice.

Nerves and excitement shoot through my fingertips, my stomach.

"Annie?" I hear Colt's voice.

My face grows warm, and my stomach is overwhelmed with butterflies.

"Hey. Yeah, I'm in here," I say inelegantly as I dry my hands and throw the paper towels in the trash, trying my best to act casual.

I turn to face him, unsure of where to put my hands, so I awkwardly tuck them in my armpits.

We can't do this, I think to myself as his handsome face with his strong jawline appears before me.

Something happened to Colt when he was away at college. He grew out of the boy and turned into a man.

"Do you have a girlfriend? Like, a real girlfriend?" I ask him point-blank. I know I should have asked him this before we kissed last night but I allowed my heart to get ahead of my head. I allowed my own wants to push away any thoughts of what's mine and isn't mine.

"A girlfriend?" Colt's taken aback.

"Yeah, the one who's on your Instagram account. Jordan—I think that's her name."

Colt sighs deeply. "It's complicated, Annie."

All the nerves leave me, and somewhere inside me, the feelings I had as a child—the fear, the hatred I had for the people my father had affairs with—turn to anger.

I shake my head. "We—no—I let things get too far last night," I whisper, so Kimber can't hear me.

Colt runs a hand through his hair and searches the floor—for words, I suppose.

"I can't do that, Colt. You know how I feel about that." My voice quivers.

Colt's eyes dart up at me. "Annie, I know. I know. I just ... I can't control myself when I'm with you." He pauses and meticulously chooses his next words. "It went too far last night, Annie, and I'm so sorry to have put you in that situation. It will never happen again. And she's ... she's not my girlfriend. It's just complicated, is all."

Flashes of Colt touching my breasts, me straddling him come to mind. Want and love and madness flood my thoughts, my heart.

"Good," is all I say when, in reality, I'm not so sure my heart is convinced of that.

"Um, I need Tupac's collar," he says. "Did I leave it here?"

"I'll check the surgery room." I leave and retrieve the bright orange collar.

When I come back into the other room, I look up and watch Colt, who is pensive, staring at the floor, his hands at his hips. Regrets. He probably has those, just as I do. Sometimes, we do things, say things, in the heat of the moment, and all that's left are the pieces to pick up.

I push my shoulders back, tip my chin up, and hand him Tupac's collar.

"Thank you."

"You're welcome. I'll check in tomorrow and see how he's doing."

"Annie?"

Don't. Please don't. Just go.

"Dr. Cain? Logan is here." Kimber peeks her head in.

Logan, my drug representative.

"I'll let you go." Colt looks down at me and hobbles out of the room toward the lobby of the clinic where he sees Logan standing there at the counter.

Colt stops in front of Logan. Eyes him for a moment. "Colt Atwood." He sticks out his hand.

Colt has Logan beat by at least six inches.

"Holy shit." Logan reaches for Colt's extended hand, his lips slightly parted in awe.

I roll my eyes.

"How ... how's the Achilles?" Logan asks.

They shake hands.

"Healing."

Logan nods. "That's good."

Colt tries to figure out if Logan is a friend or foe. A threat.

Silence hangs in the room.

"Thank you … Dr. Cain," Colt says and limps toward the door and leaves.

Kimber sits down at her station as Logan tries to figure out what just happened.

"I mean, I knew he was from here, but I never expected to see him here, much less come out of the same clinic."

I stand in the doorway and lean on the frame.

"What do you have for us this month, Logan?" Kimber asks.

"Do you guys know him?" Logan asks, pulling out his iPad.

Kimber looks back at me. "Dr. Cain knows Colt real well. Isn't that right?"

I stare down at my hands. My dry, cracked hands from handwashing time after time. The hands that have performed multiple surgeries on all different kinds of animals with assuredness, confidence.

"I used to." My eyes leave my hands. "Same order as last month, Logan." And I retreat back to my office, shutting the door behind me.

I sit down in my leather chair and lean back. I glance at the pictures that line the wall. I remember Dr. East's pictures when he had this same office. Pictures of his wife, his children, his grandchildren, trips taken. Collected memories that sat on the shelves. Memories of a life well lived.

My shelves have textbooks. No pictures. No family. Just science sits on my shelves. Maybe this guise is an added layer of protection of the heart. A layer built with the idea that hearts are better left unloved than broken. My father instilled this in us well. I'd rather be left unloved than with a broken heart.

I guess that's what Colt helped me learn, too.

18

Prom

Anna: Age Fourteen

"It's fine, Annie. You'll be fine. Would you stop messing with it already?" Colt said as he looked down at me.

I nervously pulled at my dress. I hated dresses.

"You look beautiful, Annie," Colt whispered over the lyrics of Garth Brooks as he blared through the radio.

Conroy drove us down Waddington Road. We'd told our dates that we'd get a ride into town. Conroy would drop me off at Tess's house, and we'd go from there.

It wasn't a date. It was prom. I was going with Baker Knight, and Colt was going with Amy Teasdale.

We were freshmen. And Dillon Creek was so small that freshmen and sophomores were invited to prom because if they didn't go, juniors and seniors would have little attendees.

Besides, Amy was probably hoping to get to at least second base. She was, of course, a senior, and Colt was a freshman in a big body.

"Promise me you won't do anything stupid?" I asked Colt.

"Me? I'm not the one going with Baker."

"It's a dance, Colt. It's not like I'm stupid."

"I didn't say you were stupid, Annie." He put his hand on mine. "Stop pulling on it. You're fine, all right? And if Baker doesn't know that, then he's clearly an idiot."

"I don't know why I'm nervous."

"I can tell you why. You hate dresses. You hate to dance. And your dad's an ass."

I smiled through the tears that started to burn my eyes. I nodded because my heart couldn't find the right words to explain the brokenness of it all.

"You're going to be okay, Annie."

I had faith in Colt. Faith that he knew what he was talking about. Trust. Just like I trusted Tess.

I wanted to tell Colt it didn't feel like it. That my heart felt like it was broken into a million little pieces and that it would take superglue and wire and time to put it all back together.

Instead, all I said was, "Okay."

Conroy adjusted the radio station. "Look, I don't know what you're going through, Anna. Sometimes, in your life, you're going to be hit with some really shitty stuff. But what makes us who we are isn't the shitty stuff; it's what we do after it all hits the fan." He put on his blinker and drove toward Amy's house.

"I'll be there with you. Tess will too," Colt said.

I was only going to prom because I didn't want to let my friends down. Casey, Tess's date, was going to meet us there. He'd had some rodeo thing to be at, so he was running late.

Conroy would be driving Tess, Baker, and me while Amy and Colt would drive separately.

Colt didn't feel comfortable with Amy driving out to their ranch. I wasn't sure why. Tess had said that Colt just wanted to ride in with me to make sure I was okay after everything that had happened yesterday. I'd overheard a phone call I wasn't supposed to hear. A man in Eureka was suffering and in a lot of pain and there was no hope for him. He'd be dead in two weeks but until then the pain was excruciating. His family called my dad to end the suffering.

It was in that moment, when my dad hung up the phone, I realized I never wanted to be my father. I still wanted to help others but in ways that were legal and just. What he was doing wasn't legal. And if being a doctor meant having any symbolism of my father and this practice, then I didn't want any part of it.

Tears again started to burn my eyes. I couldn't ruin my makeup or ruin this night for Tess and Colt.

My dad's words ran inside my head. *"You'll understand when you're older, Anna."*

I'm so tired of holding myself up. Weary of continually placing all the pieces of my family neatly back together and waiting out another storm. I just wanted to be able to breathe. And the only time I could seem to do that was when I was with Colt.

Cautiously, I rested my cheek against his tuxedo jacket.

I felt the air leave us both.

This was why I could never date Colt Atwood.

He was the air that I breathed.

"She kissed me."

Tess's lips jerked up. "What'd you do?"

"I just sat there," Colt said.

"You didn't kiss her back?" Casey chimed in.

Colt, Tess, Casey, and I were at the top of the cemetery hill that overlooked Dillon Creek.

Colt shrugged. "I did a little, I guess."

Tess laughed. "You either did or you didn't, Atwood."

Colt looked at me, as if his conscience was wobbling on good and bad. "What about you?" Colt nudged me. "Did Baker make the move? You looked a little cozy with him on the dance floor."

It was just nice to have someone to hold me up, I wanted to say. Someone who had pretended to understand even though, deep down, I had known Baker just wanted a piece of ass. A piece of ass he wasn't going to get, and he and I both knew it.

"He didn't."

Casey toyed with Tess's hand. Nudged her neck with his nose as if Colt and I couldn't see what was really going on. Tess liked to pretend that she and Casey were just good friends, but everyone knew there was always more.

The way that they looked at each other.

The way her hand fit perfectly in his.

The way, when they danced, they just moved and molded together.

Our families were all best friends. This was the way things were supposed to work out, right?

"Get a room." Colt pushed his brother as we sat and overlooked the town lights.

Casey laughed. Tess giggled.

And I smiled.

Things might not be good at home, but they were good with my friends.

"I wonder if Amy and Baker knew that you and Colt were meant to be," Casey said.

"What?" I said.

"I wonder if they both knew there was no hope. That it was all just a waste of fucking time," Casey said.

"What are you talking about?" I asked again.

Casey leaned forward to get a good look at me. "You two really don't see it, do you?"

"See what?" we said in unison.

Casey smirked. Looked at Tess and then back to us. "Nothin'. You two will figure it out in the end, I guess."

The four of us sat there in silence, watching the moon kiss the land, the valley below us, our town, our people, our home. I began to think that maybe time wasn't on our side. That maybe if we let opportunities slip by, well, then, it was just up to time to turn those missed opportunities into grace.

Tess looked down at her watch. "It's late. Give me a ride home, Casey?"

Casey looked longingly at Tess, as if she'd hung the moon and placed the stars in the sky. As if he needed just one more minute of her time. "Whenever you're ready," he said.

I could tell by Tess's look that she wasn't ready. That she wanted to sit here forever with us, but her parents would be waiting when she got home. Tripp, Tess's older brother, would also be waiting, if he wasn't out himself.

Colt touched my arm, and my body ignited. I looked at him, and he was taking off his coat.

"Here," he said. "You're cold."

Dillon Creek residents—not transplants, but residents who had been Humboldt born and raised—were made with an extra layer of skin. The weather in Dillon Creek wasn't your typical California weather. In the winter, it dropped to the low twenties and rained like hell. But when the rain came, the weather turned warmer. In turn, snow rarely fell in Dillon Creek. The rain cleared up until May, and then spring would come and offer the sunlight again, although still cold and nasty on some days. Summers were mild in the mid-seventies.

Tonight was cold. It could have been because we were sitting in a cemetery with a bunch of dead spirits around us. Or maybe God was telling us it was time to go home. Either way, I was cold, and I was grateful for Colt's jacket.

"Did you have fun tonight?" I asked, stealing just a few more minutes of the night.

"Yeah. You?" He looked at me, his eyes darker and deeper in the moonlight than I'd ever seen them before. Not that I looked at Colt in the moonlight often because I didn't. But the moonlight gave off a sort of romantic darkness, gave his eyes some sort of mystic haze.

"Did you know that Baker bales twenty-seven bales of hay every day in the summer? And did you know that he also won two all-around cowboys in the Humboldt County Rodeo?" I smirked. "That boy also talks more about himself than anyone I've ever met in my life." I pulled Colt's jacket around me tighter—not because of the chill, but because of his scent. I breathed him in.

"Did you know that Amy used the word *like* four hundred and eighty-two times?"

"You counted?"

"I tried. It was probably more, but that was all I could focus on."

I wanted to say to Colt, *Are we going to spend the rest of our lives comparing others to each other?* But I didn't. Deep inside me, I knew we would.

"All right, hooligans. Let's go," Casey said as he took Tess's hand and led the way down the steep cemetery hill.

Dillon Creek Cemetery was home to thousands of bodies of deceased relatives and friends. What had started as a cemetery next to a church with a flat plot of land had grown up a hill over the years. This was the place I came to when I just needed the world to quiet down.

"Give me your hand," Colt said. "It's steep, and we can't see a damn thing."

I slipped my hand in his. His hand was warm and big, and I felt safer than I'd ever felt before. Colt and I had held hands before but not in the way you might think.

He'd held my hand on the first day of kindergarten as we walked into Mrs. Pinkerton's classroom.

He'd held my hand in first grade as we took the stage for our annual Christmas program. I'd kept my eyes on him the entire time while I sang the lyrics, too afraid to face the audience.

He'd held my hand when Grandma Cain passed away.

He'd held my hand when we lost our cat, Dinker, who was found along Waddington Road when he was just four years old.

The truth was, I needed Colt more than he needed me, and that scared the living hell out of me.

19

The Old Woman's Reflection

Erla stares back at the reflection in the window of Dillon Drugs, the only pharmacy in Dillon Creek, which also doubles as a gift shop in a pinch. She's surprised by the woman who's staring back. She has more gray than not. The creases, the folds tucked in places, make her look older than she is. The crow's-feet that run from her eyes, she moves closer to her reflection, hoping it's just the light.

Where has the time gone?

To which situation did she owe an explanation to her face, an apology, for time and stress?

Before she reaches up and touches her forehead, she hears a man's voice.

"Good morning, Erla," Dan Rigby, the pharmacist, says when he opens the door and flips the sign from *Closed* to *Open*. "Don's medicine is ready."

"Good morning, Dan."

He holds the door open, and Erla walks through, purse in hand.

Dillon Drugs smells like cider and freshly copied paper; it always has. A comforting smell nonetheless.

She wonders if Mabe is taking medication for her depression. *And if she is, should she be drinking her beer with it?*

Erla wants to mention Mabe to Dan, gauge his reaction. See if he knows something she doesn't. Of course, Dan Rigby is a professional man, who'd never breathe a word about the patients he serves. But maybe Erla can catch a glance of the twinkle in his eye when she asks, something that shows that maybe he knows more about Mabe than she does, that maybe Mabe has let him in as a confidant, a friend.

How on God's green earth will I bring her name up in conversation?

Erla's never been the gossiping type because she knows firsthand what it's like to be gossiped about. The center of others' words, speculation from rapacious people squandering and questioning the rumors that quickly spread around town after Don and she first got together. About Erla's swelling belly and how quickly they'd hit the sheets.

"Never judge a book by its cover," Gloria, Erla's mother, would always say, which leads Erla back to Mabe.

"It's two prescriptions, right, Erla?" Dan calls from the back.

She nods. "Yes, that's correct."

She toys with the odd-shaped pens at the counter, which advertise an ergonomic design for less strain, reducing the symptoms of carpal tunnel. Erla highly doubts seven dollars for a pen will help reduce those symptoms, but she would have been naive enough to buy it in her younger years, probably due to lack of life experience and maybe more hopeful, more trust in others.

Dan walks to the front counter and rings Erla up at his old-style cash register. "That will be one hundred and seventeen dollars."

Don would pitch a screaming fit if he knew how much his medications cost on a monthly basis. A smart tightwad most of his life, though in the past few years, he has come to care more about family than money. Perhaps it's time. Time that has become so important, time that has created the wrinkles in her face and the sag of her skin.

She hands Dan her debit card.

"How's Don doing?" Dan asks.

"Well." She's never sure how to answer this question. There are good days and bad days. And it could be worse. *If we just had more time*, she wants to say. But really, it's just an old woman feeling ungrateful for the time she has left, she supposes.

Erla always answers by saying he's doing well because it's as honest as she can get. It's well because it's not great and it's not bad. *Well* is somewhere in the middle.

After a few errands in town, Erla decides that it's time she go by Mabe's again. The last time, she didn't answer the door. Perhaps the last time Erla stopped by, the time she was going to come by and help Mabe with her situation, she didn't answer the door because she didn't want help. At first, Erla thought it was just plain rude. After all, she'd offered up her time, and Mabe was standing her up. But as Erla thinks about it, she was the one who'd put the expectations on Mabe. *But she should want help, right?* Her place was a mess. This beautiful, old Victorian and lush gardens had all gone to hell in a handbasket. *Doesn't Mabe see it? Doesn't she want out?* So, Erla has decided she's going to Mabe's to apologize. It's not Mabe's fault after all.

Mabe was always so brilliant with roses and orchids. She'd created her own hybrids and grown the most magnificent flowers you'd ever seen. But now, her yard is desolate and barren. As if all the love has left her home, all the passion, all the color, has dissolved to nothing.

Twelve straight years, Mabe won best in show at the annual Garden of Color held in Eureka. It was open to the entire county of Humboldt. Then, her husband and daughter died. She never entered the show again.

Erla can see how death and love can strip away the passion for life. Erla supposes she can compare it to Devon.

She just fell from their life. As much as Don and she didn't want to accept it, they had to. They just had to let her go in hopes that she'd find her way back.

Mabe's garden is now a wasteland. Like a cemetery to beauty and color that once thrived.

Erla makes her way up the steps to her porch. The paint on the house reflects its age, its wear. The once-vibrant yellow has faded to a dingy, dirty shade of ugly. And if the house were power-washed, just as John did every year when he was alive, the paint would most likely dissolve into nothing, leaving the house more broken than it had been before.

When Erla knocks, she notices Mabe's mailbox to the left of her front door overflowing. Bills and advertisements stick out awkwardly. Erla knows it's a federal offense, but she takes the mail from Mabe's box and neatly stacks it in her arms.

No answer.

She knocks again.

She waits.

Still nothing.

She taps her foot, nerves growing.

Erla knocks once more and waits.

Nothing.

She tries the doorknob, and to her surprise, it's unlocked.

Opening the door, she notices nothing's changed. The state of the house, if anything, has gotten worse.

"Mabe?" Erla calls out. "It's Erla." She looks down at her armful of mail. "I have your mail."

But it's so eerily quiet that it scares Erla.

"Mabe?" She finds a small, empty space on the dining room table amid the stacks of boxes, both medium and small.

Mabe used to always keep an impeccable house.

Maneuvering around boxes, Erla looks in the living room. "Mabe?"

Nerves begin to build in her stomach. She makes her way down the hallway to the office. More boxes. Some opened. Some not opened. The opened ones are mixing bowls and some sort of blender, all brand-new. Two vacuums out of the box. Three tablet things.

Pads or something like that, Erla thinks to herself.

Don always uses a computer, so that's what they've always stuck with. Erla can't keep up with the latest technology, but Mabe always has.

Erla leaves the office and walks farther down the hallway to the bathroom. She flips on the light. The bathroom, so far, is the only place that doesn't have boxes. Nothing out of place, except a pill bottle that's open and on the counter. She picks up the bottle, and on it reads Mabe's name with the word *Ambien* underneath it. The bottle is empty, which makes for a quick, disturbing thought.

"Jesus, Mabe, what have you done?"

Leaving the bathroom, the pill bottle in her hand, she heads back down the hallway. And when Erla reaches the kitchen, she sees a set of purple flats, toes pointed up toward the ceiling.

Panic like she's never known before rouses in her chest. "Mabe!"

Her stomach still clenched tight, she fumbles with her phone, trying to dial the numbers 911. Erla grabs for Mabe's wrist to get a pulse.

Thank God.

"Nine-one-one, what is your emergency?"

"Stella, it's me, Erla." She tries to keep her fragile control. "I found Mabe unconscious, and you need to send Will, the EMT, right now to Mabe's house."

She hangs up, not listening to what Stella has to say.

She hears the fire whistle sound, which signifies lunch and emergencies in Dillon Creek, and it's not noon in Dillon Creek, so Erla knows they're on their way.

It's a weird thing, she thinks—cradling her oldest friend, her cousin in her arms, someone who's seen most of her ups and downs in life, someone who's been through hell and back with her, and there's nothing Erla can do to save her.

She's shaking, Erla thinks, feeling a slight tremor. But she quickly realizes it's herself who's shaking, not Mabe.

"You stay with me, Mabe Muldoon. I'm not ready to let you go. We still have so many *yets* to do, do you hear me? You hang the hell on."

Will comes screaming through the front door.

"In here, Will! The kitchen!"

Will comes around the corner, his bag in hand. Randy, his assistant, is behind him, carrying the stretcher on his back.

Will comes to Mabe, and Randy helps Erla to her feet.

Testing her vitals, Will says, "They're weak, but she's still with us."

Thank God.

Erla steps out of the way but not before handing Randy the empty pill bottle of Ambien. "I found this in her bathroom."

Randy takes it and shoves it in a bag.

Will and Randy load Mabe up on the stretcher and get her out of the house.

Erla stands on the porch and watches. *Somehow, it feels safer here*, she thinks, her heart too tender to bear what they'll do to her. The things she might see. Memories that she'd rather not have.

"Are you coming?" Will shouts as he closes one of the doors to the ambulance.

But without a second thought, Erla calls out, "Yes." She shuts the front door behind her and gets into the back of the ambulance with Randy's help.

Dear God, I want this to be a story that we look back on and laugh about. Right now, it's too sad to even muster the thoughts. But give us this story later.

Her mind spins away with anxiety as they make the twenty-minute trek up to Eureka where the hospital is located. Will is keeping an eye on Mabe's vitals, an oxygen mask resting on her face. Her eyes have fluttered open a few times, but it's not enough to be considered conscious.

"Will she be all right?" Erla asks Will.

"I think you found her in time. But only time will tell."

What if I hadn't stopped by Mabe's today? What if I hadn't followed the tiny voice inside my head that said to stop by, to apologize?

Erla can't stand the thought of Mabe lying on the floor, dying by herself. She's spent far too much time by herself.

Erla promises Mabe in the ambulance that she'll never have to die alone, and Erla will make sure of that.

Did she take all the Ambien?

What was the quantity on the bottle?

When was it prescribed?

Did Mabe try to kill herself?

No, of course not. There's a logical explanation, right?

Don.

Erla forgot about Don. He'll worry about Erla. Why she's not home. Maybe get confused.

She left her purse and his medication in Mabe's house. "Can I borrow your phone, Will? I need to make a call."

Will hands her the phone, and she dials Clyda's number with Will's assistance. The new phones with no buttons really mystify her.

"Clyda, it's Erla. It's a long story, but I need you to go get my purse at Mabe's house and go check on Don. There's been an accident with Mabe, and we're on our way to the hospital."

"Oh my word. Yes. Of course. Do you need me there?"

"No, no. I can handle it. But will you do those two things for me?"

"Of course."

"Thank you. I'll call when I have an update."

"Okay. Take care."

"Will do." Erla hands the phone back to Will before she ends the call because she's not sure how to end it. Old ladies can do that. Act perplexed, and it's all done for them, especially when it comes to technology.

Still with Mabe's hand in one of hers, she traces the lines on Mabe's face that reflect wisdom. Lines that signify a life lived.

"Do you want to give in, Mabe? Throw in the towel?" she asks her, not expecting her to answer.

And she doesn't.

No, it's not what she's done. It's what she's willing to do to put her heart at peace. That is a tricky feat. This, Erla knows, from experience. Don and she have had a real good life. But when Devon left their life, Erla felt like she wanted to die for a time, and the one to pull Erla out of it, along with Don, was her Scarlet.

Mabe didn't have either.

20

One-Way Ticket

Colt

Dad is awake and sitting at the table, coffee in hand, reading the *Dillon Creek Echo.*

"Morning," I say, dripping in sweat from my morning physical therapy.

"Morning," Dad says.

Mom comes inside from the outside. "Did you two hear about Mabe Muldoon?"

Dad looks up from his television set. "No. What happened?"

"Apparently, Erla found her on the floor in the kitchen, unconscious."

"They take her in?" Dad asks.

"Yeah, but no word since. I should run up to see her."

"Don't jump to conclusions, Laurel," my dad says.

"Paying her a visit, Daryl, isn't jumping to conclusions."

Dad goes back to the television and sips his coffee.

Mom turns to me. "Wedding today," she says. "It's a wonderful day to get married."

"Who's getting married?" I lean against the counter.

Dad's *MASH* plays quietly in the background.

"Oh, a couple from Arcata. Came across our venue on Facebook."

"Need any help today?"

She sighs. "Before the guests get here, sure. But after they arrive, please keep yourself scarce. You know I mean that in the most loving way possible."

"What your mother is saying, Colt, is that you're too famous for our own good," my dad says.

Rob walks in, holding a cup of coffee.

"Think I can get on a horse today, Rob?"

He shrugs. "Do you think it's a good idea to eat kale with peanut butter?"

"No."

"Then, no. It's not a good idea. So many things can go wrong on a horse, Atwood."

"Really, Colt, there isn't much to do," Mom says.

Tan comes walking through the back door. "Colt, a word." Tan's voice has changed octaves. It's his serious tone.

Tan walks into the living room, and I follow. He has both phones in hand.

"Jordan is on her way up here."

"Wait. What? Why?"

"Apparently, she's been blowing up your phone, and you haven't responded, so she's texting me now."

Shit. "She's the last thing I need up here."

"You, me, and baby Jesus," Tan says. "She'll be here in a few hours."

"What the hell's she flying up here?"

"Company jet."

"Fuck."

I've got to take her to a hotel. She can't stay here. I don't want her to meet my parents. Meet my family. This … this isn't like Jordan.

"Look, stay as low-key as possible. The media is used to you and Jordan, and it seems like Dillon Creek really respects your privacy, so lie low until she leaves town. You two in a new town might signify house-hunting or marriage. So, just stay quiet until you convince her to leave."

"I could just break it off with her completely and tell her to go home." I run my hands through my hair, trying to think.

"Oh, you want a goddamn Armageddon to happen? Come on, Colt; you know how she gets. She's half-crazy, and she'll do whatever it is to get what she wants." He pauses. "And maybe … just steer clear of Anna."

My defenses go up. "Why?"

Tan looks at me and drops his hands to his sides. "It's obvious, man."

"What is?"

His upper lip curls back. "Seriously? That you're in love with her."

His words meet me in the gut.

"Why are we here, Atwood?"

"To rehab my Achilles."

He laughs. "You can rehab your Achilles anywhere. We have state-of-the-art facilities in Los Angeles. New York, where you own your penthouse. We could have gone anywhere in the world, really, to rehab, and you chose Dillon Creek."

I go to speak, make some shit up because the truth is steaming from Tan's mouth right now.

"Don't try to cover up the truth or make excuses. Hell, I don't know why you hold back, keeping her a secret in our world. We live a different life in LA, yes. Maybe you're shielding her from it, or maybe you're trying to be the Colt you used to be—I'm not sure. But one thing is for certain; you're in love with Anna. Jordan is on her way up here, and our goal is for you to keep Jordan quiet. Don't let her explode. Just with the trade, we want to keep everything as quiet as possible—unless it's good. Okay?"

Tan has always had a way of keeping things simple.

Am I shielding Anna from this life? The life of flashing lights, money, people, lies, deceit, the truth, and me? Deep down in my subconscious, am I protecting Anna from me?

There's a knock at the back door.

My heart drops. I look at Tan.

"Go time."

"I'll go pack my shit. Wait, what am I going to tell my parents?"

"That you have a batshit-crazy woman coming to visit you and you need space." He laughs the annoying *I'm so funny* laugh. "I'm kidding. Look, I can keep the media and the public off your back, but I can't keep your family from the truth."

The knock is just Juniper Jones and she's looking for my mother. "In the barn, Juniper."

"Thanks, Colt." She turns and walks back toward her van.

"Jordan will arrive in an hour at the Rohnerville Airport in Belle's Hollow. Said she'll have a car come pick her up." Tan looks up from his phone.

I laugh. "Yeah, unless she's going to steal one, then I'll go pick her up."

Tan types this out—not the car-stealing, I'm sure, but the part about me picking her up. "Got it."

After I throw some clothes in a bag, I hop in Casey's truck, which is parked back in one of the barns since he's gone with the Bullfighters One tour. I think Cash has driven it a total of three times. He won it for Bullfighter of the Year last year. Brought it home and then left again when the tour started up. It's a nice truck. Similar to mine in LA. I don't drive mine much because I hate LA traffic.

I pull out of the driveway and head down Waddington Road to Grizzly Bluff to State Route 211 to US 101 south.

It's a fifteen-minute drive to Belle's Hollow.

I pull up to Rohnerville Airport. There's one cattle gate that protects the land from the public. No one works the gate, so if you don't know the code, you're shit out of luck. I texted Giffin, the caretaker of the airport, before I left. I get out of the truck and type in the code he sent me. The electric lock pops open, and I pull the gate open, drive through, and close it behind me.

Rohnerville Airport consists of sixteen privately owned hangars. The planes that land here are no more than six-seater aircrafts—unless it's fire season. Then, you see the big CAL Fire tankers coming in to fuel up and go on to Redding usually or more inland when we have the summer wildfires.

There's one main building where air traffic control is housed, and it's usually Giffin who's operating. I pull Cash's truck just off the taxiway, turn off the truck, and walk into the building.

"Well, look what the cat dragged in." Giffin comes around the counter to shake my hand. "Mighty good to see you, Colt. Sorry to hear about the injury."

I shrug. "Thank you, Giffin. It's good to be back home."

There's something about small towns and big dreams. Once they're achieved, really, there's no place like home. A place where you can settle into your own skin.

"So, the flight you're waiting on is coming in about a half hour."

"Great. Thank you."

"Have you decided?" Giffin walks back around the counter. "Where you're going next year?"

"Honestly, I haven't. Just trying to rehab this injury and get back on the court."

I haven't thought about where I'm going. Pete, my agent, said we'd reconvene mid-summer. I haven't given any thought to where I'll live if I move to a new team.

"Well, anyway," Giffin says, "it's good to have you home."

The scanner on the desk starts to sound.

Giffin walks to the desk and puts a headset on. "Go ahead, 223."

I walk to a bay window, which opens up to the runway and the mountain of redwood trees that surrounds the airport.

Rohnerville Airport sits on top of a small mountain. The background though shows hills of redwood trees, giving off the idea that you're in the middle of nowhere when you're not. Belle's Hollow sits behind us.

Anna crosses my mind, as she always does. Slips into my mind and stays there. I want to text her. Check in with her.

My phone chimes.

I pull my phone from my pocket.

It's Anna.

Anna: How's Tupac?

Me: Good. He hates the crate, but after one more day, like you said, I think he'll be fine.

Bubbles appear as Anna types.

They disappear.

Start again.

Disappear.

Start again.

She's conflicted with words, like what she does to my insides. I need to tell her about Jordan before she sees me in town with her. Before she can jump to any conclusions. It's just a difficult relationship to explain.

I look back at Giffin, who still has his headset on.

Giffin looks at me and pulls the talking piece back. "It's going to be about twenty more minutes before they land. Got stuck in traffic." He laughs at his own joke.

Landing a plane in Humboldt County on the first try is like getting a hunting license for an endangered species. Because we're so remote, the fog lives in the trees around us. Although summertime has been okay, but you just never know. Today is one of those days where the fog is coming in and out like waves.

I walk outside, my insides doing shit that makes me want to puke. I touch the number one contact in my phone, and it's calling.

"Hello?"

"Hey." It's Anna. Her voice gives me relief.

"Hey. How are you?"

"Could be better." I chuckle. "Listen, I need to tell you something. And I know I don't owe you an explanation, like you've said, but I do." I let out a sigh.

Anna doesn't say a word.

"Jordan is an on-again, off-again thing. I … I can't call her a girlfriend. Maybe I did in the beginning, but now, we're just friends with benefits." I wait for her words.

Still, she says nothing.

"I mean, we're not friends with benefits now. We used to be." I sigh again. Run my hand through my hair. "What I'm trying to say is, Annie, you're not the other woman. You never have been. You never will be. She's coming up for a visit. Annie, I have no idea why. I haven't talked to her. She reached out to Tan. Anyway, I'm at the airport to pick her up."

Anna is quiet.

"Annie, please say something."

"Will you take her back to the ranch?" she whispers.

"What? No." My head jerks up from my hard stare at the ground. "No, we are staying in town." *Fuck*. I know how the word *we* might sound. "I … I'm just trying to keep her quiet."

"Why?"

"Because I don't want her coming after you."

Anna laughs.

Anna has always been able to stand on her own two feet. Defend herself. But she's never met Jordan Landry.

"Why would she come after me?"

"To hurt me."

"Why would she want to hurt you?"

"Because she's never been told no before." I sigh again. "Once she sinks her claws in, Annie, it's like she owns you." I shrug my shoulders in mock resignation. "But you're the only woman I've ever been in love with. And she knows this."

The dead air on the line becomes loud.

"Say something, Annie," I whisper.

"I can't."

"Why?"

"I don't have words. I have to go now, Colt."

"Anna, wait."

"What?"

"I'll see you around." I chicken out. I don't say it. I don't say that I love her because that will only make things more complicated for her when Jordan is here. It'll just fuck everything up.

"See you around," she says.

21

Huevos Rancheros

Anna

Surprise siphons the blood from my face. I feel it and become instantly wide-awake.

I want life to go back to the way it was before Colt. It's never been the right time for the two of us. Ever. Maybe that's fate or God's way of saying, *Not this one.*

"Are you all right?" Kimber asks, staring up at me from her computer.

I nod.

"No, you're not. But it's okay. We haven't taken our friendship to that level yet. And I get it. I'm younger than you. You probably think I wouldn't understand. And maybe I won't, Anna, but maybe I will. You need to talk about shit more. It's like you walk around here with a stick stuck up your ass. Deep in thought. Always thinking. You've got to give yourself a goddamn break and not be such a tight ass. I mean, don't get me wrong; your ass is great, but, Jesus Christ, lighten up. Besides, who do you think I'm going to talk to? You know as well as I do that the big mouths of the town are Pearl and Delveen."

I start to laugh. I laugh so hard that tears form in my eyes, and I can't tell if they're sad tears or tears of laughter. I hold my finger up, so Kimber will give me a minute, and then I stop. This could go really badly for me or really good. Maybe she's right. Maybe I am a tight ass, not money-wise, but maybe I do need to goddamn lighten up.

I take a deep breath and lean on the counter. "Colt and I made out in my office. It was hot, and I've never felt so loved and so vulnerable and so scared at the same time. We've made love once. Before we both left for college. The night Conroy and Tripp died. I was terrified. He was confident. We both grieved. Grieved in different ways. But Colt lost a brother. Aside from his father, Colt envied Conroy. So, I needed to be there for him. He wouldn't let me. He shut the door on life. Shut me out and played basketball like you wouldn't believe. He bottled up all that sadness, all that anger, all that emotion and played the game of basketball so beautifully that I knew I could never break that. I didn't want to. But in turn, I don't think he's ever processed his own grief." I pause to breathe. "And now, Colt is bringing home a woman named Jordan Landry." I tap my fingers on the counter, almost afraid to meet her eyes, but I do anyway. "How is that for word vomit?"

Kimber is leaning back in her chair, taking it all in. "I think you and I both know the truth, Dr. Cain."

"The truth? And what's that?"

"Colt didn't come back home to rehab his Achilles. Come on. He came back for you, and if that isn't evident—because he's a billionaire and he could have gone anywhere—then you have another thing coming. And I don't know who this Jordan Landry chick is, but Dillon Creek ain't having that shit in our town." She pauses. Leans forward and rests her elbows on the desk. "Everyone knows it's always been Colt plus Anna."

I shake my head. "Kimber, it's never been the right time for us. Ever. And one thing I've never wanted to do is ruin our friendship. We had a bond I thought no one could break."

"Had."

"What?"

"You said *had*." She shrugs. "Maybe you already lost the friendship because the love got too big."

I feel the weight of the silence that sits in the clinic, the weight of her words. "We can love from afar. Sometimes, things just aren't meant to be."

"And maybe it's the way you're looking at it. Maybe you need a different perspective." Her eyebrows rise.

"Have you ever thought about law school?" I ask, shaking my head, a slight smile forming.

"No, but I grew up with Charlie and Wade, so, you know, I had to be the voice of reason with those two."

Charlie and Wade are Kimber's brothers.

I go to walk away but turn back to face Kimber. "I'll try not to be such a tight ass. I'll try to loosen up."

"And I'll try not to be so nosy."

"No, you're not nosy. You care. And I see that. So, thank you."

"You're welcome. Now, let's get to doctoring." Kimber's phone chimes. She picks it up. "Oh, no." She looks up at me. "Did you hear about Mabe?"

"No. Why? What's going on?"

"Erla found her on the floor in her kitchen. Black and blue, like someone had beaten her up."

"What?" My mind reels with confusion. *Who in their right mind would hurt our beloved Mabe Muldoon?*

Kimber shrugs. "That's what Lou heard down at The Whiskey Barrel this morning from Toby Lemon."

I laugh. "Toby Lemon? And you consider him a reliable source?"

"Sometimes."

"Well, I'm sure the truth is in there somewhere."

I finish up with the last patient. Bones is asleep in his bed when I come out of room three, following Delveen and her dog, Birch, a cross between a pug and dachshund—tucked underneath her arm.

I often think Delveen talks just to hear her own words. And right now, she's talking about how close she and Mabe are. And how she's worried sick after the mugging.

We get to the counter, and Kimber's there.

I touch Delveen's hand. "I'm sure Mabe is going to be fine, and I'm almost certain they'll find what happened."

"And find her mugger, too." Delveen nods, her eyes as big as saucers. "I'm scared to death we have a mugger on the loose in our small town. I called Chief McBride at home and told him there ought to be a manhunt with helicopters, lights, and sirens, searching for her attacker."

"And what did he say, Delveen?" Kimber asks, looking rather entertained.

"He said it wasn't a mugger. And then I said she was black and blue, for God sake. How can it not be a mugger? And then he said that while he couldn't disclose any personal information, I could rest assured that Mabe is safe and the town of Dillon Creek is free of muggers, attackers, and Unabombers."

My face scrunches. "Unabombers?"

"Bobbie Joe Seedy told me that there was a bomb found under her porch. Might be linked to some attacks on the East Coast."

Birch whines in Delveen's arms.

I wonder if Delveen is set up to fail on a daily basis. The whole town knows she has a hard time keeping her mouth quiet. I think it's an impulse that she can't control and that she's addicted to chaos. Delveen seems to be the type to worry just for the sake of worrying. If she's not in a constant state of panic or worry, well then, apparently, she's not living.

"I'd say you should take the good word of the Chief, go visit your friend, and find out the truth, Delveen." Kimber hands Delveen some paperwork. "Sign here, please."

I give Birch a pet on the head. There's nothing wrong with Birch. Delveen brought her in because she said she was acting funny. "No charge, Delveen. Just give her extra love and belly rubs today."

Bones is still passed out in his bed. He doesn't even budge when Delveen and Birch leave.

"I'm leaving," Kimber says. "I'll get everything locked up out here. You going out the back door?"

I don't want to go home. I don't want to go and be alone. My mother is at a meeting, and my father is most likely still working. Amelia is never home, and Adam is probably at The Steeple.

I can't move my things into my place until Thursday, and it's Tuesday now.

"Don't worry about it. I'll lock up. I'm going to finish up some stuff in my office," I say.

"Okay." Kimber grabs her purse from underneath her desk and shoves her phone in it. "See you tomorrow." After she gives Bones a good belly rub, she stands and turns to me. "Remember how I said you should loosen up?"

"Yeah."

"That means, don't work late. Go out to dinner with Tess. Have a drink or two."

I smile. "Got it."

She nods and leaves, shutting the door tightly behind her.

This time, the bell on the door startles Bones, and his head shoots up. His ears are more like a German shepherd than an Australian shepherd, and it makes me laugh.

"What is it, boy?"

He looks at me, back to the door, and back to me.

"Come on, goofy. Office."

When I sit down in my leather chair, my phone starts to buzz. I look at the number. *Unknown*, it says. I rarely pick up unknown numbers. Probably a drug company calling, wanting the clinic to test their new drugs. How they get my cell phone number is both irritating and frustrating.

Maybe it's impulse, maybe it's curiosity, or maybe it's just the need to give them a piece of my mind, but I answer.

"Hello?" My tone is rushed. Hurried.

"Anna?"

"This is she." I delve through the mail on my desk. Glance at my watch.

"It's Sam. Sam Houston."

I draw a blank and feel embarrassed. "I'm sorry. Who?" A tactic to pause time, so I can rummage through my brain killed from all the science and math I suffered through college.

"Huevos Rancheros? Marta and Jesus?" the man says.

Immediately, I start to laugh, and my mind burns with memories.

"I assume by the laugh, you remember me."

"I don't know how I forgot. Sam Houston. How the hell are you?"

"Well, I'm really good actually. Dr. Houston now."

"Ah. Of course. You didn't let Dr. Ferguson, our professor, scare you off, I see." I rest easy in the familiarity of his voice, his deep tone.

"Nah. He almost did. But there was this beautiful blonde who had this laugh, and I just … I just couldn't leave her to the wolves."

"Oh, but you did." I smile. Bite my lower lip and stare at the wall, remembering the professor's scornful tone during his lectures.

Samuel, as he told me his name on the first day of college in General Biology, left after freshman year, as a spot had opened up at Yale.

"Guilty. But I'd really like to see you again. I'm driving up to Seattle. A job interview at Seattle Western."

"Specialty?"

"Hearts."

I know he doesn't use the scientific term because he wants me to remember it.

"No surprise there."

"Yeah." There's a sigh. The guilty one. "So," he says, changing the subject, "when I pulled up the map, I noticed Dillon Creek. I couldn't … I couldn't drive past and not stop."

It's quiet for a moment.

"You go by Sam now?"

"Sounds less biblical than Samuel. Less dated. It's hard to get a date with the name Samuel, you know?"

"You never had a problem finding a date, Sam."

Dark brown hair, green eyes that are the color of limes.

"I had to work hard with you. Something about some Atwood kid."

I push Colt out of my mind. "When would you be coming by?"

"Tomorrow."

"Tomorrow?"

"Tomorrow."

I glance at my patient schedule tomorrow. It's a full day. "It's a Wednesday. I'm available for dinner, if you'd like."

"That would be wonderful. Any places you recommend to stay in Dillon Creek?"

"Are you a bed-and-breakfast kind of guy, Sam Houston, or an eat-sleep-and-leave kind of guy?"

"Depends."

"On what?"

"The company."

His suggestion intrigues me.

"Well, there's the Shaw Inn and The Gingerbread Mansion in Dillon Creek. Both are more bed-and-breakfast types. There are a few hotels in Belle's Hollow, which is about fifteen minutes away, if you don't get caught behind a tractor on the 211 when leaving town."

"I'll call around."

"All right, Sam Houston."

"All right, Anna Cain. I heard you were a veterinarian."

"From who?"

He laughs into the phone. A slow, throaty laugh. "I'm really bad at the flirting thing. I looked you up on Facebook. Saw some graduation photos on your timeline."

"So, you were stalking me?" I smile into the phone.

"More like testing the waters. I didn't know if you'd become a waitress at Huevos Rancheros or fulfilled your lifetime dream to … well, I'm not quite sure. By the way, waitressing is a good job, but I just saw so much talent in you."

Now, I laugh.

We got tipsy one night after midterms. They were brutal. I declared my job after college would be a waitressing job at our favorite restaurant just off-campus. I confessed to Marta, the owner, that school was too hard and that I'd make a fine waitress.

"No!" she said. "You will finish college, and you will do big things. This is my dream, not yours."

"I wonder what happened to Marta and her husband Jesus?" I say to Sam more rhetorically.

They came to the States in the 1970s. Walked through the long, lengthy, and expensive process of becoming American citizens. When they got their citizenship, Sam and I brought them flowers.

"I hope they're retired now and living comfortably in Florida or Arizona and travel to Maine or New Hampshire for summers. I hope they're snowbirds and that they don't have to worry about money," Sam says.

I'm brought back to all the memories Sam gave me in our short time together. His compassion to help others. His generosity. His love for people and his curiosity of the human mind. What makes a person whole. He's a deep thinker, too.

"It will be good to see you tomorrow, Sam Houston," I whisper into the phone.

"It will be good to see you tomorrow, Anna."

"Until tomorrow. Drive safe."

"Good-bye, Anna."

"Good-bye, Sam."

We hang up.

After freshman year, Sam left. He said his father had gone to Yale, and that was what his father wanted. I know Sam wasn't sold on the idea. And Sam was the first boy, aside from Colt, that I connected with. We took three quarters of Chemistry and General Biology together. On Friday nights, we would eat at Huevos Rancheros. And when he left, I knew it was for the best. He was smart and charming, and I always expected him to do great things in this world. Honestly, I never thought we'd meet again. He's from Connecticut. His family is well-to-do. We exchanged e-mail addresses when he left. E-mailed a few times. But life got busy. I suppose it was one of those things—not our time. But I smile to myself.

How did he find my number anyway?

Colt comes into mind. I try not to wonder what he's doing with Jordan. Instead, I Google Dr. Sam Houston.

22

Was It Suicide, Mabe?

Dillon Creek Pizza
Last Tuesday of the Month — Noon Sharp

A few weeks have passed since Mabe's incident. But nevertheless, The Ladybugs have never missed a meeting in forty years. Even after the earthquake of 1992.

Dillon Creek took the brunt of the shaking. The earthquake registered at a 7.3 on the Richter scale. The next day, two aftershocks hit, registering at 6.6 and 6.5. Twenty-nine homes were destroyed, and one hundred twenty-six were damaged, including Cranky Carl's old Victorian. Fifty-one businesses were damaged, including The Rusty Nail, which moved off its foundation.

After the massive destruction of their beloved town, The Ladybugs still met at Dillon Creek Pizza on the following Tuesday.

Delveen eats her salad with beets. Pearl drinks her Diet Coke. Clyda looks at Erla, and nobody talks about the missing person in their group.

"Okay." Pearl's voice wobbles from emotion. She sets her Diet Coke down on the table. "If nobody is going to talk about the fact that we're missing our fifth Ladybug, then I will. What in the hell happened, Erla?"

Erla has been quiet about the matter. Mostly because it isn't her business to tell and Pearl and Delveen have mouths bigger than the state of Texas.

Erla looks up from the tablecloth. Stares at the two pairs of eyes staring back at her. Clyda, of course, knows the whole story because Erla couldn't keep it from her, nor was there reason to.

"If you want to know what happened, you'd better ask Mabe yourself," Erla says, staring particularly at Pearl.

"I've tried. She's not talking."

"Well then, I suggest you learn to keep your mouth shut, and people might learn to trust you."

Pearl is appalled by this news.

Delveen says, "Erla's right, Pearl. You do have a big mouth."

Clyda now is caught off guard. "Delveen Marie Constance, you know damn good and well that you've got a mouth just as big."

Clyda raised the Atwood brothers—Daryl, Larry, and Bob. You ask anyone in town, and they'll say that her sons were the most well-behaved boys because Clyda never settled for mediocre politeness, and they were a bit scared of the switch she threatened them with. All three boys grew up to be great husbands and fathers, so she had done something right.

"Hold your tongue, Clyda Atwood. I do not have a big mouth." Delveen is seething now.

Clyda slaps the red-and-white-checkered tablecloth and hoots. "Either my hearing is getting worse or you're just plain stupid to think I'd believe that line of crap."

"Settle down, ladies," a voice sounds from behind them.

It's Mabe. With a cane and at a slow pace, she makes it to their table. "I haven't missed a meeting since I was inducted into this group, and some health shit doesn't scare me, so let's get on with it."

Mabe makes her way to her spot next to Erla. She sets her cane against the wall behind them and sits down.

Relief spreads throughout the group.

The Ladybugs have been worried about their friend. Really worried.

Erla smiles the biggest. She hasn't seen Mabe since the day after she returned home from the hospital. Mabe was sent home with an in-home caretaker from the hospital. She's since left, as Mabe is up on her feet again.

Mabe sighs. "Long story short, I almost died. But I'm back."

Junie, the owner, approaches the table. "Mabe? Something to drink?"

The whole table goes quiet, hanging on Mabe's answer.

"Water, please, Junie."

The whole table and even Junie quietly sigh with relief.

"You got it."

Erla touches her cousin's hand. "I call to order the meeting of the Dillon Creek Ladybugs, Club Number 227."

There were many rumors swirling about Mabe for a few weeks. Whether she'd tried to commit suicide or not. Whether she had been mugged. Though Delveen is still certain a masked mugger is running the streets of Dillon Creek. The rumors have subsided, and townspeople moved on to new things, such as ... *Who is the new woman Colt Atwood has been seen with?*

"How'd you get down here, Mabe?" Erla asks as they walk out of Dillon Creek Pizza.

"I flew."

Erla is confused by Mabe's humor. Maybe because of what she saw with her friend that day.

Is it dementia? Is she still taking the Ambien? Or has she just lost it?

Mabe smiles.

Clyda, Delveen, and Pearl have left, leaving Mabe and Erla out front with awkward silence and nothing to fill the void but the birds and the occasional car driving down Main Street.

"I got a ride from Pixie."

Erla nods. "Do you need a ride home? I brought my car today. Have to run into Eureka and do some errands."

"That would be nice. Thank you."

Erla's car is right in front, the passenger door closest to them.

"Do you need help getting in?" Erla asks.

"No, I've got it."

She watches Mabe slowly ease her way into the seat, and Erla walks to the driver's side, opens the door of her 1967 Cadillac, and gets in.

It's a short drive, only one block, and it's quiet between the two, the old friends, the cousins.

The question has been burning in the back of Erla's mind since she found Mabe on her kitchen floor. It's kept her up at night, pacing her own kitchen, worried about Don, too. It's kept her stomach queasy and uneasy.

Erla puts her car in park.

The question needs to be massaged into a conversation, right? It needs to be slowly brought in with tact and respect, Erla thinks.

To hell with it.

"Mabe, I need to know if you tried to take your own life with the Ambien." The queasiness spreads throughout her body. She cannot take the question back. Besides, she's not sure that she wants to.

In the stillness of the car on Berding Street, the two women only find solace in the truth that hasn't come yet.

Erla doesn't look at Mabe, doesn't want to put pressure on her, but she also expects the truth.

But she can't help herself and steals a glance.

Mabe is biting her lower lip, toying with the tissue in her hand. She goes to say something but stops herself.

Erla restrains herself from saying anything. She wants to make this easier on Mabe. She sees the pain in her eyes, the weight on her shoulders.

"I … I don't know." Mabe looks to Erla.

Due to confidentiality, Erla didn't get to see the results of any toxicology tests. They did keep Mabe in the hospital for a week and a half. Erla doesn't ask about the tests. She gave Randy the empty bottle, and that was it.

"Secrets keep us sick, Mabe," Erla whispers. "You, of all people, should know this."

It's the same line Mabe fed Erla when Devon stopped calling. Stopped visiting. Stopped all communication.

Mabe noticed, and in the living room of Don and Erla's house, Mabe said, "Secrets keep us sick."

Mabe stops toying with the tissue. "All of my family is gone, Erla. Don't take it personally. My husband. My daughter. I'm not sure that I wanted to die; I just wanted to stop hurting." She stops talking for a moment, and a single tear slides down her face. She begins again, her voice rusty and broken from emotion, "I feel like there's a hole in my heart—a big hole—and the only way to fill it is with things. Buying things, drinking my beer, taking Ambien to wash out the memories that play in my head when I try to sleep at night. Truly, I just wanted everything to stop. That's all."

Erla stares at her cousin and then to the road in front of them, watching the McGuthrie children make their way down the road with their bicycles.

"I know," Erla says. Because the truth is, Erla does know. She knows exactly what that feels like.

Don and Erla didn't have one child; they had two. One just couldn't survive outside the womb. Devon was a twin. And although she didn't get to spend any time with Lisa, Erla held her on her chest. Touched her tiny fingers, her tiny toes. Erla can still remember what she smelled like. If heaven had a smell, it would have smelled like Lisa.

"I don't want you to die, Mabe. I want you here with us."

Erla knows this is selfish, but so is suicide. So, she holds her ground. But the questions cross her mind. *Would it be better for Mabe to cross over? Would she stop hurting so much?*

"Today, I'm okay. And that's the most honest answer I can give, Erla. I hope you can understand."

"What about the boxes?"

Mabe smiles. "Can you help me with those? I'd like to find homes for all the things I've tried to fill the void with."

"Yes, I can help you with that." So, Erla gets out of the car and walks over to the passenger side where Mabe has the door open.

Mabe is sitting there, feet out. "Getting out of the car is a bitch."

They laugh as Erla helps Mabe from the car.

Erla reaches behind her and grabs her cane.

They make their way to the porch of the large house. The house that used to be filled with laughter, love, and people. And now what stands there is the same large house filled with boxes, and memories that have since faded into stories untold. Memories that hurt too much to remember.

Mabe looks to Erla, grateful she's here. Grateful she didn't walk away or give up. "And thank you for not saying anything to Pearl and Delveen."

"I did tell Clyda, Mabe, just so you know."

They reach the front door.

"Clyda doesn't have a mouth the size of Texas, so we're good." Mabe opens the door to her house.

They walk in hand in hand and begin the work that needs to be done.

All we're guaranteed is today. Just twenty-four hours—nothing more, nothing less, Erla thinks as she squeezes Mabe's hand.

23

Sexiest Man Alive

Colt

I finished my morning workout with Rob and showered, and I'm now back at The Gingerbread Mansion, where Jordan is staying.

Usually, out-of-town guests stay here. It's a ten-thousand-square-foot old Victorian that the original owners—Mel Copeland's parents—renovated. I haven't been in here in years—that is, until yesterday.

I slept on the couch last night. Made some excuse to Jordan that I wasn't feeling well. She wasn't happy about it. I think she knows something is going on.

Tan calls as I'm opening the door to her room. He only calls me if it's important.

"Are you sitting down?" Tan asks.

I'm sitting on the couch in Jordan's room. "What?" I sit down, just in case.

"Nothing bad. But are you sitting down?"

"Yes, I'm sitting down now." I run my fingers through my hair, and it makes me think of Anna.

"*Mayhem Magazine* just called. They've named you Sexiest Man Alive." He giggles and then laughs.

I smirk. "What?"

"*US Monthly*. You. Sexiest Man Alive."

I run my left hand over my face, trying to clear my mind. "What'd you say?"

"I asked if they had the right number. I repeated your name, just to be certain." He laughs again, this time so hard that he pulls away from the phone.

It makes me laugh. "Are you shitting me, Tan? Seriously?"

He's still laughing.

"You're fucking with me."

I give him a minute.

"No, no. I'm not kidding. I'm laughing because they asked to come to Dillon Creek to do a photo shoot." He's hysterical now. He can't speak but manages to say, "Remember *Health and Men* and the photo shoot we did in Los Angeles?"

I do. It was awful. I'm not a model. God didn't have any intentions of making me a model.

"Drop your jaw but smile."

"Less smile."

"Look up only slightly."

"Try not to look so constipated."

"Put your hands on your hips. No, your hips, not your waist."

"Never mind, just stand there."

"No, less Superman, more Colt Atwood."

"Forget it. That's a wrap."

I don't know how the photographer did it, but he pulled it off. My mom called after the cover went live. She asked why I only had underwear on. I tried to explain to her it was a Speedo, but she didn't get it.

"Don't worry; I'll explain you have to have a shirt this time. Laurel told me about the underwear cover," Tan says, still trying to contain his laughter.

"I'm so glad I could entertain you today, Tan." I cover my face with my hand. "When do they want to shoot the cover?"

"Next week. I'll get the details."

"What about the boot?"

"They'll work around it, Vinci said—the assistant I talked to today."

"You're sure it's me they want?"

"Dude, I'm sure. But you know what this means, right? Once they make the announcement, this will blow up. People will want interviews."

"No interviews. I've got to focus on rehab and getting better. I'll update my social media."

"You sure?"

"Yeah. Gives me something to do."

"Okay. I'll call Vinci back and confirm the details." It's quiet for a minute. "Where's the she-devil?"

"Sleeping. I think."

"Hey, Colt?"

"Yeah?"

"Don't do anything stupid. Not before the new contract."

I thought Tan knew me better. I thought he knew I was a man who was loyal to his word. "No way in hell, Tan."

"All right, man, we'll talk to you soon. Bye."

I hit End and stare at my screen saver—a picture of Anna and me in the first grade at our Christmas program. She's wearing a red-and-black-checkered sweater with black pants. Her hair is down, and she has big blue eyes and only a slight smile. I'm wearing an awful cream sweater with a knitted pattern, and my hair is combed to the right. I hated anything that involved singing and dancing. Anna hated anything that involved being in front of a lot of people. And she hated dresses, growing up. Nora had forced her to wear a dress for the first day of kindergarten, and Anna sat in the biggest mud puddle she could find when it was all over. I don't have many memories from when I was that young, but this one I remember because of how brave she was and how much I admired that in her.

"Hey," Jordan says, sauntering out from her bedroom in nothing but a towel. Her hair wet from the shower. "Feeling better?"

"Not really. Not sure what's going on."

She eases down next to me, and her tits under the towel brush against my arm.

"Come on, Colt. I need something from you. I've missed you. Haven't you missed me?"

I could lie. Tell her I missed her. But then she'll expect more, and I can't give her more. I don't want to give her more. Not anymore.

"Is it the blonde?" Her eyes move to my phone.

Fuck. The picture is lit up.

"You're adorable in that picture."

"Is the blonde the same one you've been seen in this godforsaken town with?"

"What the fuck, Jordan? Why the twenty questions?"

"Is that why you're sick?" she asks, allowing the towel to fall back from her chest, exposing one of her tits.

"Listen, leave her out of this. Let's be real. Why are you here? Why did you come to Dillon Creek?"

"I came to Dillon Creek to take back what's mine."

"What is yours in this town?"

"You, Colt Atwood."

"We've never had that type of relationship, and you know that."

"I want more."

"I can't give you more right now." I coldly look at her in the eyes.

"Right now," she says and pulls the other side of the towel away from her chest, exposing both of her breasts.

I look away, and she crawls on top of me and throws her towel to the side.

"Can't or won't?" she asks.

Housekeeping comes through the door. The young housekeeper looks up and immediately panics. "Oh my goodness, I'm so sorry. I'll come back later." She quickly shuts the door behind her.

Jordan leans into my ear. "I'm so wet, Colt. Please."

"Get up, Jordan."

But she takes my hand and puts it to her wetness.

"Stop." I yank my hand away, lift her up off me, and stand. "I can't do this with you anymore. It's over."

I walk to the sink in the bathroom and wash my hands.

Before I walk out the door, Jordan says, "It would be a shame to find out that Anna's dear old dad is a gay man living on the down-low in a small town, wouldn't it? I wonder what this small, stupid, little town would do to a man like that."

Shock yields quickly to my fury. How I put up with this woman for years has all of a sudden become a mystery. Now, I know why she defends criminals—because she's a bad guy. It becomes crystal clear to me.

I turn around, and my stare meets hers. "Jordan, let me be clear. You have a problem with me? That's fine. But leave the Cain family out of this. Do you hear me?"

Jordan glares at me with burning, reproachful eyes.

"Pack your shit and leave town, Jordan. Don't come back. I'll have Tan deliver your things." I turn and leave.

I make it down the stairs, and I run into Mel, the current owner.

"Colt, how are you? So good to see you home." She reaches in for a hug.

"Hey, Mel." I give her an awkward hug.

"Are you leaving?"

Yes. Thank God. "Yes, just on my way out."

"Well, you come back, all right? Hey … how's Anna? I've been meaning to get down to the clinic."

"As far as I know, she's good." Guilt turns in my gut.

"All right, well, you have a good day, okay? And tell your mother I'll see her next week for the school board meeting."

"I will," I say and make it out of there before someone else stops me.

I want to stop by the clinic and see Anna's face. But it's not a good idea when Jordan is still in town. That's all the Cain family needs—Jordan Landry snooping in their business. I get in Cash's truck and drive home to the ranch.

24

Sam Houston

Anna

I'm in between patients. It's Wednesday, about noon, and the fire whistle sounds just at the same time my phone signifies a text message.

> *Sam: Have you seen the trees up here?*

> *Me: You're close?*

> *Sam: I couldn't sleep. I left earlier than expected.*

> *Me: Where did you decide to stay the night?*

> *Sam: The Gingerbread Mansion. Is it a real mansion?*

> *Me: Yes.*

Bubbles appear, then disappear, and then appear again.

> *Me: Where are you?*

Sam: A place called Willits.

Me: You're about two hours from here.

Again, bubbles from Sam's end appear again.

Sam: I'm really excited and extremely nervous to see you. Is that too forward?

I start to type, then stop, and start again. A tiny smile spreads over my face.

Me: I'm excited to see you, too. It's been far too long. And too forward? What do you mean?

Sam: It will be good to see you, is all.

Me: And you know how to get here? US 101 to the Dillon Creek exit and take a left at the Stop sign. Go over the bridge and head down State Route 211 about five miles. You'll run into us. :) Drive safe.

Sam: I will. ;)

Kimber comes in my office, and I jump.
I set my phone down on my desk. "Hey, what's up?"
She looks at me funny. "Cranky Carl is here with Jinx for their twelve o'clock appointment."
"Thank you," I say quickly.
Kimber nods, staring at me, most likely trying to figure out why I'm so jumpy.
"I'll see you out front." She walks back down the hallway.
I take a big deep breath in and think of Colt. Our conversation yesterday.
"I don't want her coming after you."
I'm not scared of Jordan. I've never been scared of anyone. No, that's not true. I was scared of Colt at one time.
After I came back from North Carolina, my heart in my hands, scattered in a million pieces, I tried my best to move

on. In the days, the weeks, the months that followed, I was scared of what I'd do when Colt called or texted. I was scared that I'd rush back to him to help him pick up his own pieces. But he never did. It wasn't until months later that he finally texted me and said, *I miss you.* I prayed every day for God to give me the strength to not respond. Truly though, I think it was my own free will and also my stubbornness, playing the memory over and over and over again of Colt making love to another woman, that ensured my fingers never did the dance across the keyboard. That my anger and my broken heart never got the best of me, but they eventually did. Only once did I text him.

My phone chimes once more.

It's Sam.

Sam: I don't have the mullet anymore. I might look a little different.

Me: I didn't mind the mullet, Sam Houston.

Sam: I know. See you soon.

I smile and set my phone down on my desk. I go down the hallway to my next patient, leaving Bones to his nap in my office.

"Room two," Kimber calls, hearing my footsteps.

"Thank you."

"You're welcome."

Carl is sitting in the chair with Jinx, the cat, on his lap. An ugly cat with patches of hair missing only due to his ownership of the block he ruled.

If you ask Carl why he named him Jinx, he'll tell you, "Look at him. He's ugly as sin. A walking joke."

Though Jinx, to me, didn't look like a joke at all, but if you catch him on a day when Cranky Carl is extra-cranky, you might see Jinx's face change. I've seen it. Once.

"Hi, Carl. How are you doing today?"

"Hey, Dr. Cain. I'm well, but Jinx here isn't so well."

I take a seat across from Carl. "What seems to be the problem?"

"He's not eating."

"How about water? Is he drinking water?"

"Yeah."

"May I?"

"Of course."

I take Jinx from him and put him on the exam table. Listen to his heart. Lungs. Jinx sits down in a crouching position and purrs. "Lungs and heart sound good. Did you change anything? His food?"

"I did. Larry at Wilson's Grocery switched up the damn cat food." He waves his hands in the air, frustrated. "I had to get Jinx some off-the-wall brand. Who the hell knows what's in it? Larry said his supplier couldn't get the other brand for two more weeks."

I stroke Jinx's coat. He purrs and digs his face into my hands. "Well, he's feeling okay. But you're probably going to need to drive to Eureka or Belle's Hollow to get what you're looking for. And if you do decide to change his food indefinitely, then do it in increments. Has he been able to produce excrement?"

"What?"

"Does he have the ability to produce excrement?"

"What the hell does that mean?" Carl tucks his hands into his pockets.

"Poop. Can he poop?"

Both the corners of Carl's mouth turn up. "Oh. Well, how the hell do I know? He does his excrementities—or whatever word you used—outside."

I try not to laugh. Not at Carl, but the way he's so stuck in his ways.

I pick Jinx up and hand him back to Carl. "Well, if I were you, I'd get him the food he's accustomed to and slowly add the new food to his diet. Give it a week, and then if he's still not feeling well, bring him back in. That should fix it though."

Carl nods. "Well, I ain't driving to Eureka or Belle's Hollow every few weeks, so unless Larry gets the old food in, Jinx will have to settle with this new crap." He rolls his eyes and stands. "Thank you, Dr. Cain," he grumbles.

Carl's come a long way.

"Oh, how do you like the house?" he asks.

"I move in tomorrow. Tom should be done with everything."

"Tom's a good man," Carl says.

I'm caught off guard by his statement. Carl doesn't really say anything nice about anyone.

Then, he whispers loud enough for me to hear him, "And you're a good doctor."

"Thank you, Carl. I appreciate that." I touch his arm.

I open the door for Carl and Jinx, and we head down the hallway.

"How is he?" Kimber asks, reaching over the counter and giving Jinx extra love.

"I think he'll be okay."

"What do I owe you?" He grabs his wallet out of his back pocket.

"Thirty dollars today," Kimber says when I hand her the chart.

Carl gives Kimber cash.

"Would you like a receipt?" Kimber asks.

"Nah." Carl shuffles toward the door, but Bones comes running down the hallway and catches up to Carl and Jinx.

Bones sits.

Carl smiles brightly. "Hey, buddy."

He puts Jinx down, and Bones doesn't budge. He waits for Carl to give him the rub he does behind the ears.

Bones makes a groan sound deep within his throat.

"Attaboy," Carl says, and Jinx rubs up against Carl's legs.

Bones has always had a soft spot for Carl.

Carl gives Bones one last pat, picks up Jinx, and leaves, calling behind him, "Good-bye, ladies."

"Good-bye, Carl," we say.

I'm nervous, and I shouldn't be, right? It's just dinner.

I told Sam I'd walk down to meet him; it's only a block to pick him up at The Gingerbread Mansion. I haven't set foot inside that place since I was a kid. I guess I just haven't needed to.

I always imagined the first time I had sex, it would be at The Gingerbread Mansion. Maybe on prom night. But my first time wasn't at the mansion, nor was it on good terms. I lost my virginity on the worst night of my life, but somehow, Colt made it feel all right. Made everything feel okay even if it wasn't.

He took care with my body. Made sure to kiss every inch of me. Gave extra attention to my hip bones that stood out when I lay before him. It was as if we'd done that before. It wasn't awkward or weird or uncomfortable.

He looked in my eyes as he crawled on top of me, pushed my hair from my face, my cheeks flushed with passion and want, and said, "I love you, Anna Cain." His look was hooded.

I know he loved the way my body felt because he told me so, made sure to put his mouth around my breasts as I watched. I paid close attention to his body as well and took pleasure in touching him, just as he touched me. Then, he slipped the condom on and slowly pushed inside me. I winced.

"Does it hurt?" he asked. "Are you all right?"

I'd never had sex with someone, but it did hurt at first. Then, he told me to climb on top, so I did. He put his thumb at the top of my folds, where the tiny knot was. And as he applied a light pressure, I rocked, and it hurt but felt wonderful, all at the same time.

When I was about to release, he took my head in his hands. "I want to watch what I do to you, Anna."

And with that, I climaxed, and so did he. While I was sore, he gently took me three more times that night and into the early morning. Once in the shower.

I'd never felt closer to a man in my life, not like that.

That night and the morning after was the fallout of Conroy Atwood's and Tripp Morgan's deaths.

Our night had been built on grief and years of friendship and love. And love in the sense that our relationship went deeper than lovemaking. Love in the sense of the word. It's an action after all. It's taking care of one another, even when we're broken.

Push these thoughts away, Anna, I tell myself. The ones I keep locked inside.

I look in my mirror and put in my pearl earrings that my great-grandmother Eledice gave me. My cheeks are flushed pink.

Late this afternoon, I decided that Bones and I would stay at our new house. My parents have a dinner to go to, Adam has a visiting musician from Italy at The Steeple, and Amelia is out of town. I haven't moved anything in yet, but I figure all I need is an air mattress and a sleeping bag and a coffeepot—with coffee, of course.

Just have a good time with Sam Houston, I tell myself. *It's just dinner and the musician at The Steeple in town. Friends. Old friends.*

Bones lies at my feet in the bathroom. I apply some lip gloss and then step back to look at myself in the mirror. I'm wearing a light-blue sundress and a white cardigan, my grandmother's pearls, red lipstick, and the gloss. My blonde hair is down, and I try to remember the woman I am. A woman who has needs that consist of a man's hands. It's not like I forget, but rather, I tuck it into my scrubs and pretend I don't need it. I drop my head to the right and try to laugh a flirtatious laugh.

I'm not made to flirt.

I roll my eyes, shut the bathroom light off, and walk down to the kitchen. I give Bones his dinner before I go. Grab a bully stick. I bend down to his level, and he stares back at me. His rust-colored eyebrows and his amber-colored eyes stare back.

"It's been a long time since I've gone to dinner with a man, Bones. How do I look?"

Bones sniffs my entire face and gives me a tiny lick.

I smile and take his head in my hands, my face against his neck. He rests his snout on my back. "I don't know how I got so lucky with you, buddy."

I pull back and stand but not before I put a kiss on his head.

"Look, keep watch, and I'll be back early." I look into the living room to make sure the air mattress and sleeping bag are still in place and that Bones hasn't pulled the sleeping bag to the floor yet for his own keeping. His bed sits next to mine. "Be good."

I leave the kitchen light on over the stove and shut the door behind me.

The walk to The Gingerbread Mansion is quiet. It's a little before six p.m., and during the summer, the fog usually rolls in about four in the afternoon. But not today. The sky is full of blue, and the sun is almost warm. Northern California gets to be seventy degrees, and we all want to die. Most of us anyway.

The Gingerbread Mansion is a big yellow house with orange trim. It's a Victorian home, built in 1895, and it's been a staple in Dillon Creek since then.

When I reach the mansion, I make my way up the stairs to the porch and open the door. All the scents and the feelings of my childhood come back to me.

"Anna, how are you?" Mel Copeland approaches me.

I turn to her. "Hello, Mel. I'm well. How are you?"

"Keeping busy." She nods. "Are you here to see Colt?" She motions upstairs to the second level of rooms. "He left this morning."

My stomach clenches. *In the morning. Did he stay the night with Jordan? Stop!* "No, actually, I'm here to see Dr. Sam Houston."

"Oh. The surgeon?" Mel looks confused.

A man comes downstairs, fixing his sleeves. His dark brown hair is cut short on the bottom and longer on top.

"Mrs. Copeland?" a customer calls from the other room.

"I will see you later, Anna. And don't be a stranger," Mel says, touching my arm with her hand.

I nod and watch the handsome man.

He's not the gangly eighteen-year-old boy I met freshman year, the Samuel Houston I remember with a boyishly adorable face and a genuine smile.

He's somehow become a man with a strong jawline and the same green eyes that would burn holes in lies.

Now, I'm worried that I'm somehow underdressed, pulling at the sleeves of my light sweater. All of a sudden, I'm hot.

I look up again, only to see his smile.

"Anna." He reaches me after saying my name. His scent of a cologne, which smells expensive, gets lost somewhere inside me.

"Sam."

I reach up on my tiptoes and put my arms around his shoulders while he slides his hand around my waist. Sam has always been a gentleman.

We release, my hand somehow caught in his.

"You've grown up." I try to keep things light and airy, like two old friends having dinner, which is what this is.

"You look beautiful, Anna."

His hand lingers in mine for a bit too long. I take it back and pretend that my ear needs attention, doing something, anything to distract myself.

"You do, too. I mean, not beautiful in the womanly sense, but in the manly sense." I sigh. I look around the foyer and the sitting room next to it, which are both now empty somehow. "Shall we go grab a drink and then dinner?" I could use one. A drink, that is.

"I would love to," he says. Sam walks toward the front door and opens it for me.

"Thank you."

He shuts it behind us.

It's quiet for a moment between us. I'm not sure what to say, and I'm completely caught off guard by the way he looks, just because he's so grown-up.

"Tell me what happened after you left Davis," I say as we begin our journey two blocks to Main Street.

We kept in touch through e-mail for a little while. Social media was just becoming a thing. Besides, I don't think Sam and I had time for it. We were too committed to our studies.

He slips his hands into his pockets. Looks at me with one closed eye, the summer sun beaming behind me. "I'd rather hear your story."

I shrug. "Well, let's see. I finished with an undergrad degree in animal science and completed the Doctor of Veterinary Medicine program, and then I moved home."

"Why'd you move home?"

"Dr. East, the town veterinarian at the time, gave me an offer I couldn't refuse."

Sam listens. "And how do you like being home?"

I think about it. Bite my lip. "This place will always be home, no matter where I go."

"But how do you like being home?"

"It's familiar. It's routine. I'm glad to be home with Tess."

I don't bring up Colt. Though, when we were younger, I told Sam about Colt. I'm almost certain Sam knows where Colt is in life, if he follows any sports.

"How is the infamous Tess Morgan?"

I laugh, thinking back to the first time Tess came to visit me at Davis. "You know, she's never forgotten that."

Sam laughs, and I like the way it sounds. I've missed the way it sounds. How does that happen? How do you miss something you didn't know you'd missed?

"I swear, I didn't know it was the dean's house, or I wouldn't have let her puke in the bushes." He laughs it off.

I laugh. Look up at him and then up ahead toward town. "What about you?"

"Well, I finished my undergrad and immediately went into medical school."

I wait for him to continue, but he doesn't. "That's it?"

"I guess so."

"You guess so? It's either the end or not, Sam Houston. There's no *I guess so*."

"Did you keep up with our tradition and go to Huevos Rancheros every Friday night?"

The ease of our conversation is making me feel more comfortable. Our back-and-forth banter and our wit have always been our thing. I settle into our words.

"I tried to." I shrug. "It was just different without you."

We reach Main Street.

"Sam Houston, welcome to Dillon Creek. The Whiskey Barrel is this way." I point to the right.

I'm sure we'll get extra sets of eyes on us. If Colt and I do anything in this town without each other, the whole town knows. But Sam is an old friend. I'd like to say that it's different, that there's nothing between us.

We make it to The Whiskey Barrel, a place the Atwoods haven't set foot inside in just over seven years. It's not a middle-ground place because it's owned by the Morgans, Tess's parents.

Dave Lubbock walks up to us from behind the bar, cautiously eyeing Sam. "Anna." He nods to Sam.

"Dave, this is Sam Houston. He's visiting from …" And then I realize he didn't say where he lived. Originally, I know he's from Connecticut, but he said he was just passing through.

"Connecticut." Sam reaches out and shakes Dave's hand.

Dave likes this. He might be a bartender, but he's got more brains than most in this town.

"What can I get you two?" Dave asks.

Sam looks at me and grins. "Coors Light?"

I roll my eyes and smile. "Your jokes are not funny, Sam Houston."

I drank four Coors Lights one night, and I threw up all night long. I hadn't drunk much at home before I went to college.

"I'll take a glass of red—the Ménage à Trois, please, Dave."

"Maker's Mark and water on ice, please, Dave, is it?" Sam says.

Dave throws the stained towel over his shoulder. "Yes, sir. You've got it. I'll be right back." He turns to go but stops. "You're the doctor, right? Some sort of heart surgeon?"

Sam looks back at me. His eyes wide. "Um, yeah. How … how do you know that?"

Dave lets out a robust laugh. "Welcome to Dillon Creek, man. Where everybody knows your business."

Dave leaves to get our drinks, shaking his head.

"I'm from Stamford, Connecticut, Anna. There are well over a hundred thousand people there. This"—he looks around The Whiskey Barrel—"isn't something I'm used to."

"Try growing up here." I laugh, crossing my arms.

Dave brings our drinks.

"Thanks, Dave," I say.

"Thank you, Dave," Sam says and puts the bottle to his lips.

"So, Doc, I've got a question for you," Dave says, leaning against the bar.

"Shoot, Dave." Sam sets his beer down.

"I've been havin' some chest pains, but my wife makes this spicy chili that I just can't say no to. You think it's just heartburn, or you think I've got somethin' more goin' on?" Dave rubs his five o'clock shadow.

Dave's a bigger guy. Potbelly, a tuft of peppered hair on top. He was a logger before he got injured by a falling log, and the Morgans hired him as their main bartender. Though his alliance stands with the Morgans, I think he still has a soft spot for the Atwood boys.

"Well, I'd say, cut out the chili first, and if the problem persists, you should schedule an appointment with your physician."

Dave presses his lips together. "Sound advice, Doc. Thanks." He looks at me as I set my glass down, feeling the alcohol meet my head. "Atwood seen the good doctor yet?"

"Shut up, Dave."

Dave shrugs, limps away.

"Ah, Colt Atwood. The man who broke your heart."

I take a sip of my wine to disguise the way his name makes me feel. "Stop."

Sam smiles. "So, you're saving animals now?"

I nod. "Yep."

"Anna." Sam rolls his eyes. "You realize I know you well enough to know when you're feeding me a line of bullshit, right?"

"What?"

"You were at the top of our classes. I didn't even know a hundred and two percent in a class was possible. Anna, you could have been anything you wanted to be. Why'd you choose veterinary medicine?"

"Why not? At any rate, it's harder because animals can't tell you their symptoms."

Sam smiles, looks back at me, and settles his elbows on the bar. "What's your first love?"

"What?" Clearly, I don't know where he's going with this, and maybe he thinks I do.

"What's your first love, Anna? What ... what makes your soul breathe? What puts fire inside you?"

I nervously laugh to buy myself time. *Do I know the answer to his question? Do I know the ramifications if my answer doesn't align with the fire inside me? What if I give him the safe answer? The one people expect.*

Dave returns to us. "Doctor and Doctor"—he laughs—"you both good?"

"Yes, thank you, Dave," Sam answers for both of us. He used to do that in college. And I didn't mind because it was one less decision I had to make. It was one less thing I had to think about, worry about.

Dave walks down the bar to Toby Lemon, whose head is on the bar. Poor guy. He's had too much to drink. "Hey, Al. Take Toby upstairs and let him sober up, would ya?" Al is waiting tables.

"You didn't answer my question, Anna." Sam drinks his beer and carefully sets it back down on the bar.

I wonder if he takes this much care of the hearts he operates on. The heart, after all, is a very complex organ but probably not to Sam. As far as I can remember, Sam has always been able to separate life from death. Able to look at situations with a bird's-eye view. Able to construct the situation for what it is, the pieces of what exists and what doesn't exist. He just looks at life differently.

I take a big breath in and chase it down with wine. I set my glass down on the bar and give him the most honest answer I have, "At first, I did want to be a doctor. Then, I didn't. Then, I thought, just for a moment, I'd be a surgeon. Then, I didn't." I pause. "I chose the path that was safe. I chose a path that would pay the bills and allow me to give back in some small fraction."

I can feel Sam's gaze upon me, and I pick my eyes up to meet his.

"Does it put fire in your bones?"

"Good surgeries do. The positive outcomes do. So, yes, I suppose it does."

Sam is now peeling the label of his beer bottle.

"What about you?" I whisper. "Does having people's lives in your hands put fire in your bones?"

Sam looks at me and then back to his bottle. "Yeah, it does. But so do you."

His words catch me off guard, and I swallow the hot feeling that forms in my throat and on my cheeks, which are now probably pink. It could be the wine. It could also be Sam Houston.

25

Clyda Atwood Is Dying

Anna: Age Nine

First Christian Church was quiet. It was peaceful when I made my way in. The smell was musty and godly. I wrapped my arms around myself and ran to the first pew. Sat down. My heart pounded against my chest, and I couldn't tell if it was from the running I had done, coming down here, or the fact that Clyda Atwood had had a heart attack right in front of us and I was terrified.

I'd thought she'd died on the spot until my dad rushed to her, felt her neck for a pulse, and put an ear to her mouth.

"Call 911," he'd said.

That was a good sign, right? That Clyda Atwood still had a pulse.

We had been at Portuguese Hall when I took off running down to the church.

I took refuge on the bench seat and allowed my body to melt into the wood. An uneasy feeling grew inside me from the thoughts that spun out of control in my head.

Will Clyda die?

She's the matriarch.

What will happen to the Atwood family?

Clyda's husband, Borges, had passed away three years ago.

Maybe Clyda was suffering from a broken heart.

The soft warmth from the candle that burned at the front of the church made the truth pour from my mouth.

"It's me, God, Anna," I whispered so lightly that I wasn't sure God could hear me, but I continued, "If this is your way of repaying me for the two cuss words I said last week, well then, that's just wrong." Tears started to tempt my eyes. "Look, I'm sorry. They … they just slipped out, and I couldn't control it. When that hammer hit my finger, it made me want to scream." I paused, almost waiting to hear from God himself. Even knowing full well that God never spoke to me, I listened anyway. "Please don't take Clyda Atwood right now. She's a real good lady, and I know the Atwoods would be lost without her."

Besides, there are other people I wouldn't mind you taking, I said in my head, too afraid to admit this in the house of God and all things holy. As if lightning would strike me dead or something like that.

"Anyway, I just … I just feel like someone needs to plead her case. We need her here." I paused, again waiting for some sort of sign that God was listening.

Pastor Mike eased down next to me in the pew. Stared up at Jesus on the cross. My eyes were about to explode with tears, so I gave myself the okay to let them roll down my cheeks.

"Clyda Atwood is going to die, Pastor Mike, and it's all my fault."

The weight of the church's silence sat around us like morning fog to the redwood trees.

"How is Clyda's heart attack your fault, Anna?"

I twisted my fingers into a ball until my fingertips turned white. "She was eating my brownie, Pastor Mike." Tears welled up again. "I just know I added too much baking powder, and now, I have to tell Colt and his family that I killed Clyda. And she's a real good lady." My voice was caught somewhere between the fear in my throat and the sadness I felt in my heart.

"Is Clyda dead?" he asked.

"Well, no, not yet."

"And what makes you think she's going to die?"

I shook my head, trying not to remember her face when her head had hit the hardwood floor. She had been awfully white. I couldn't answer his question because I didn't have an answer.

"Can I suggest something to you?" he asked, looking down at me. His hands neatly folded in his lap.

And from this angle, I swore Pastor Mike was wearing a halo.

I shrugged. "Sure, I guess."

"I think our Father calls us up when it's time, but I don't think that happens until our bodies are ready or when unexpected things happen. From the studying that I've done the past twenty-five years, I know God gave us free will to do as we wish. God can't control if we eat what we shouldn't or put bad things in our bodies. We control that." He was quiet for a moment and then said, "Sometimes, our bodies are predisposed to illness, and he can't control that either."

"But God can perform miracles. I mean, look at Mary Gable. She had cancer, and now, she doesn't."

Pastor Mike tried not to smile. "What makes you think Clyda had a heart attack?"

I still twisted my fingers. "She grabbed her chest, Pastor Mike, before she fell. That's a heart attack." I caught another tear before it fell.

I knew what he was thinking. *Yep, she killed her; she's right.*

He was probably going to condemn me to hell now that he had conducted his own research and knew that I was a cold-blooded killer. I probably wouldn't be able to come back to this church.

"Can I ask you another question, Anna?"

"Go ahead," I said and pushed my sweaty hands against my jeans to dry them.

"What makes you think you're that powerful to make someone have a heart attack?"

I'm not, was my initial thought response.

But I supposed it wasn't me. It had been my action of adding too much baking powder.

But when Pastor Mike said it like this, it started to resonate with me.

How could a nine-year-old kid kill an old woman with baking powder by accident? And how could I be that powerful?

I looked up to Pastor Mike. "So, you don't think it was the brownie?"

He smiled. "No, I don't, Anna Elizabeth Cain. In fact, *if* it was a heart attack, there isn't one single instance that can cause it. Usually, several things cause heart attacks." Pastor Mike winked at me. "I don't think Clyda Atwood could die of a heart attack anyway. I think it's going to take a lot more than that to kill that woman."

I reached up and made sure my face was dry.

"Anna?" It was my brother.

I turned and saw Adam standing there, scared to death.

"What happened to you?" He walked down the aisle to the pew.

"Pastor Mike," Adam said.

Pastor Mike stood. Looked at both of us. "Take Anna home, will you? She'll be all right. She just needs a good night's sleep."

Adam nodded and stuck out his hand. "Come on, Anna."

I took his hand, and we started to leave the church.

"Pastor Mike?" I turned to look at him.

With his hand in his pocket, he juggled some change with his fingers. "Yes, Anna?"

"Thanks. Thanks for everything."

"Do me a favor, Anna?" he asked.

"Yeah."

"Before you look to blame God for everything, ask God for the right lenses to view the world. You might get a different perspective."

I stared at him long and hard. I couldn't understand what he meant by lenses. But I did know that Pastor Mike had made me feel better just by giving me a way to look at things a little differently.

I wrinkled my nose. "Yeah, okay."

"And remember, fear can be the keeper of our souls if we allow it. Walk with God and not with fear."

He lost me on that one, but Adam's grip tightened, and I knew it was time to go.

I tossed and turned in bed and waited for my father to get home from Eureka. He'd gone in the ambulance with Clyda. I'd gone from a nine-year-old girl to a nine-year-old murderer back to a nine-year-old, scared that her best friend, Colt, had lost his grandma.

Hearing murmurs outside my door, I knew my father was home. He knocked softly and opened my door. Quietly made his way to my bed and sat down. Reached up and pushed my hair from my face.

"Anna, are you awake?" he asked.

I nodded and left my eyes closed. Pictured Clyda's head hitting the hardwood floor again, her pale face lying there against the wood.

"Are you all right?" he asked, stroking my forehead.

Tears began to burn in my eyes again. I'd worked it out in my head that I wasn't a murderer, but still, I couldn't stop the tears.

"That frightened you."

I nodded, eyes still closed. Terrified to ask the next question, but I knew I needed to. *If she is dead, I need to know, so I can figure out a plan to help Colt through it.* "Is Clyda dead?"

"No, she'll be fine after a few weeks of rest."

My eyes opened and stared up at my dad. "She survived a heart attack?"

My dad gave me a curious look. "What makes you think she had a heart attack, Anna?"

I looked the other direction. Tried not to remember how she'd grabbed her chest and fallen. I looked back at my dad and shrugged.

"Exhaustion," my dad said. "Extreme exhaustion and dehydration. She needs plenty of water and lots of rest, is all."

My dad's eyes changed, and I knew it was because of the tears that began to slide down the side of my head. Tears of relief. Relief that Clyda would be okay. Relief that Colt and the Atwoods wouldn't have to bury Clyda in the ground, like they had Borges three years ago and how sad that had been to watch them go through all that.

"Honey, what's wrong?"

It's a long story, Dad. One only fit for a pastor who knows about fear and murder.

"Just relieved," I said because, after all, it was the truth.

My dad searched my eyes. He knew there was something more, just like when I looked into his eyes and saw that maybe he needed more of something, too, more out of life.

But what did I know? I was just a nine-year-old kid.

"Dad, will you stay with me until I fall asleep?" I asked.

"Always."

And he lay down next to me, and I curled into the crook of his arm and fell fast asleep.

The truth was, I didn't have to tell my dad anything, and he trusted that if and when I was ready, I would. But not tonight. I was too tired.

26

Russell, the Dog

Pearl sets her water down after taking a sip at The Rusty Nail. "If you ask me, I think there's something fishy going on with that whole mess."

Delveen nods, taking a bite of her chicken sandwich, which sets Erla off. Delveen is not a chicken-sandwich-eater; she's a salad-eater with beets, and this doesn't sit well with Erla for whatever reason. She knows it's petty, that it's absurd to allow this to bother her, but it does.

Clyda hasn't arrived yet, and Pearl apparently thinks it's all right to talk about her friend's grandson and use the word *mess* in the same sentence.

Mabe gags of her salad with fat-free dressing.

"You ought not to throw stones until you know the full story," Erla says to Pearl.

"Truth isn't throwing stones, Erla," Pearl says.

"Did you see Colt in town with the new girl?" Erla asks.

"Well, no, but Tony did from his shop window. So did Mabe. Didn't you, Mabe?" Pearl puts down her fork.

Mabe rolls her eyes. "So what, Pearl? Doesn't mean a damn thing."

Erla looks at Mabe and doesn't dare ask the question in front of Pearl and Delveen, but Mabe can feel it from her stare.

"According to Mary Gable, that new gal is one of a kind. Came into the Mercantile, barking orders like a drill sergeant," Pearl says.

"Can I get you anything else, ladies?" Merry asks. She looks around the table. "Where's Clyda?"

"Running late," Erla says after she wipes her mouth.

Merry tops off their water. "Okay. Well then, I'll bring the bill."

"Thanks, honey," Mabe says.

Clyda comes into The Rusty Nail, carrying her purse and a notebook, and sits down at our table, stunned speechless. "That Rita Lewis has to be out of her goddamn mind." She shakes her head, using her finger to push a curl from her face. "Sorry, Jesus," Clyda huffs under her breath.

"Clyda," Merry says when she returns. "Can I get you anything?"

"Just a glass of your homemade iced tea would be great, Merry. Thank you."

"You got it," she says and leaves again.

"She wants a goddamn Picasso by tomorrow."

Everyone knows that Clyda is a beautiful painter and artist. Since she's gotten older though, her hands have gotten shakier and her fingers arthritic. Ruby is an old friend, and that's the only reason Clyda entertained the idea in the first place. Clyda used to own an art studio in town, but when she got too old to run it, she sold it to a beautiful out-of-town artist named Thumbelina Thundergrass. The studio is down the alley next to Book Ends, and Thumbelina still owns the shop. She sells paintings and ships them all over the world, just like Clyda used to do in her heyday.

"She wants a ten-by-ten-foot canvas painting of Russell, their twelve-year-old schnauzer. He's a goddamn dog, and Dr. Cain had to put him down yesterday. She's planning a damn funeral for the dog. Sorry, again, Jesus."

"Well, in her defense," Delveen starts, "they've never had kids."

Clyda drops her head only slightly to the left. "It's a dog, for Pete's sake, Delveen, not a person. Who has a funeral for their dog and invites the whole goddamn town? Damn it, Jesus, I'm so sorry for the foul mouth today." Clyda is frustrated.

Merry returns with Clyda's tea.

"Oh, thank you."

"Ruby's schnauzer, Russell, died?" Merry asks. "It's about time. He was twelve." Merry places her hand on the back of Delveen's chair.

"Amen, Merry. And now, she wants a funeral," Clyda says after taking a sip of her iced tea.

Merry says, "A funeral?"

"A funeral," Clyda says.

"For a dog?" Merry clarifies.

"Thank you, Merry. Yes, for a damn dog," Clyda says.

"We love our Grizz we got from the Atwoods, but we wouldn't have a public funeral for him," Merry says.

"That's right, Merry," Clyda says.

"Anyway, let me know if I can get you ladies anything else," Merry says to the group and walks away.

Clyda finishes off her tea. "Well, I'd better get home. I've got a lot to paint before tomorrow," she says as she stands.

"All right, well, call me later," Erla says, touching her friend on the shoulder.

"I've got to go too," Pearl says, throwing a twenty down to the table.

"Me too," Delveen says, doing the same.

Erla stands, as does Mabe.

"You coming over today?" Mabe whispers as the other women leave. "I could use some more help."

"You got the stuff I asked for?" Erla asks.

"Two bottles."

"Perfect."

Mabe takes a box from the living room and begins the process of going through it the way Erla suggested.

Do I need it? Can I use it? Mabe asks herself.

Erla wrote the phrase down on each box, perhaps knowing she might forget. Mabe is definitely getting more forgetful with age.

Do I need it?

Can I use it?

If not, throw it away.

It's been nineteen days without alcohol for Mabe, though she doesn't think it's an addiction or some sort of disease like her cousin Joey had back in 1972 and died from, but it was something Mabe used to pass the time, take the pain away from losing her husband and her daughter.

Mabe opens the box.

It's a box full of brand-new baking items—an order she doesn't remember placing, but she must have, right? A wooden rolling pin, three baking tins, an upside-down cake mold, a cookie sheet, and four cookie cutters of different shapes. Mabe keeps everything in the box and sighs deeply. Why on earth she thought she needed these things is beyond her.

Did I really try to kill myself with the pills? What if someone had coerced me while I was in a drunken stupor and I don't remember?

It isn't a farfetched thought, but Mabe Muldoon doesn't take direction from anyone if it isn't wanted, so Mabe pushes that thought to the back of her mind and considers that she might have tried to take her own life.

"Hey, Erla?" Mabe calls to the dining room.

"Yeah?"

"Have the Dillon Creek yard sales already happened this year?" Mabe can't remember. Her memory isn't what it used to be.

"Yes," Erla calls from the other room.

Mabe considers hanging on to it for next year, but instead, she marks the box with the word *Donate*.

"I've almost got the stain up from the hardwood floor." Erla peeks into the living room where Mabe is.

She looks back at her cousin. The person who's always been there. Who's never given up on her.

Erla pushes a wayward silver-colored strand of hair from her face.

Erla has always been beautiful. She used to leave men in their tracks in her prime—their prime—and it's no wonder that Don scooped her up as soon as he could. And Mabe was normal. The kind of woman who is forgettable to ninety percent of the population but unforgettable to John. Mabe's heart aches at the thought of him, but she swallows her hurt.

Death can be crippling, she thinks to herself as she opens another box. This one is full of family relics, and all the air in her body just leaves. She pulls out their wedding photo. Nobody knew, except for Erla, but she was twelve weeks pregnant with Francine. Mabe runs her hand over the frame.

When did I pack these things up and put them in a box?

She can't remember.

When did I try to erase the past? When did I try to replace my memories—my most cherished memories—with sadness?

Mabe isn't one to cry, but she feels the tears start to sting her eyes. She's had more feelings, more tears, and more sadness in the past nineteen days than she's felt in an awfully long time. For the first time in a long time, she has begun to feel. It doesn't feel great, admittedly, but she's felt, and that is saying something. Nineteen days ago, it was easier to pick up the beer she kept hidden in the detached garage.

Oh, no, she thought. *The detached garage.*

Worry makes her bite her lower lip, and her stomach grows queasy.

She'll need to tell Erla about that, too. So many memories she put in the garage, and she'll eventually have to tell her secret. The one she swore in the silence of the night that she'd never tell anyone. The one secret that has divided a town, the one secret Mabe Muldoon knows that no one else does, all because she was where she wasn't supposed to be on that oddly cool summer night on a country road, where everyone slept.

"Don? I'm home." Erla sets her purse down on the counter and waits for him to call back. She listens quietly.

"Don?" she calls down the hallway, and she hears the shower running.

Why on God's green earth would Don be in the shower right now?

Erla walks into their bedroom and into the bathroom. "Don?"

"Yes?"

"Why are you in the shower?"

"Because I'm dirty."

"From what?"

"Gardening. Why?"

Erla sighs and leans against the doorframe. "You know you're not supposed to shower without me home, Don."

"Erla, I'm a grown man, and I'll do what I want."

This is the part that tugs at Erla's heart the most. His strive for independence. She doesn't want to take that away, but in the same token, she wants to keep him safe, keep him on this earth as long as she can.

Relief meets Erla's chest because somewhere down the hallway, it tightened with fear that somehow, maybe, he was confused. Thought it was morning time. Erla worries too much. Thinks the worst in every situation. It's easier, right? To be prepared for the worst. But if the worst doesn't come, then relief surely would. Maybe it has been a lifestyle that Erla has grown accustomed to. The lifestyle of worry, fear.

Perhaps it isn't healthy, but Erla can't think of another way to do things.

"Did you take your medication I'd laid out for you this morning by your bedside?" Erla looks back to his side of the bed and knows she's setting him up, but she prefers the word *testing*. Testing his memory.

"Cognitive difficulties," the doctor said—another symptom of Parkinson's.

"Do you see it there?" he asks.

Sometimes, he's so with it. He understands everything around him. Savvy. It's like he's the same Don from ten years ago.

Erla smiles. "No, dear. Good job." She hesitates and debates on asking him if he needs help getting out of the shower. But she doesn't.

She turns and leaves the bathroom. She begins to put his gardening clothes in the hamper, checking his pockets, only to find his medication in one of them.

Her heart seizes.

Erla pulls the one small yellow pill from his pocket and tries to breathe.

The shower turns off, and she thinks quickly, placing it on the dresser instead of the nightstand to protect his ego. If she put it back on the nightstand, they'd both know he didn't take it.

Don walks out in his towel.

Erla tries to act casual by putting his jeans in the hamper. She hopes he notices the pill on the dresser, and he does.

He looks at Erla, who's pretending to grab something from her own nightstand.

Don picks up the pill and takes it with one swallow.

Erla walks to Don and kisses him on the cheek. "How about dinner?"

"Yes, that will be nice, dear. But I need to get to work."

It's impossible for Erla to control her erratic pulse now. *Maybe it's more than the Parkinson's*, she thinks.

Though the doctor explained dementia doesn't usually come about with the disease, she's beginning to believe it might.

"You retired, remember, Don? Years ago."

27

Chickens Are for Gardens

Colt

"Hello, Colt. My name is Tatum, and I'm from *Mayhem Magazine*. Congratulations on your win." She reaches in for the handshake.

"Nice to meet you. Thank you." I shake her hand. "How was your flight?"

She looks back at her crew of five, who are unloading equipment from a Mercedes van.

"Drove. No way in hell was I going to let American Airlines fuck up my equipment."

Tatum doesn't remind me of a Tatum. I've met two Tatums in my life, and both were blonde and blue-eyed. This Tatum has short, spiky brown hair, both her ears have gauges, brown eyes, and she seems like she doesn't take any shit from anyone. She's taller than most women and built like some sort of ballerina.

Tan approaches us. "Tatum? What the hell!" He comes in for a hug. "I didn't know you worked for *Mayhem*."

Tatum laughs and gives him a hug with both arms. "It's been a minute, Tan. So good to see you. Yeah, I lost my shit with Estelle Cary, you know, the singer. She is the biggest bitch I've ever met in my life. What a diva." She rolls her eyes. "She almost assaulted Greg." She motions to a man over by the van, lifting a big light out of the back. "This was the end of the day by then." Tatum shrugs. "So, I told her that her music sucked and that she'd be better off singing to deaf monks."

I wonder how much shit Tatum had to take from Estelle for her to flip her shit.

Tan laughs. So does Tatum.

"I put *Reimer Magazine* in a tough spot. They had to let me go. I understood. Besides, I was getting burned out on photographing movie stars." She looks at me. "No offense."

I shake my head. "None taken. I'm not a movie star. Who and what do you photograph now?"

"Anyone or anything I want."

"Do you guys need any help unloading?" Tan asks.

She looks back at her guys. "No, I think we're good. We're going to scout the property, if that's all right?"

"That's fine. Just stay away from the far left. There's a bull named Abe that's meaner than hell," I say.

"Got it. No far left. Abe's an asshole." She gives me a thumbs-up and checks her watch. "It's four thirty now, so we'll start shooting at about six when the sun isn't so bright." Tatum looks me up and down. "Are you going to wear that?"

"No. I have suits set aside that we received from Gucci and Armani," Tan says.

"Perfect. Which assistant sent them? Bao or Lauden?"

"Lauden."

"Nice." Tatum bites her lower lip. "You'll look swass, Colt. I mean, not that you don't now."

"I'm sorry, what?" I ask.

Tan laughs. "It means, super cool, Colt. I swear"—he looks at Tatum—"you can do a whole lot with a kid from the sticks, but change his words? Not even a chance."

"Okay, then, I'll let you guys get to it. Colt, nice to meet you. And we will see you soon."

"Yeah, you, too." I wave.

Tatum turns and walks toward the van where she grabs her crew, and they head to the right side of the ranch.

"Where'd you meet her?" I ask as Tan and I walk back to the house to get changed.

"Bad breakup actually. I was friends with her ex, Amber, and Tatum and I just clicked. When they broke up, Tatum won me. Pulled her out of a dark place after her split. She got mixed up with the wrong people, nearly lost her career. Have you seen her photos?"

"I'd have no idea if I had."

"Her photographs are frozen moments of time where emotion and beauty are caught in the rawest of times." Tan holds his hands out, pretending to capture a frame with his fingers. "Has Jordan left town yet?"

The mention of her name makes me grow sick. Sick because I feel a bit guilty for the way I treated her. We both knew our expiration date had since passed. If we'd had sex that morning, it would have only prolonged what we both knew was inevitable. But I shouldn't have treated her like that. It is on me to apologize, and I will as soon as the shoot is over.

"No idea." And frankly, I don't give a shit.

We walk inside, and Mom is preparing dinner.

"Figured the photography team would need dinner before they left."

Tan says, "Aww."

I roll my eyes. "Mom, these people are from LA. Home-cooking isn't in their vocabulary."

Mom gives me the eye. "Well, I'm sure as heck not letting them visit the ranch, photograph my son—not in underwear—and not feed them a good meal."

I bend over and kiss the top of her head. "Thank you, Mom."

"Now, Tan, you're sure, no underwear, right?"

"Scout's honor, Laurel. I have two suits and his jersey."

"Good. That's all I need—Colt's picture on the cover of whatever magazine while I'm sitting down at Curl Up and Dye with old ladies ogling my son again."

"Mom, it will never happen again."

"You bet your bottom dollar it won't, Colt Atwood."

Calder walks in the back door. "Well, if it isn't the Sexiest Man Alive." He reaches in and tries to pinch my nipples.

"Dude." I smile. "Don't be jealous." I pop a tomato in my mouth from Mom's salad.

"Leave it, Colt. Have you even washed your hands?"

"Come on, SMA," Tan says. "Let's go get changed."

Before we're out of earshot, I hear Calder ask Mom, "Did you hear about Anna going on a date with some heart surgeon?"

I stop and listen. Hold my hand up to Tan to give me a minute.

"Pete said something downtown today at Nelson's."

"I'm sure it was nothing. They're just old friends or something."

Mom. Always the optimist.

I try to focus on her words because all I'm beginning to see is red.

"Hey, man. Don't let that get under your skin." Tan heard it, too. "Besides, you did just pick up your girlfriend-slash-friends-with-benefits from the airport and stayed the night with her."

"But I called Anna and told her about it."

"Did you ever stop to think that maybe her dinner with Mr. Heart Surgeon was completely platonic, and that's why she didn't tell you about it?"

We walk to the back bedroom, and Tan grabs a black bag labeled *Colt Atwood*. He unzips it. I take off my polo shirt, pull off my jeans after sitting down and taking off the black boot that I have to wear for a few more days, and stand in my underwear as Tan hands me the white button-up shirt. I try to let go of any thoughts of Anna doing things with a man who isn't me.

He's right; I know.

It's platonic, I tell myself and try not to wonder what the great surgeon looks like.

Besides, Anna and I have a past together. Raised from the same roots.

But what if those same roots make her feel stifled? Stuck? What if those same roots make her feel like she needs out?

"You like her, Anna, don't you?" I ask Tan.

"It's hard not to, Colt. She's what every feminine man dreams of when they go to bed at night." He laughs. "A best friend."

Tan hands me the pants.

"These pants will fit over the boot?" I ask.

Tan nods. "I told them they'd better design a suit that could fit over a big black boot."

I slide them on. "Feels like silk." I've never been caught up in all the hype about fashion and shit. Just give me a pair of shorts and a sweatshirt. Some of the NBA players get all decked out. I just don't want to. I have better things to do with my time. "Have I worn a Gucci suit before?"

"Two years ago to the ESPYs."

"It didn't feel like this." I can appreciate a suit that feels right, feels good.

"I think they've changed some of their fabrics."

"Does Gucci make basketball uniforms?"

Once the suit is on, I look at Tan.

He fans his face. "Yeah, I see it. The honor of SMA has been rightfully given. But your zipper is down."

I zip up my zipper.

I'm not into selfies. That shit is cheesy. But I ask Tan to take my picture anyway. Anna follows me on Instagram. Maybe I'll post it, but maybe I won't.

Let her do what she needs to do, I think as the voice of reason returns. *The things you guys share is the only thing no one can take away. And that's time and memories.*

The other side chimes in, *Fight for her. If you don't, you'll lose her forever.*

And you'll also look like a self-involved asshat.
Tan takes a picture.
Hands me my phone.
I delete the picture.
"All right, let's go give 'em the SMA."

"Thank you so much for having us for dinner, Mrs. Atwood."
Tatum goes to shake my mom's hand.

"Please, we don't shake hands in the Atwood family,"
Mom says and reaches in for a hug.

"Night cap at Dillon Creek Pizza?" I ask.

"Isn't there a bar downtown?" Greg, one of the camera
guys, asks, looking at his phone.

His words are met with silence, and Mom, Dad, Calder,
and I exchange glances.

"We could," I say.

"Colt—" Mom says.

"Nah, let's go. It'll be fine," Calder says.

Mom sighs.

"Early morning workout," Rob says. "Don't forget."

"You're not coming?" I ask.

"I'll drive," Rob says.

Calder pinches Rob's shoulders like he's been in the
family for the last twenty-eight years.

"I'll keep an eye on them, Mrs. Atwood—I mean,
Laurel," Rob says.

Dad pipes in, "Don't be starting any old shit downtown,
Colt and Calder."

After everyone gets in the Mercedes van, Rob drives it to
The Whiskey Barrel.

Calder and I exchange glances, as if asking each other if
this is the right move or not. We haven't set foot in the bar
ever. When we turned twenty-one, I was gone, and I know

Calder wouldn't have gone by himself. He gets ballsy when he drinks, and that's probably why he doesn't do it that often.

We're almost to town when one of Tan's phones rings.

"This is Tan." He listens. Nods. "Yes. Wonderful. Great. Thank you. Okay." He hangs up. "That was Liz at *Mayhem*. The announcement for Sexiest Man Alive is going live tomorrow."

"She must have loved our unedited images," Tatum says, looking out the window.

Calder tells Rob to park across the street from the bar.

Parking on Main in the evening, unless there's a play at Dillon Creek Repertory, is open.

We unload, and it's Tatum, Tan, Rob, Calder, Greg, Steve, Levi, Torch, Eric, and me.

Calder takes the lead, and I follow. I've had two beers, nothing enough to give me the *I don't care* mentality. Besides, it's the Morgans who turned their backs on us, except for Tess.

I think about Anna and the Cains and how the Morgans put them in the middle of the shit.

Calder opens the door, and the scent of old beer and cigarettes comes dancing out into the street. We pile into the bar, and with Calder and me at the lead, the whole bar grows quiet.

Dave, the bartender.

The Sanborn brothers who live just up the road from us.

Lyle and his girlfriend, Twila. Anna and I went to high school with them.

Tony and Pixie.

A group of kids not from Dillon Creek, who are bellied up to the bar.

And for the first time, it crosses my mind. *Are they quiet because of who I am, or are they quiet because everyone remembers what happened that night, thinking of what side they took and the line we all had to draw in the sand?*

I take a seat at the bar, closest to the door.

Calder, Tan, Tatum, and the rest of the crew follow my lead.

"Showstopper," Tatum whispers. "What the hell did you do, Atwood? Doesn't your town know you?"

And now, I know. It's the line that was drawn seven years ago.

"Town history runs deep," is all I say.

Dave waits a few minutes before he comes up to us.

"You're brave, showing up here." Dave's eyes dance between Calder and me. He cleans a pint glass. "What the hell did you do, bring LA with you?"

"You know, add a nice shirt, shave your face, and you might have a look going," Tatum sarcastically says to Dave.

"Dave, this is Tatum, Tan, Rob, Greg, Steve, Levi, Torch, and Eric. All we want is to show our new friends what Dillon Creek is about." I try to keep the peace, but I can feel my brother's tension.

Dave lets out a robust laugh from the pit of his stomach.

If you ran into Dave at Wilson's Grocery, at Nelson's, or at The Rusty Nail, he'd chat it up. You wouldn't know what side he was on. But come into the establishment that helped save his life and his loyalty with the Morgans ... well, it might be a different story.

"What can I get you guys to drink?" He sets the pint glass down in its rightful spot.

We give him our order.

The jukebox begins to play Merle Haggard's "Mama Tried," and the company in the bar returns to the normal level of chatter.

"Mr. Atwood?" I hear.

Calder and I both turn.

A kid who looks to be barely twenty-one has a black Sharpie in his hand.

"Should have known," Calder says and turns back around.

"Would you sign my shirt?" He's nervous, I can tell, and he isn't from here.

I smile and take the Sharpie from his hand. "Where are you from?" Nobody asks for my autograph in Dillon Creek.

"Eureka. My buddies and I are just having some drinks. I lost a bet."

"How so?" I motion him to turn around, so I can sign the back.

"They bet I was too chicken to do it. Ask you for your autograph."

"What's your name?"

"Drew. Drew Giles. How's your Achilles?"

I sign it. "It's attached."

He turns back around, and I hand him his marker.

"Have you made your choice of where you're going to play?" he asks.

"Not yet." And then I ask him, "What would you do?"

He shrugs, smiles, drops his head. "Man, I'd run as far away from home as I could. But mostly, I'd take the deal that gave me the most money."

"Is money important to you?"

He tilts his head, as if I were asking him a trick question. "Isn't it to everyone?"

My mind finds Anna's face in my memories of the night Conroy died. She wrapped her body around mine and tried to help stop my body from shaking. Shock does that to people, and somehow, I thought I was immune. I let her see that side of me. *If Anna were gone tomorrow, if she died or married Heart Boy, would money make a difference?*

"Not in the least, man. If I had a choice between money or happiness, I'd choose happiness."

He smirks.

"What?" I say, taking a swig of my beer.

"Mr. Atwood, that's"—he's trying not to be rude—"easy for you to say because you have the money."

"Then, I've lived the best of both worlds, right? Is that what you're thinking?"

Calder turns and looks at Drew and me. "That's deep shit, man."

Tatum turns, too. "Trust me, kid. Money isn't everything."

Drew nods. I can tell he's at a loss for words, so I let him quietly leave the situation. "Nice meeting you, Drew."

"Nice to meet you, Mr. Atwood. Thank you for signing my shirt."

"Call me Colt."

He uncontrollably releases a high-pitched giggle. "Thank you, Colt."

When Drew turns around, I see the words I wrote on his back.

Chickens are for gardens. Drew Giles is the tiger.
Colt Atwood #14

28

Still You and Me

Anna

"Drive safe," I say to Sam Houston, who's standing in the doorway of the clinic. It's just after eight in the morning.

"I will." His eyes linger on mine. "Anna," he sighs. "I'm really glad I stopped to see you." He nervously shoves his hands in the pockets of his jeans.

Sam has on black-rimmed glasses that make him look more like Clark Kent. It works for him.

"Me, too." *Me, too? Couldn't you say something more meaningful, Anna? Really?* "Let me know how everything goes in Seattle. I've never been there before."

"Really? It rains there a lot."

I hold up my hands. "I was raised in Humboldt County. You realize it rains here three hundred days out of the year, right?" I smile.

I want to touch his cheek. Feel his skin beneath my fingers. His clean-shaven face and strong jawline give off a level of confidence that wreaks havoc on my insides.

"Good luck with the interview."

His lips turn inward, and his gaze moves upward. "About that. Well, I sort of already got the job." Sam Houston meets my gaze again.

"What?"

"I … I don't know. I didn't want to freak you out. I just wanted to be casual—like, *Hey, just making my way up to Seattle. Thought I'd stop and see you.* Not, *Hey, I got a job, and I'm moving to Seattle. I need to see you.* You know?"

The corners of my mouth turn upward. "Need to see me?"

Sam smiles like a boy. "Yeah." I see him collect his own thoughts and try to put them in a sentence. "Look, Anna, I've thought about you every day since I moved away from you. And I told myself, *Get yourself settled. Get established. And then find Anna.* That was my five-year post-graduation plan at least. So, this is me, settled and needing to see you."

I think my cheeks are pink, and I'm really glad that Kimber isn't in yet to witness this so she could tease me later. "Well, you have my number." Butterflies stir in my stomach.

Sam looks at me with purpose and conviction. "I do." And he hesitates at first, but then he moves in. His lips touch my cheek in a way that's soft and needful, all at the same time. "Good-bye, Dr. Cain."

Still attempting to catch my breath, I say, "Good-bye, Dr. Houston."

"I was thinking," he calls as he climbs into his Mercedes Coupe, "the next time, we can meet in Davis. See if we can pay a visit to our favorite Mexican joint." He shrugs. "Even if it isn't there anymore, there's still you and me, right?"

"There's still you and me."

Sam nods and gets into his car. He drives down Main Street, and I watch him until I can no longer see his taillights in the dim morning fog.

Kimber is walking toward me, two coffees in hand, looking over her shoulder, then at me, and then over her shoulder again. She reaches me and hands me a coffee.

"Thank you."

"Is that Dr. Heart?"

My face squints. "How did you know?"

"Oh, the whole town's talking." She pauses. "And I suppose you haven't heard what happened last night at The Whiskey Barrel?"

"No. Why?"

"Come on. I'll fill you in."

We walk inside the clinic, and Kimber sets her purse in its spot. Sits down. Takes a deep breath in. "Okay, first of all, where's the picture of you and Dr. Heart kissing?"

"What?" I set down my coffee, which is too hot to drink right now.

"The photo of you two kissing."

"Okay, first of all, his name is Sam Houston. We met in college, and he stopped by on his way up to Seattle." It's the truth. "And we didn't kiss."

"Well, apparently, Colt and Calder and their entourage went to The Whiskey Barrel last night. Got hammered, and then Colt saw a picture of you kissing Dr. Heart."

"Sam. That's his name," I correct her, trying to wrap my head around all the swirling thoughts. "What were the Atwoods doing at The Whiskey Barrel?" My heart sinks.

Kimber shrugs and takes a sip of her coffee. "Mother-trucker!" She sets her coffee down and touches her finger to her lips. "That's hot. And your guess is as good as mine."

"What the hell happened?"

"All I heard is, it was a good time, and then Colt saw this picture and went ballistic."

"That's not Colt," I whisper.

"Apparently, Tess tried to call you, but you didn't answer."

My phone. Shit. I forgot to flip off the Do Not Disturb function this morning when I woke up. "But nothing happened. How could he have seen a picture of something that didn't happen?" I want to throw up. "I think I'm going to be sick."

"Not on my desk, Dr. Cain. Hit the restroom."

But I don't move because I'm not sure I can. "When's my first appointment?"

"Hang on. Let me check." Kimber scans the schedule. "Not until eleven."

"Great. Call me if there's an emergency. I'm headed to the Atwood Ranch. Come on, Bones."

"Tan? Wake up." I give him a nudge in one of the spare rooms.

I snuck in through Colt's window, the way I used to do it way back in the day, but he isn't in his bed. This thought alone makes my heart thump against my chest.

"Tan!" I give him another nudge, sitting on the edge of the bed.

"Mom, stop," he says in a boyish voice.

I lean over him. "I'm not your mother. Wake up."

Tan lifts his head. Stares at me dead in the eyes. I give him a minute, so he can regroup.

He wipes his eyes. "Oh, hey, Anna."

"Where's Colt?"

His eyes grow shifty, and he bites his lower lip. "That's a really great question."

"Tan, don't give me shit. Where's Colt?"

Tan drops his face into his pillow and says something inaudible.

"What?"

He says it again.

"Tan, you realize I can't hear you, right?"

He picks up his head. "I know. I don't want you to hear what I'm saying."

"Where is he?" I take his head and hold it in my hands.

Tan sits up in bed and pulls his covers up to his chest. "Anna, in his defense, he was hammered, and no one could stop him."

My heart is beating so hard right now, and my stomach is in knots. I'm not sure I can say anything, for fear of puking.

Tan closes his eyes. "He's at The Gingerbread Mansion. Room two." He shakes his head.

As I get up, I hear Tan rattle on, "Sexiest man alive … hangover … angry with himself …"

Tan stands. "Anna? For what it's worth, Colt is in love with you, and I'm not sure his heart will ever get over you." He pauses, and I stop walking, turning back to face him.

"I didn't know Colt before Conroy died, but sometimes, I'd hear him crying in the shower—and only when he'd get drunk, which was very, very little. There was one other time I'd seen him like I saw him last night, and that night, he talked about Conroy and I think that's part of his problem— he doesn't know how to grieve."

"No, Tan, he does. He just hasn't wanted to. See, I did know him before. I watched his heart break, and I never saw him put back the pieces. He doesn't want anyone's help. He just wants to forget it ever happened."

Tan nods as his phone begins to vibrate across the nightstand. "This is going to be a shitstorm today," he mutters to himself.

I sneak back out of Colt's window, but when I'm midway through the window, I see Daryl staring at me from the outside.

"You realize we have a front door, Annie, right?"

"Oh, yeah. Hey, Daryl." Embarrassment colors my tone, and I want to disappear.

I hop down.

"You okay, Annie?" he asks.

My eyes begin to sting. He was once a tall, handsome man before Conroy died. He's still handsome, but he's just grown thin and gray in these past seven years. He's asking if

I'm okay. The man who lost a son. The loss that separated best friends, families, a community.

I want to lie and tell him I am. I want to lie and tell him that my heart is pounding out of my chest because I love Colt so much that I know letting him go is the only way to let him heal. I can't be his miracle. He needs to be his own miracle. Not a woman. Not basketball. Not booze.

He needs to meet his grief.

"How did you do it?" I whisper as a tear begins to fall. "How'd you get over Conroy?" I want to know, so I can help Colt.

Daryl drops his head and flicks his lip with his tongue before meeting my gaze. "I haven't. I … I don't think you can get over a loss like that. But …" He pauses. "I keep showing up for life because I have a wife and four sons left who need their father." He nods to shake off the emotion his words brings.

I realize I've spent these past seven years running away from a man and hiding behind what I saw to protect my own heart.

Quickly, I bring him in for a hug. "I need to find Colt." And I walk to my truck.

"Hey, Anna?"

I stop and turn. "Yeah?"

"When you find him, tell him to stop running."

Slowly, I nod.

Daryl waves, takes his gloves off, and walks back to the house.

I get in my truck and head to The Gingerbread Mansion. Bones is nervous as he keeps his eyes on me. "I'll be okay. Don't worry, buddy."

When I get inside, there's no one downstairs, except for a couple having coffee in the parlor. I make my way upstairs, my heart almost exploding with beats.

Don't throw up. Don't throw up. Don't throw up.

Room two is just ahead. When I reach the door, I take a deep breath and listen.

Silence.

I reach for the doorknob and give it a twist, and the door opens without any resistance. Silently, I walk into the foyer of the room.

But it's when I hear muffled cries that my breathing quickens. My hands drip with sweat.

I round the corner and see a black boot sitting on the floor by itself. A whiskey bottle sits on the bedside table. It's almost gone.

The thing about life is, it doesn't stop coming. It unveils itself as it unfolds, sometimes quickly, sometimes slowly, and yet, in times like these, when our hearts are sure to shatter, they don't, but it would feel so much easier if they did.

I've seen this scene before. I'm not sure if it's my mind playing tricks. Her legs are wrapped around his middle, and this time, they're in bed. I can't look away, and I watch how his muscles contract with each push.

"Colt?" I call to be sure what I'm seeing is my own living nightmare. No. No, a nightmare would be losing my mother, my father, Amelia, and Adam. Bones. *Losing Colt might be my refuge*, I tell myself, *maybe my mind's way of protecting my heart.*

The thrusts stop.

Only slowly does he turn his head.

I see the pain in his red-rimmed eyes. Colored by the drunkenness of the night before and blurred with the drinks from this morning. The wreckage of his past—the losses he's suffered, the pain he's endured—meets my eyes right now in this moment.

"Anna?"

It reminds me of the time when we were eleven. When he pulled me from the creek. Somehow, I'd gone under, and he pulled me to safety. When I came to, his high-pitched "Annie?" was covered in terror, just as it is in this very moment.

How do we begin to overlook these moments? Indiscretions? How do we begin to forgive?

I see what my heart is doing. It's trying to override my mind. The right decisions, the just decisions, and yet I still hang on with forgiveness.

Colt pulls the sheet to protect me, not himself, not wanting me to see what he was doing with the woman on the bed. Not wanting me to see him for who he is right now. Not the young boy Daryl and Laurel raised to be respectful, unbroken, and strong. But now, standing before me is a broken man, who is using his own body to mask his pain.

He won't say anything. He can't say anything because he knows his words won't mean anything.

A single tear streams down my face. "For the record"—my voice quivers—"I did not kiss Sam Houston." I swallow. Lick my lips. "He's a friend from college, and he was on his way up to Seattle." A lump forms in my throat. "I ... I don't know what happened to you after Conroy died, and I feel like we lost the old Colt that day, too. But this"—another tear streams down my face—"isn't you. I hope you find yourself. Because the guy I know ... doesn't hide from anyone."

I look at the woman in the bed, who's covered with a blanket now. She's the woman, Jordan, from Colt's Instagram page. "I wish you had known the real Colt Atwood because if you had, he certainly wouldn't be breaking both of our hearts right now." And with that, I turn and walk out of Colt's life, just like I did seven years ago—except this time, I said what had needed to be said.

"Come on, Annie. You've got to eat something," Adam says from his container of Chinese food that he picked up in Eureka on his way to my house.

"I can't," I say weakly.

I haven't eaten since I left The Gingerbread Mansion this morning. I went back to work and served my patients, and here I am, at my empty, brand-new house that I haven't moved into yet, too scared to go home and tell my parents what happened.

Adam reaches for his glass of wine. The thing with my brother, Adam, is, he shows up. Even when I think I don't need him.

"Here's the truth as I see it." He takes a sip and sets his glass down. Crosses his arms and leans back against the wall. We're sitting in the living room, on the floor. "You're the strongest woman I know. You got that from Mom. You're also the most stubborn and intelligent woman I know, aside from Mom. This situation will not break you though, Anna. When Conroy and Tripp died, yeah, I saw you feel your way through it. But you did it with grace and dignity. You will get through this, Anna. It's just going to take time."

I play with the corner of the broccoli and beef container. "You know what hurts the most?"

Adam takes a bite of his magic beef—also known as Mongolian beef, but it never tastes the same, so we just started calling it magic beef. "I'm scared he won't heal himself, and he'll lose everything he has."

Adam shrugs. "Sometimes, that's what it takes to start over. We all have to find a bottom, right? Whether it's emotional or physical. If he hasn't found a bottom, he's got to keep digging, Anna."

My eyes start to sting, but the tears don't come. They're all gone.

"Eat. Drink some water. No wine until you finish your dinner, dear."

I barely smile and watch my brother eat the magic beef. "Thank you," I say.

"For what?" he says with a mouthful of food.

"For being here with me."

"That's what brothers are for, right?"

"Only brothers like you." I open the container of broccoli and beef. My stomach turns, but I know I have to eat.

Adam hands me a plastic fork. "Attagirl." He smiles. "Did I mention, you're stubborn?"

"Yes. Yes, you did." I launch my fork into the container and take a small bite.

"Hey. Sorry I'm late," Tess says, coming through the back door. "Did you save me some magic beef?"

Adam pushes over the container as Tess joins us on the floor.

"How's our girl?" Tess looks over at me.

"She'll survive," Adam says.

I watch my best friend, who lost her only brother seven years ago. I watched her family suffer, too. I think that's why Adam and Tess are tight—because he was there for her when Tripp died.

Maybe that's why the Morgans don't hate our family. Because we made ourselves available to both families—the Atwoods and the Morgans. We didn't choose a side. We didn't draw our loyalty to any one side. We just gave love.

I watched Tess grieve. It was hard for me to leave for Davis. I wanted to defer my enrollment for a semester, but she wasn't having it.

She said, "Anna, I'm going to grieve whether you're here or not and I'll be okay."

There's a knock at the back door, and I look at Adam and Tess, as if to say, *Did you invite someone else?*

But they both shrug.

I get up and walk to the door. It's Tan.

I open the door and sigh. "Look, Tan, if you're going to be a resident of Dillon Creek, you can't knock. It's assumed that if you're coming to the back door, you know us well enough to just walk on in." I hold the door open.

"I'm not staying, Anna. I just wanted to say good-bye and apologize again. And to give you this." He hands me a white envelope.

"Why are you apologizing? You didn't do anything."

"But I did. If I had pushed Colt to get some help prior to his shit sandwich, then maybe he wouldn't have hurt you again."

"Did … did he tell you anything?"

Tan shakes his head. "No, but he's a mess. I have never seen him like this before."

The truth is, I haven't either.

I muster whatever I have left in my depleted body and say, "He needs to process his brother's death, Tan. Until he does, he's not going to be able to survive the tough stuff. I'm just a bandage for his wounds. I'm comfortable. I'm what he had to help him most of his life … but I can't fix this one."

"You're right. I can't argue with that." Tan holds up his hands. "We're taking the jet back to LA tonight. Anyway, Colt wanted you to have what's in the envelope."

I motion my hands toward me. "Come here. We also don't leave Dillon Creek without hugs." When Tan reaches down for a hug, I whisper, "Do me a favor? Don't try to fix him, just offer advice only when he asks for it. Okay? And he likes Cheetos. So, when he's having a rough time, give him those."

I feel Tan's smile against my cheek. "Thank you."

We release, and I wave good-bye as he heads toward a car that's most likely being driven by a driver.

I shut the door and glance down at the envelope. I bring it back to the living room where Tess and Adam are talking.

"What's that?" Adam asks.

"Tan gave it to me. From Colt."

I open up the envelope. Inside is a check for one hundred thousand dollars, and it's signed over to me from Colt from *Mayhem Magazine*. "What the hell is this?"

Tess and Adam look at each other and then to me.

"I told you she wouldn't have seen it," Tess says.

I look up from the zeros. "Seen what?"

Tess takes a sip of wine and looks at Adam. "Colt won Sexiest Man Alive for the year. This is probably his payment."

"This is fucking bullshit. He can't just throw goddamn money at me." I go to rip up the check, but Tess stops me.

"Anna, you know Colt. There's got to be a reason. He knows how you are about money. He knows you better than you know yourself," Tess says.

Next to the check, there's a note from Colt.

Anna,

This is payment for never charging us for our dogs and their care. Please, use it as you see fit at the clinic.

Colt

I cover my mouth, so they don't see my lips quivering. I look up at Tess and Adam. "I can't accept this."

Adam takes the check, and Tess takes the note.

"Seems to be, this is for services rendered," Tess says.

"I'll hold on to the check until you're in your right mind," Adam says.

My phone chimes, and I pull it from my back pocket. It's a text from Sam.

Sam: Hey, beautiful. Just wanted to let you know I'm here, sleepless in Seattle.

Sam Houston and our good-bye this morning seems like it happened years ago. Inwardly, I try to smile, but it's hard.

29

Moths and Fear

Anna: Age Sixteen

"Anna, I don't think this is a good idea." Colt scratched the back of his head, unsure of what we were about to do.

"It will be fine, Colt. At some point, you've got to walk through the fear."

I took him by the arm and led him to Cranky Carl's moth refuge. Who would have thought that Cranky Carl had a thing for moths?

"You're going to be fine. Unless you die of a heart attack. My dad even said you cannot die and that moths don't have teeth." I laughed. "Come on."

We pushed the door to the moth refuge, which opened to a room that was separated by glass. On the other side of the glass were thousands of moths.

I felt Colt's muscles tense under my hand. "Would you feel better if you closed your eyes?"

"No."

"Okay then, take my hand."

His hand slid into mine, and it was just like it had always been, but it fit more perfectly than I remembered. His fingers, like spider legs from a daddy longlegs, curved into mine.

Friends, I told myself. *Just friends. Best friends.*

I led him through another door that opened up to the moth enclosure.

The flutter of their wings kept an ever-so-slight breeze.

Colt's body tensed again. "I—" But he stopped, and his hand grew sweaty. He leaned down and whispered into my hair, "I'm afraid if I talk, the moths will fly in my mouth."

I tried not to laugh. I didn't want to make Colt feel like his fear wasn't valid. The only brother who helped with this was Conroy. He was the one who had set up the meeting with Cranky Carl. It was his idea.

When I asked if he wanted to come along, he said, "This is a job for his best friend, not his oldest brother. Besides, I think, by being with you, it'll push him even more."

"Can you feel my heart?" Colt asked.

I put my hand to his chest, and the pounding was so fast that I couldn't get a count. "The good news is, panic can't kill you. How do you feel?"

"Like a lunatic." He smiled, and I smiled.

Somewhere in this moment of his fear, I fell even harder for Colt. Maybe it was because he was walking through the fear, and I got to be by his side. Or maybe it was because I was watching the small pieces of courage build him into something bigger. Or simply, maybe it was because I got to see a vulnerable side to him even if it was a fear he kept hidden from others.

A moth landed on his nose.

"Holy shit. This is bullshit."

"Does it hurt?" I asked.

"No."

"Does it tickle?"

"No."

"Do you feel it?"

"No."

"Do you see it?"

"No."

"Then, what are you scared of right now?"

Colt was quiet for a minute. "That … that I can't control anything, I guess." He breathed heavily. "And maybe the eyes they have on their wings."

"So," I started, "it doesn't hurt. You can't feel it. And you can't see the wings right now because it's so close. Why are you scared?"

"Control."

"You can't control the situation, and that's what terrifies you?"

"Yeah, I guess."

Several moths landed on his shoulders. His head, our hands. My shoulders. My head. My face. Different colors, different shapes, different sizes.

Colt looked down at me, our hands still joined.

"Are you scared still?" I asked.

He nodded his head. "This sucks."

"What's the worst thing that can happen, Colt? They bite you? That they kill you?" I laughed.

Colt grimaced and stifled a laugh as another one landed on his nose.

"Fear experienced together is better than alone, right? I can help you walk through it, but ultimately, it's your fear, and the only way to get past it is by working through it."

"They aren't going to kill me," he said quietly. "They aren't going to kill me." His breathing was quick.

"Close your eyes," I said.

Colt closed his eyes. "They aren't going to kill me." He swallowed, and I saw his Adam's apple bob.

"Sometimes, you just have to trust the process, Colt."

He smiled and peeked out of one eye. His grip on my hand tightened. "Tomorrow, we'll do the same thing with spiders. Aren't those your biggest fear?"

"Not on your life. Spiders can kill you." But spiders aren't my biggest fear. Losing Colt is.

We both laughed, and Colt's shoulders relaxed. His breathing wasn't so shallow.

Colt and I held hands, and everything in the world just seemed right.

3o

Better Bones

It's a Tuesday in September, months have passed. Erla has a hard time remembering which day is which sometimes. She blames it mostly on retirement or just time passing in general. But she always remembers the month—perhaps her own test to prove she's still with it.

Her alarm sounds at the normal six in the morning, but she has an uncanny ability to wake two minutes before her alarm every morning. Except for Sundays. Sundays are saved for Jesus and forgiveness, and she allows herself an extra half hour of sleep for wellness even though it never works. She wakes at 5:58 a.m. and tosses and turns until six thirty on the dot.

But not today. Because it's a Tuesday.

Erla throws her covers back and slowly gets out of bed. Summer mornings are better for her bones. Then, the air is just a tad warmer in the mornings.

She looks over at her husband, who's sound asleep, and she wonders how much time they have left together. Erla Brockmeyer has spent more time with Don in her life than she has without, and that's saying something.

Millie is deaf and blind and at Don's feet. Millie has loved Don since she was just a pup. Sure, she loves Erla, too, but

Don is the one who feeds her tiny pieces of salami when he thinks Erla isn't looking. Both sound asleep—Millie on her back and Don on his side, facing the window—Erla wonders what life will be like when they're gone. This thought makes her stomach turn and twist, and she fights the urge to cry, something she hasn't done in quite some time. She supposes that's something—crying—goes away as people age. Maybe it ages the heart, provides more calluses, more bruises, so when people grow older, they can handle the biggest of blows.

Erla puts on her robe and slowly makes her way out to the kitchen, passing pictures on the wall in the hallway. Still, she mulls over why Devon left. Swept Don and Erla under the rug and forgot about them. Like lost luggage or an overlooked food order. Left them high and dry with no explanation. This makes Erla's heart ache the most. With Don, she's spent a lot of great years, and they have many good memories; they've had a great ride. But with Devon, everything ended so suddenly and without explanation. Their relationship with their daughter had been good, Erla can conclude.

And with Scarlet, things were wonderful. It still is though, from a distance, which any relationship is hard three thousand miles away. She knows her granddaughter is busy, especially now, with the divorce. She's spoken with Scarlet. Don, too. People grow apart. She understands that. Divorce isn't something that Erla agrees with, but if the shoe doesn't fit, don't wear it. It's uncomfortable, and it can have long-lasting effects.

She sure wishes Scarlet and Devon could make a trip out—before Don gets worse. Erla doesn't want to worry them though. No, she couldn't. Besides, Devon, according to Scarlet's letter, is on assignment in South Africa. They'll have plenty of time when Devon returns. But admittedly, Don is getting worse.

Just last week, Dr. Cain said Don's in stage three Parkinson's. Progression from stage two to stage three was only a month. Don took a fall a week ago and banged up his elbow real good. Erla can't leave him unattended at home anymore. That's something Don would have noticed a month ago, putting his foot down about being independent and taking care of himself. But maybe he hasn't noticed, and Erla doesn't dare ask which, too scared of the reality of his answer.

Don's balance has gone from poorer than average to not good at all. His judgment is off-kilter. When Erla suggested a walker, Don flipped a lid. So, he spends a lot of the day sitting in his recliner, looking out the window or watching his true-crime shows.

Erla stops when she gets to the coffeepot, listening for Don.

Is he awake already? She puts her chin to her chest, waiting for sound.

Nothing but silence.

But a nagging feeling tells her she needs to walk back and check on him.

Don't be so overprotective, Erla. He's fine.

But she can't help it and walks back into the bedroom anyway.

Millie is up at Don's head now, curled into a ball, sleeping. Must have been the dog because Don is still in the same position she left him in.

Erla walks back down the hallway, pours her coffee, goes to the living room, and sits in her chair. Their view from their chairs opens up to the beautiful garden Don used to keep. With Erla's knack for flowers and Don's in-depth knowledge of plants, they did make a garden look beautiful together. But now, since Don hasn't been able to get outside anymore, per the doctor's instructions, it's only the perennials that have come back without care and extra attention. Erla hired the Sawyer boy to mow the lawn, which Don grumbles about so she makes sure that he comes when Don is at his physical therapy in Eureka.

"I can mow the damn lawn, Erla," he always says.

She's learned not to argue with him, per Dr. Cain's instructions, but empathize instead, saying, "I know you can,

Don. I can clean the house, but I'd rather spend more time with you."

Erla sips her coffee and takes in the morning sun. Morning sun in September in Dillon Creek isn't common. Fog usually weaves in and out of the surrounding redwood trees and lies like a blanket down the streets of their town. So, the sun this morning feels well with the soul, keeping the sadness of Erla's current predicament quiet.

If Erla could do it all over again, in the fashion that she has done it, she would. In a heartbeat. Though she wishes she had spent more time with Devon. Not so much in a rush. Not made her participate in pageants like she did and made her do dance and ballet. She wishes she had allowed her to make her own choices and not been so uptight about what others thought.

Yes, if she were to live life all over again, those are the changes she'd wish she had made. Time, after all, is the only thing she can't take back.

"Erla?" Don calls for her.

She jumps, feeling a thousand needles prickling her skin with fear. She sets her coffee down and walks to the bedroom.

Don is sitting up, his feet dangling over the bedside. Erla rushes to his aid.

He looks at his wife with forlorn eyes. Maybe it's regret she sees or frustration.

"What is it, Don? Are you all right?"

"I can't stand."

This is the moment Erla realizes that she cannot care for Don by herself, and this thought is met with not only defeat, but also heartbreak. She understands that their lives will be lived as Don and Erla Brockmeyer *and* the caregiver or just Erla alone while Don is in a home. Their lives will never be the same.

"Stay here. Don't move."

Erla runs to the phone on the wall in the kitchen and dials.

"Laurel, it's Erla. I'm sorry to bother you this early, but, well"—her voice chokes, and she tries to swallow the fear and sadness—"it's just that Don is having trouble getting out of bed. Can you send Calder over?"

"He'll be there in a few minutes. Don't worry, Erla."

"Thank you, Laurel. I just … I just didn't know who else to call." A lump in her throat begins to form.

"Would you like me to stay on the phone with you until Calder gets there? Never mind. Scratch that. I'm coming with him."

Erla doesn't answer, and she doesn't cry either. Erla Brockmeyer is made of stone and steel, and she isn't letting one big setback break her into a million little pieces without a fight.

The phone line goes dead.

Moments later, Calder opens the front door. "Mrs. Brockmeyer?"

Erla comes rushing out, trying not to look too terrified or too much of anything. But this is the first time Don hasn't been able to get out of bed.

"He's in here."

Calder follows, as does Laurel.

Calder Atwood, in many ways, reminds her of Don when Don was in his late twenties. Strapping young man. Tall. Strong upper body. Full of muscle and strength. A rancher—which is what Don wanted to be initially, but he decided on an engineer, only because his father had told him he couldn't make a sufficient income and that the hours of a rancher were ungodly.

"Hello there, Mr. Brockmeyer. How are you doing this morning?" Calder says.

"Not so well, Calder. Not so well. Can you move me to the chair right there?" Don asks.

Erla put a chair by his bedside for situations like these. Ones where he has trouble catching his balance, so the chair gives him a place to sit down and find his footing.

Balance. What a small word with such big meaning.

Calder acts as though he's done this before. "I'm going to reach around your chest and pick you up, and then I'll set you in the chair. Okay, Mr. Brockmeyer?"

"That will be fine, Calder. Thank you."

Calder does as he said and sets Don in the chair against the wall.

Erla notices one of his legs is extremely stiff, a side effect of Parkinson's. A stage four side effect, not a stage one, two, or three.

Calder sits on the side of the bed and starts small talk with Don.

Erla's eyes fill with tears.

"Erla, let's go in the kitchen and make Don something to eat," Laurel says.

Erla looks back at Don, who gives Calder a smile as he tells a story of a fox that was a recent visitor at the Atwood Ranch.

"Yes, yes, that will be good," Erla says and leads the way to the kitchen, and Laurel follows.

She remembers when Laurel and Daryl lost their son Conroy. It was an awful day, an awful month, an awful year for all of them. They lost two tremendous boys that day.

She took food every single day for a month. She baked and cooked and baked some more. Seven years later, she is almost certain they still have banana bread. Things were different for them then—Don, Erla, Devon, and Scarlet.

Devon was still in their lives.

Scarlet still called on a daily basis.

And Don wasn't sick.

How quickly things can change.

Erla is certain that Laurel might feel a little better than she felt seven years ago, but her guess is that life has changed and that she's learned to cope with a new normal.

"Can you grab the yogurt from the refrigerator, dear?" Erla says to Laurel.

"Absolutely." Laurel walks to the refrigerator while Erla takes the homemade granola that Don likes so much.

Laurel sets the container of yogurt on the counter. "Have you called Dr. Cain?"

Erla puts some granola in a bowl and sighs. "No, not yet."

"I would. Just so he can check Don out. Make sure it's not a stroke or anything more."

Anything more. Don is slowly dying of Parkinson's.

Anything more. What does that mean? Erla asks herself.

A quick death or a slow death—Erla isn't sure which is worse.

But she nods. "Yes, that's probably a good idea."

Erla dusts her hands off before she walks over to the phone where she called Laurel from earlier. She watches as Laurel takes the initiative to mix the yogurt and granola together before she dials Dr. Cain's home number. Laurel has always been Clyda's favorite daughter-in-law. But there's never been a doubt in Erla's mind that Laurel is her favorite, too.

Erla picks up the phone as Laurel grabs a spoon from the drawer, puts it in the yogurt, and walks it back to Don.

She dials the Cain residence.

"Hello, Nora. It's Erla Brockmeyer, and I'm so sorry I'm calling so early."

"It's no trouble, Erla. Is everything okay?"

"Is Dr. Cain there?"

"Yes, just one moment."

Whispers are exchanged, and Dr. Cain gets on the phone. "Good morning, Erla. What seems to be the problem?"

No, Dr. Cain. Everything is not okay. Everything is going to hell in a handbasket, she thinks to herself.

"Well, I think so," she lies. "Don couldn't get out of bed this morning, so I called the Atwoods, and Calder and Laurel came over to help move Don. He's okay for now, but if you wouldn't mind, could you come over and take a look at him before you go into the office?"

"I'll be there in less than five minutes."

That's the thing with residents of Dillon Creek. We take care of our own, Erla thinks.

"Oh, thank you so much, Dr. Cain."

"It isn't a problem."

Erla retreats back to the bedroom where Laurel, Don, and Calder are.

Don is eating his yogurt and telling a story about the bear who broke into the trash can ten years ago and made a ruckus in the garage behind the house.

Don smiles at Erla. The same smile he gave her when they got married fifty-four years ago. The same smile he gave her when Devon was born. And the same smile he gave her when Scarlet was born.

Joyful days, Erla remembers. She tries not to cry.

Erla doesn't tell Don that Dr. Cain is on the way. She wants him to stay in this moment where the disease that he has isn't eating away at his mind, his body. She wants him, just for a minute, to forget about all that is wrong and unjust and unfair with the world.

"So, Chief McBride says with a Taser, 'I'll cover you. Go get your blanket.' And I say, 'No, give me the Taser, and I'll cover you, so you can go get the blanket.'" Don laughs.

Laurel and Calder laugh.

It's like his disease doesn't exist, and Erla's heart explodes into tiny pieces of love for the man she fell for all those years ago.

"All right, well, we're going to go, Don." Laurel stands from her perch on the bed next to Calder. Gives Don a quick hug from the side.

Calder reaches out his hand to shake Don's. But Don can't reach out, and the realization and the happiness of the moment shift yet again. It isn't that Don won't reach out; it's because he can't.

Calder instantly understands this and pats Don on the back. "No more line dancing with Mrs. Brockmeyer, all right?"

Don laughs back the sadness that has reached his face. "No, sir."

Laurel and Calder go to leave just as Dr. Cain comes in the room.

"Hey, Laurel, Calder," Dr. Cain says.

"James," Laurel says. "How's Anna?"

Concern is reflected on Dr. Cain's face. "She'll be okay."

Calder and Dr. Cain exchange a handshake.

Erla remembers, a few months ago, there was a debacle down at The Whiskey Barrel. Though her memory isn't the greatest, or maybe what she heard wasn't the clearest, but Erla has always said that Anna and Colt were made for one another and that it would just take time and a whole lot of patience. Erla and Don's marriage hasn't always been perfect, but she can count the unresolved issues they've had in the last fifty-plus years of marriage, and that's a zero.

"Don, how are you feeling this morning?"

Dr. Cain has always had the best approach with his patients. It's never been a doctor-patient relationship—unless of course, the confidentiality piece is considered, then, yes—but it's more of a friendship, and that's why they've kept with Dr. Cain despite the rumors they've heard quietly whispered about him around town.

Rumors and gossip are just as ugly as lies. The only difference among the three is the tellers and the keepers. That's why Erla and Clyda get so frustrated with Delveen and Pearl, but maybe that's why God keeps Erla and Clyda front and center of The Ladybugs—to perhaps coax the women to be better humans. But Erla swears, in church one day, she caught Delveen playing a video poker game in the Lord's house when she sat just two seats down.

"I'm not doing so good this morning, Doc."

Relief meets Erla's chest when she hears Don's words. Finally, he's being honest with Dr. Cain about the way he feels.

Usually, it's, "Feeling good. I look worse than I feel." Or, "Look better than a law-breakin' man behind bars."

Dr. Cain listens to Don's pulse. Checks his lungs. Examines the leg. Feels his lymph nodes in his neck. Looks in his eyes with a flashlight. Why? Erla isn't sure, but she sits patiently and waits.

"Well, you should feel like a million bucks because on my side of things, everything looks and feels okay. Aside from the leg." Dr. Cain takes off his stethoscope.

Erla knows there's more Dr. Cain is thinking about. He's been their doctor for as long as he's been in practice in Dillon Creek—after Dr. Heister retired.

Erla notices Don's reflection in Dr. Cain's glasses, and for a moment, she thinks she sees a much younger Don. Don from his mid-thirties with a broad chest, strong jawline, hair a dark brown—not gray and thinning like it is now.

"But I think we need to have a conversation about daily routines."

Erla knows where Dr. Cain is going with this. She's already considered it.

"I think, Don, you and I both know that Erla can't take care of you on her own."

Don bites his lip as he processes the words. He nods.

"I think we also know that we have two options for the well-being of both of you, right?" Dr. Cain looks to both Erla and Don. "Either you hire in-home care or Don might have to move to Crest View."

Don has never been an easy sell. He's a researcher, hardheaded, stubborn. But he's also a smart man, and he knows when to throw in the towel. "I know," he says and looks at his wife. "I know."

Erla doesn't move, nor does she want this for them. She should fight back. Resist.

Isn't there something with all the technological advances in the last twenty years that will keep us independent? Erla asks herself.

She doesn't dare breathe these words out loud, for fear that it will put false thoughts into Don's head. And Lord knows, he doesn't need those. He has a hard enough time with keeping up with the facts.

"I'll send you a list of in-home health care professionals when I get back to the office."

Another thing Erla appreciates about Dr. Cain is that he doesn't have his secretary do things like this for him. He does it himself, and Erla believes this is a true sign of a great physician. Though, too, she knows that Dr. Heister's shoes were hard to fill all those years ago, but Dr. Cain did it with grace and humility, and that's another reason he's such a great physician.

All Erla can say is, "Thank you, Dr. Cain."

"Let's see if you can stand now," he says to Don, not asking, but telling.

Dr. Cain holds out his hand, and Don uses one hand to steady himself, allowing Dr. Cain to help him with the other hand.

"You'll need a walker, Don. Just so you don't worry your wife."

Don is reluctant but knows that this will give his wife peace of mind.

"I'll have Broadway Medical in Eureka deliver one today."

Don straightens his pajamas. He shakes Dr. Cain's hand. "Thank you."

Before Dr. Cain leaves, he makes sure that Don changes his clothes and makes it to his recliner out in the living room.

Don sits there as Erla walks Dr. Cain to the front door.

"I cannot thank you enough," she says.

"It's no worry."

"Send me a bill, would you?"

"No, I won't. You know that. I'm just one neighbor looking out for another neighbor, just as you did with us when the kids were little and Nora and I were having trouble. You and Don took them for a day. We help each other, Erla."

She supposes this is true, but it is hard for her to be the recipient of help without reimbursement.

"I'll call over to Broadway Medical and send you that list of in-home care providers."

Erla nods and thanks the good doctor again.

She quietly shuts the door and walks toward her unpredictable future, toward the man she loves and will always love, even when all that is left of him is ash.

"Erla," he calls to her.

She walks to the living room and sits in the matching recliner next to Don.

He stares out the window and watches the birds. "I don't want to die like this."

Erla begins to pick at her nails—something she does when she's nervous—and she swallows the lump in her throat. "What would you like to do, Don?"

He smiles as a hummingbird comes to the window. "I want to pass with dignity." He sighs. "When I get to a point where I can no longer move, I want you to give me enough pain medication to set me free."

Don doesn't use the word *die*. He's trying to protect his wife, her weary heart.

Erla continues to pick her nails but stops and stares at her husband. "I cannot imagine life without my Don."

Don carefully reaches out his hand, and it shakes as he waits for her hand. "We still have some time." He moves his eyes from his wife and back to the hummingbird. "We should call Scarlet," he says.

"Yes, and Devon, too."

"I'll make the call today," Don says.

"Don? I want to go with you. I'm not sure I can do this life without you."

"You need to. For Scarlet and Devon, you need to."

Erla knows, but it still doesn't take away the awful pain she feels in her heart right now.

"What time is it?" Don asks.

Erla looks at the box above the television. "It's just after seven."

"Oh, I'm running late this morning. I'd better get ready for work."

Erla realizes in this moment that from now on, she'll get to enjoy her husband, the love of her life, in tiny increments of time. But what's been proven to her over and over again is that real love is always worth fighting for.

31

Colt

It's September, and while I should be celebrating, I'm in a room full of people who don't give a shit about anything but themselves. Except for Tan, my parents, Casey, and Calder. And Pete, but I think Pete also cares a whole lot about money.

The only ones missing are Anna and Cash. He's on the road again with Bullfighter One.

"Please"—Pete stands on the bar of the high-rise penthouse he rented for the night—"let us celebrate the top-paid athlete in the National Basketball Association right now with Colt signing a four-year contract with the Golden State Wolves for two hundred fifty-seven fucking million dollars."

I'll be able to return to the court in March, right before playoffs.

Tan is no longer my publicist but my friend. Tan fired himself after we left Dillon Creek. I shouldn't have put him in that position in the first place. It's hard to separate friendship and business. When you become emotionally invested is the time you need to cut ties.

But Tan is here with me as my best friend, and Shanna Devorak is my new publicist.

They say that time is patient, and in that, we must meet the passage of time with understanding.

That's what Sean said, my counselor that I decided to see after my blowup at home at The Whiskey Barrel. I sent the Morgans a check for any damages done. Apologized to Dave via a phone message because the Morgans wouldn't take any of my calls.

I called Anna once. She didn't pick up and rightfully so. I couldn't put her through it anymore.

I go through this fucking song and dance when I think of her. All my regrets. If I'd just gone home and not told Rob to take me to The Gingerbread Mansion. I don't remember that night; this is just what I'm told. But the one thing I do remember is the look Anna gave me when I turned around in room two and looked her straight in the eyes, willing her to see the man that I'd become. Settled on. Not a reflection of the parents who had raised me. A direct result of burying pain.

Several people walk up to me. Some I know by name and some I don't. Some I know only by facial recognition.

"You must be on top of the world," one man says.

"Yeah, yeah. It's a feeling I can't quite wrap my head around." And yet, I would turn all this money, all this shit in, for just one more day with Anna. I can't wrap my head around it because I don't have any feelings toward it.

Drew Giles's words play in my head as I stand here and stare at the sea of people all here for me, the money, the fame. That's the thing about money. Everything is made of plastic; it's dispensable and replaceable. People pretend to be whoever you want them to be. Women, men—they're all the same. But if you're lucky enough to grow up in a town like I did, where genuineness runs deep, and wholeness is a quality that most residents have, you know that you've found a place to retreat to. And here, I've spent the last seven and a half years running from a place that's always been my home. But little do I know that I've been running from myself, from my brother's past, trying to fit a mold that anyone can fit into.

Ernie, a reporter for the *San Francisco Examiner*, is here. "Colt, looking good without the boot. Do you have a minute?" he asks.

I set my water down. I haven't touched booze since the morning after The Whiskey Barrel.

Drew Giles's words sink into my thoughts. *"Man, I'd run as far away from home as I could. But mostly, I'd take the deal that gave me the most money."*

Here I am, taking the deal with the most money the NBA has ever offered and far away from home, and I want neither. If I had a choice between NBA or Anna and home, I'd choose Anna. I'd choose home. I'd choose the only things that have ever made me whole.

"So, how do you feel, Colt? You've just signed the biggest NBA contract in history."

Do I give him what he wants to hear, what the world wants to hear, or do I give him the truth?

I pick my water up, take a big gulp, and ponder what the truth will do. What harm it might cause with my parents. They worked hard to get me to where I am. My mom driving me down to camp every summer. Watching me on the road. Watching me struggle.

But would they want me to be happy? Would I make them prouder for standing in my own truth or feeding this reporter a bullshit answer that he's heard a million times?

I set my water down, clear my throat, and stare at a tiny black scuff mark on the wall. "There are two things that make the world go round, Ernie, and that's money and love. Wouldn't you agree?"

Ernie's not sure how to answer this. After all, this is an interview he's giving. But he thinks on it. "Well, I suppose we don't need money to satisfy our need for love. But I think we all need love to some extent. I mean, you can live without money and still be happy."

I did a few interviews with Ernie when I played for LA against the Golden State Wolves. Ernie is like-minded, and I've always liked the way he speaks. It isn't polished or full of bullshit.

"Publish this right here, Ernie: *Anna Elizabeth Cain, nothing in this world is worth more to me than you. It's always been you. And I'll wait until forever for you, Annie.*"

I look at Ernie, who's not writing any of this down. He's just staring at me.

"Did you get all that?"

"That's … that's beautiful, man. I hope you get her back." Ernie scratches the side of his head and looks down at his notepad. "But I can't take this back to the office. I need more."

I shake my head. "You're the only reporter I'm giving this to. Publish it. I won't talk to anyone else."

"Really?"

"Really."

"Okay." Ernie scribbles down the quote and shoves his notepad in his back pocket. "Thank you, Colt, for your time."

Another reporter approaches me. "Hi, Colt. My name is Cate Rodgers, and I'm a reporter from the *San Jose Mercury*. A minute of your time?"

"No comment," I say and go to find Tan and Shanna.

As I walk away, I look back at Ernie, who's now talking to the other reporter, and I hear her say, "No quote? This is the best day of his life, and he's not willing to talk?"

Ernie smiles and nods. "I guess some things are worth a lot more than this moment, Cate."

"Did he give you a quote?" she asks.

"There are two things that make the world go round, Cate, and that's money and love. Wouldn't you agree?" Ernie asks.

Sly dog.

Cate looks confused. "What the hell are you talking about? Hey, if this is a pick-up line, tell your boss I'm suing."

"Read the *San Francisco Examiner* tomorrow, Cate." Ernie walks away, leaving Cate more puzzled than when she found him.

Shanna walks in with a newspaper. "Between Sexiest Man Alive and now this quote from you, I'd say you're America's number one bachelor." She hands me the paper.

I take the last bite of toast and set the paper down. It took a while to get my appetite back. I lost about fifteen pounds of muscle but have gained it all back.

Rob is sitting with me, and we're ready to go train. After the incident at home, I've never been more focused on my health physically. My workouts are three to four hours a day.

Sprints.

Agility.

Weights.

Shooting.

Long-distance running.

Stationary bicycle.

TENS unit.

Ice.

Massage.

Emotionally, I'm coming around with Sean. I didn't realize I'd put up walls after Conroy died. I shut everything off, just like a light switch. Even in my childhood with my parents and brothers, I'd put up walls because it was easier to accept the world as it was and not deal with all the expectations and shit that came with it.

I didn't know that, in order to heal, I used others and the love of the game I always felt solace in to fill the holes inside me. Jordan was a hole-filler. A person I used to feel better about myself—not just with sex, but she stroked my ego, too.

Sean explained it to me like this: "Some people go the healthy way and feel through it to get through it. Others turn to sex, alcohol, drugs, physical pain maybe, but you turned it all off. Everything. You used the love of basketball and women to fill the holes."

What Sean helped me uncover is that it does matter to me who was driving the night that Conroy and Tripp were killed. I was angry with Conroy. Angry with Tripp. My mom is the only one who grieved out loud. Walked through it instead of around it. My dad dives deeper into the ranch, buries his head in his work. Cash drinks too much, and Calder is quiet, just like me.

How do runners recover from something like this? It's been seven and a half years, and to think about my oldest brother still wrecks me.

The last words he said to me when I accepted the full ride to University of North Carolina was, "I knew you could do it, little brother. Now, go show the world."

Sean said, too, that maybe the way I play ball is my way of showing the world what Conroy always saw in me.

I come back to reality. Rob and Shanna are talking about my schedule.

"We'll be done at two thirty this afternoon," Rob says to Shanna.

"Great. Then, I'll have him after his appointment with Sean until tonight after dinner."

I stand and take my plate to the sink. "What's on the docket this afternoon?" I turn my head back around, only to see Rob and Shanna exchanging a doe-eyed glance.

They both break out of it when they see me staring at the two of them. I don't ask what's going on between them because whatever they do off the clock is none of my business. I think forbidding dating in the workplace is just a bunch of bullshit anyway. I put my dishes in the dishwasher.

"Let's see, interview with *Sports Unlimited* about life after the injury." But after that, Shanna grows quiet. "And *US Monthly* wants to do a story about the line you gave the *San*

Francisco Examiner." She winces, knowing what I'll say. She shrugs when I give her the look. "I told a friend I'd ask."

Rob looks at me and sets his dry rye toast down. Folds his hands in front of him. "What would it hurt, Colt?"

Rob never speaks up about anything personal. It's always been about my physical shape.

I look between Rob and Shanna. "No."

"What do you think would be so bad?" Rob asks. "That they uncover a love story that's been there since you guys were, what, four? A love story that everybody knows and everyone's talking about. 'Who is Anna Cain?'" Rob uses air quotes—something I've never seen him use.

"I don't want to screw up her personal life, Rob."

"You already did when you mentioned her name to the *Examiner.*"

Fuck. Fuck. Fuck. I never thought of that.

"Shit!" I pace, placing my hands on my hips. "I've got to call her. Apologize. Motherfucker. And it's already published. Shit!"

My heart pounds as I pull my phone from my pocket. I hit up her number.

I know she won't pick up. She hasn't picked up since I left Dillon Creek. I also know on the seventh ring is when I'll get to hear her voice—unless she hits Ignore, which is usually on the fourth ring.

Ring one.

Ring two.

Ring three.

Ring four.

Ring five.

Ring six.

Ring seven.

"Hi, you've reached Anna and Bones. We can't get to the phone right now, but leave your name and number, and we'll get back to you as soon as we can."

Beep.

"Hey, Annie. It's Colt." I let out a big breath. "Look, I gave a quote to the *San Francisco Examiner* last night—" I stop. I can't leave this on her voice mail. "Can … can you just call me when you get a minute? I promise I'll keep it brief. Okay, um, bye."

Rob and Shanna stare at me, their mouths open.

"What?" I ask as I shove my phone back in my pocket.

"You left her hanging with that call," Shanna says. "You can't do that to a woman, especially with the history you two have."

Panic sets in my chest. "Should I call her back?"

Shanna says, "No, you can't call her back because then you're going to look like a total douche."

"Why?"

"You never leave two back-to-back messages." She gawks.

"Why?"

"Because you'll look too hard-up. Now, what you do is, you write her a letter. You put it in the mailbox and make sure, at the end of the letter, you write, *Love, Colt.*"

I look at Rob. "She's good."

Rob looks at Shanna. "I know."

"Do you need my help writing the letter?" Shanna asks.

"No, I don't need your help writing a love letter."

Rob stands. "All right, let's go work out, Atwood."

"Don't forget; I get him at two thirty." She takes a drink of her coffee and picks up the article.

We leave The Harrison just before nine for Arco One, the new arena I'll be playing in come March.

It's late, and I can't sleep, so I pull myself out of bed and search for a notebook or a lined piece of paper. "Shit. Why don't I have any paper?"

Finally, I find a steno pad in my office, which Shanna uses more than I do. I sit down at my desk and start the letter to Anna.

Dear Anna,

Your first thought is never yourself.

It's Adam or Amelia, your parents, me.

Your first thought is how you can give good to the world.

You'd rather run on science, the truth, because science is always right, and the truth is far better than false pretenses.

I think you became a veterinarian instead of a doctor because you were terrified you'd turn out to be your father, and that is the single biggest fear you've had since we were kids. But you're you. And there's only one you.

There are so many things that make you just as beautiful on the inside, and you need to know that you aren't your father and that you deserve to be happy, Annie—truly and genuinely happy. Because your happiness brightens the world. And your smile brings light to everyone. I hope you see that in yourself.

I can't take back any of this, just like I can't take back our memories together since we were kids.

I can't take back the time you fell off your bike and skinned up your knee so bad that you made me swear not to tell a living soul that we used your dad's tools to pull the tiny rocks from your knees.

I can't take back making love to you the night before I left, and that's a memory I know will stay with me for a lifetime.

I can't take back the moments we laughed so hard that soda came out our noses and the moment our sophomore year when I stopped breathing as you came down the stairs in that light-pink dress. You are the most beautiful thing I've ever seen.

Something died in me when Conroy died. Something awful ached inside me, and I kept pushing it down, trying to numb it out with things that weren't healthy. I dived deeper into oppressing it, so I didn't have to feel it. I'm not making excuses for my actions or the way I treated you, Annie. I just want to explain how messed up I was.

When I saw a picture on someone's phone of a woman who looked like you kissing another man, I lost it. Maybe it was my mind seeing only what my preconceived notions were. Maybe I only saw what my mind was willing to see.

You will always be my other half. You will always be my rainbow in the storm, the smile that pulls me from the depths of despair, the color in my life. But you can't save me. No one can, as you said. I have to be my own miracle.

All of this is to say, I'm sorry. I mentioned you when I was interviewed by the San Francisco Examiner, and you might get inundated with calls and by strangers on social media. I want you to know that all the money in the world doesn't come near the happiness I feel with you. I didn't think about the repercussions of using your name in that article until someone pointed it out to me. And for that, I am sorry. But I won't apologize for telling the world that I'm in love with you because that will never change.

You were my first love and my last love.

All my love,

Colt

32

The Phone Call

Anna

I'm staring at the missed call and message from Colt when my desk phone starts to ring. "Hello?"

"Have you seen the *San Francisco Examiner*?" Tess asks.

"No. Why?" I'm sitting at my desk at the clinic, and it's just before eight. "And since when do you read the *San Francisco Examiner*?"

"Since Delveen told Pearl. And Pearl told the world that Colt had mentioned your name."

My cell phone vibrates across my desk. "Why is *The New York Times* calling my cell phone?"

I hit Ignore.

"Have you read the article?" Tess asks.

"No! What does it say?"

"I don't know. I haven't read it yet."

"Tess! You can't call your best friend and ask if she's read something that you haven't read yet."

I Google *San Francisco Examiner*, only to roll my eyes when the daily newspaper requires a membership to read it.

"I know; I know. I'm sorry. I just wanted to make sure you were okay."

"Okay? Why?" I whine into the phone. "You're scaring me."

"Pearl said it was sweet. And for her to use *sweet* in a sentence, it must be."

"Where do I get a copy of the *San Francisco Examiner*?" I ask more rhetorically.

"I'll ask Principal Brown. I think he might get it."

"Call me back."

"Will do."

I hang up my desk phone. My cell phone vibrates across my desk again. This time with *USA Today*. I hit Ignore.

My phone vibrates again. Losing my patience, I pick it up this time.

"Hello?" I say, impatient.

"Hello. Anna Cain? This is Cybil from *The New York Times*. I'm calling to see if you have a moment to talk about the Colt Atwood quote."

"The what?"

She's quiet for a moment. "Colt Atwood. He used your name in a quote with the *San Francisco Examiner*."

"I'm sorry. I'm sorry. What?"

"I take it, you haven't read the article yet?"

"No. No, I haven't. I'm sorry, Cybil, but no comment. I'm sure you understand."

"I do. You have my number if you change your mind."

"Good-bye." I hang up the phone.

"Anna, you here?" Kimber asks.

"In my office." I sigh, watching Bones sleep on his bed. I rub my eyes.

"Hey." Kimber stands in the doorway. "Have you re—"

"Ugh." I put my head in my hands. "Apparently, I'm the last person on the planet to not have read it."

Kimber pulls the *Examiner* out from under her arm. "Here." She smiles and walks to Bones to give him morning love. "Happy reading," she says as she leaves and goes to the front office.

"What page?" I call out.

"Sports section."

I hold up the newspaper and turn to the front page of the Sports section. On the cover, the headline reads:

Atwood Signs with
Golden State Wolves—
Four-Year Contract for $257 Million

I read through the article, where the reporter, Ernie Rodriguez, talks about information I've already read. Then, it reads:

> *When asked how Atwood felt about signing the biggest NBA contract in history, his answer was simple: "Anna Elizabeth Cain, nothing in this world is worth more to me than you. It's always been you. And I'll wait until forever for you, Annie."*

I set the newspaper down on my desk. Bones picks up his head, tilts it to the left, and stares back at me. "Don't give me that look, Bones."

I can't catch my breath, and my office grows inexplicably small.

Bones gets up, stretches, and casually walks over to me. He sits and puts his paw on my knee.

"Don't."

He whines and drops his head. I think Bones is an old man who was married for many years to the love of his life and that he was reincarnated just for me. He knows the way of my heart before I do.

"Don't you like Sam?"

Sam and I have been on a few dates in the past month and a half. He came here for a weekend, and I recently took a weekend trip to Seattle.

But it got hot last night. We'd finished dinner in downtown Seattle and gone back to his place. We'd drunk wine, and we whispered promises I wasn't sure I could keep. I was saved by his pager from the hospital when he was called in for an emergency surgery.

He kissed me good-bye, and I left the next morning when he was still at the hospital. I guess I just panicked.

I got into town late last night. While Colt had been celebrating his contract, I'd lost myself in another man's arms. His mouth. His body. And not just any man. Sam Houston. The boy that I had fallen for after Colt. Both times.

Two times, Colt had left.

Two times, he'd broken my heart.

Two times too many.

Sights that I'll never be able to get out of my head.

Bones whines again, but now, he's at the door, signaling he needs to go out.

"Okay, boy." I get up—leaving the newspaper on my desk, my phone, all lines of communication—and take him out to the alley behind the clinic.

"Hey, Doc," Toby Lemon slurs. "Did you read the *Examiner*?"

Even Toby reads the Examiner? *Damn it.*

"Yes, I have, Toby. Thank you."

Bones does his business.

"If you ask me, you need to ditch the doctor and marry Atwood."

"Yeah? Why's that, Toby?" I cross my arms.

He shrugs and wavers back and forth, unable to stand completely straight. "Been watching you two since you were wee little. Ain't nothing that makes you two smile brighter than each other."

I want to say, *Toby, you realize that you've been drunk our entire lives, right?* But I don't because if you'd had his life, you might drink to oblivion, too.

"I pay attention." Toby taps his finger to his forehead.

Toby Lemon hasn't always been the town drunk.

When Toby was at Humboldt State University, he met Jenny Radford while taking their general education classes.

In 1967, when Toby was fresh out of journalism school, according to Clyda, he cleaned up real nice and was well dressed. He and Jenny Radford, a teacher at Cuddeback School, were scheduled to be married the following summer.

Toby was a reporter for the *Dillon Creek Echo*. There was a fire east of Dillon Creek on Highway 36. Ike Isner told Toby to cover it. Said it was a house fire. According to pieces of information given after the fire, Toby was the first one on the scene.

It was the old Radford house, just past Carlotta. Back in those days, you lived with your parents until you married. The Radfords had nine children, and the house was too old and too dilapidated to withstand the flames. And communication moved like molasses. When a fire truck did arrive, Toby had brought out three children—three children who could not be revived. The entire Radford family succumbed to the fire that night, including Jenny.

Toby Lemon retreated into himself. He was never the same, and he never wrote another article for the *Dillon Creek Echo* or any other establishment again.

But the tragedy of it all is that Toby never could process the loss of Jenny, her family, her siblings that he pulled from the wreckage, so on that September night, Toby Lemon died, too.

People grieve differently, and I think that's why the residents of Dillon Creek take care of Toby Lemon—because they're family.

"Toby," I say gently, "what makes you think I should marry Colt?"

"Because," he slurs as he turns and begins to walk down the alley, "true love, the kind that we all wish for, doesn't come around twice." Toby looks down at his feet. At the shoes he's walked miles in—an offbeat faded brown filled with time, wear, bad memories, and no memories at all—that take him where he needs to go.

Toby's words bury themselves deep within me along with his story he's never told.

Bones is at my feet and ready to go back inside.

"Good-bye, Toby."

"G'night, Dr. Cain."

Good night?

We walk through the back door and back into my office. Bones continues the rest of the way down the hallway to the front office. I walk to my desk and look down at my phone, seeing seventeen missed calls.

"Hey, Anna?" Kimber calls from her desk.

I set my phone down and walk up front.

She's holding her hand over the phone, so whoever is on the other end can't hear. "*USA Today* is calling to see if you have a comment on Colt's quote."

It's both unnerving and irritating. These reporters are relentless.

"I do." I take the phone from Kimber. "Listen, this is my place of work, and I'm too fucking busy to deal with shit like this when I have animals to save. Good-bye."

I hand the receiver back to Kimber, and she smiles as she sets it down in its cradle.

"Killed it, boss," Kimber says.

This isn't Colt's fault. But one thing is for sure; I don't like the spotlight at all.

Ben Taft comes in with Radar, his twelve-week-old kelpie.

"Hey, Dr. Cain. Hey, Kimber," he says as Radar toddles behind him.

Bones gets up and does the sniff test as Radar tries to play.

I realize I work with animals because it is harder and they need someone to be their voice. Maybe I became a veterinarian so that I wouldn't be like my father, but perhaps, in the end, he couldn't hack being a veterinarian because his heart was too tender for the fur. One thing my father has is a heart of gold. Amid the undercoat of infidelity, maybe he did things beyond his control to cope, too.

Radar does a side hop to my feet, and I pick him up.

Bones lets out a low growl—not a scary one, but a *hey, you're mine, and he doesn't belong to you, so why are you holding him* growl.

"How long's the neuter take, Dr. Cain?"

"We'll keep him for the day, and you can come pick him up at about four thirty this afternoon."

"Sounds good."

We make small talk for a few minutes, and when Ben reaches the door, he turns back to me. "Hey. Dr. Cain, I don't mean to pry, but did you read the *San Francisco Examiner?*"

What is with this town and that paper? We're four and a half hours north of San Francisco, for God's sake.

"Some of it."

Ben nods. Looks down at the tiled floor and then meets my gaze. "Sometimes, you've got to put all your eggs in one basket, or the wolves will get them."

I drop my head, trying to understand what message Ben is giving me.

"Take the bait," he says with a look that wills me to understand.

Still, I don't get it.

"Take your chances because the good far outweighs the bad."

"Have you been in love before, Ben?" Kimber asks.

Shit.

"Once. And I let her go."

"Why?"

"I let all the other noise get in the way of us." The old rancher chews on the side of his cheek. "Ain't nothing better than two sets of socks sitting by the fire at night." He shrugs. "And sometimes, you've got to let go to find that out."

33

There's Been an Accident

Anna: Age Eighteen

"Anna, I need you," Colt whispered into the phone.

I tried to gather my wits about me.

"What's wrong? Are you all right?"

"No." The tone in Colt's voice changed. "It's Conroy and Tripp. They've been in an accident."

"What?" I sat up straight in bed, my spine stiff, as if someone had kicked me in the shin.

"Where are you?"

"On Waddington."

"On Waddington. Why?" I threw my covers back and shimmied on my bra, sweatshirt, and some yoga pants. "Where on Waddington?"

"Dead Man's Curve."

"I-I'll be right there, Colt."

And he hung up.

"Dad?" I tiptoed into my mom and dad's bedroom.

"He's not here, Anna. Are you all right?" She sat up and turned on her bedside lamp.

"Colt just called. There's been an accident. It's Conroy and Tripp."

"Oh my God." She jumped out of bed and threw on her robe. "I'll drive you."

Anger seethed inside me as I stared at the empty spot where my father should be.

"Where is he?" I asked as we rushed out of their bedroom and downstairs.

"Come on. We need to hurry." Mom tried to change the subject, but she and I both knew the truth.

"Is he in Eureka again?"

She stopped running when we reached the bottom. Looked up and stared at the wall in front of us.

"When are you going to understand that he's sleeping with other people? Men and women. All this is killing your heart, Mom. You're worth so much more than a man who cheats on you."

Still, we hurried out to the car and jumped in. It was quiet for a moment, and I pushed my tears back—for my mom, for Conroy, for Tripp, for Colt, for Tess, for the Atwoods, and for the Morgans.

"You know, Anna, we do things for the people we love. We do things for the person they are, not what they do. I knew your father liked both men and women from the moment I met him. It doesn't change the fact that he's a wonderful father to you, Adam, and Amelia. Sometimes, in love, our hearts love more than one person. That's what makes us human."

"But what about the church, Mom? You, of all people, should know that infidelity is a sin, right?"

She drove faster than she normally did, taking the corners quicker. "Listen, the old saying goes, *Take what you want and leave the rest.* I love God, and I love my church, but we're all sinners. We don't follow the Bible one hundred percent of the time. We all screw up. Nobody—absolutely nobody—is godly all the time. If we were, we wouldn't need the church or a book to follow.

"Honey, look, I chose this life. I knew your father was different—I guess that's the right word—but he loves his family more." She shrugged. "He always will. And I suppose, at some point, we'll have to let go. But right now, it works."

"What about what you want, Mom?"

She smiled and looked out into the darkness. Her eyes brimmed with tears, and I watched them gather, almost on the brink of falling. "I have what I want in life. I have my three beautiful children. I have my work with the church and my volunteer work. I have what I need." She took my hand in hers and kissed it. "God gives us what we need in life, not necessarily what we want. I believe I'll know when it's time to move on, but I love your father."

It was then that we saw the flashing lights, and they lit up the night sky in an explosion of color.

It was much worse than we'd thought. My mom parked a safe distance away, and I called Colt.

"Where are you?" I asked when he picked up.

The scene was a mess. Ambulance workers, the Humboldt County Sheriff's Department, Dillon Creek Police, Humboldt Fire Department.

"By the ambulance," Colt said. "This isn't good,"

I ran full speed to the ambulance and met him with the force of my body and held him. He clung to me. Like I was his way out of the pain. As if I could take away the awfulness that he felt inside.

My eyes danced over the scene.

Two bodies lay in the field, covered in a white sheet, and the only thing Colt asked was, "Is he okay, Anna? Will he be okay?"

His body began to shake, and I wasn't sure if it was just his or both of ours. The truth was, my body was growing more numb by the second as I surveyed our surroundings. Laurel fought off a sheriff to sit with her son, whose body no longer held breath or a heartbeat.

"Where's Tess?" I asked whoever was listening, my arms still so tight around Colt. I couldn't see her. I couldn't find her in the sea of people.

I didn't remember everything that happened that night, what the world around us did, but what I remembered was how it felt. Like nothing at all and everything at once, at the same time. Two worlds, two humans, two best friends, two young bodies lying in the field that night, and everyone cried.

Laurel lay with her dead son until the sun rose.

Tripp lay alone.

I pleaded with God to give the boys one more chance. Asked Him to give them a fresh start. I asked him more from the self-centered part of me that didn't want to watch my best friends feel this.

My eyes burned when the sun came up and offered a new view of our reality.

Trucks left.

People moved.

And all I could do was sit there and ask what had happened.

The bodies stayed there for an awfully long time.

Tess never showed up.

Mavis Morgan kept moving in and out of the field, yelling at whoever would listen, her face contorted by grief.

My mom sat with the Atwoods and the Morgans. Because in that moment, they sat together, cried together, tried to look at the situation clearly.

My father finally showed up, and I told him to fuck off.

Adam came with Cash. They picked up Colt and me from the grass where we lay, trying to remember a time when life didn't hurt so much.

Colt watched his brother Cash. "Why are you doing this?" he asked.

Cash took his brother's cheeks in his hands and held his face to his. "Because there's no one left to pick up the pieces, so it's my job to help the little brother."

Cash smelled of booze and cigarettes, and I welcomed the smell.

"But Conroy's gone," Colt said out loud. He said this to be sure it was a reality because I felt the same way. I waited for Cash to answer him.

"He's gone, little brother. Come on. Let's begin the aftermath."

Colt's eyes were wide.

Adam said, "Come on, Anna. Let's get you home."

I thought it wouldn't be the same and that everything would change. And that life, as we knew it, had been turned upside down. I thought it would never feel the same again.

I clung to Adam. "Somebody has to save Colt."

Adam looked at me like I was dead and said, "He needs to save himself, Anna."

"Tripp was driving," someone said.

"Conroy was driving," said someone else.

And no one knew all the details.

They had both been ejected from a Willy's Jeep. It's a jeep with no doors and no windows.

And alcohol had been a factor.

Even the investigation had legs it couldn't stand on in the form of the facts. And it wasn't how the investigators carried the investigation out; it was because of love. It was love that kept their families inside the fence and in the field. It was love that kept their hearts afloat.

But when the coroner tried to take Conroy and Tripp, everything went from bad to worse.

Laurel screamed when they touched Conroy's body. Daryl tried to hold his wife back. My dad stepped in and took her by the shoulders and explained that Conroy was only being taken away so they could look at him in more detail. Laurel understood that.

Everyone loved my dad. Even the ones who whispered behind his back.

After all, he was a good man, as far as my mother was concerned. But to me, he cared more about his own needs than his family, and that was just how I planned to look at my father until the day I died.

Died.

Death.

This all could have been prevented.

Later that night, I called Colt, and he asked me to come over.

I did, and we fell asleep on his bed and woke up to an empty, dark house where no one was sleeping.

It felt nice, and it made me ache between my legs for only Colt.

His lips trailed up my neck to my earlobe and traced over to my mouth. That was when he kissed me with urgency as the tears rolled down his cheeks.

I crawled on top of him and asked him what he needed.

He said, "Just you."

So, I slowly took off my T-shirt and slipped off my bra.

He moaned quietly at the sight of me in the dim light of the setting sun. He took my breasts in his hands and then into his mouth.

I could feel him below me.

He undid my jeans and took them off me so that the only things that separated our sexes were my panties and his nylon shorts.

He reached up and wiped a tear that had fallen, and I didn't know if I was crying for him or me or for the fact that he felt so good underneath me and I needed it. I felt selfish for it.

He pushed my panties to the side and used his thumb to gently rub my sex.

Quietly, we both moaned as I rocked on top of him, and he rubbed.

I tugged on his shorts, and he picked me up and set me down on the bed. He pulled his shorts off, and I found him long, just like his body, but with girth.

He pushed me up to the pillow and crawled on top of me without moving inside me.

"Please," I begged.

He reached in his bedside drawer, retrieved a condom, and slid it on.

Slowly, he pushed inside me, making me bigger with each slow push.

"Are you all right?" Colt asked.

"Are you?" I asked.

"With you, yes."

And that was when he kissed me in the softest way that he could as he cried.

"Turn around," he whispered, breathless.

When I did, he eased into me from behind and took my knot in his fingertips where he pushed gently and then harder, and we both came and fell onto the mattress.

We kissed and made love into the late evening, and no one bothered us. Under the covers, he put his fingers inside me, put himself inside me. He kissed my breasts and between my legs. I didn't know how long we touched each other, but in the early morning, I was sore until he made me wet again and touched his tongue to my knot until I couldn't stand it. I held his head to my middle and watched as he made me see stars.

The last time we made love before I left him, I asked him to leave the condom off.

He slid inside me and silently cried out in my ear, "God, Annie. I feel every inch of you. I'm going to come right now."

And when he did, he pulled out and held himself in the sheets.

Colt left the next day. He didn't say much, except that he was sorry. And when he kissed me good-bye, I felt him slide through my fingertips, and I felt his good-bye with awfulness.

"I love you, Anna."

I didn't tell him I loved him back. But I did, and I couldn't hang on to him, so I tried selfishly to protect my own heart from obliteration.

"I'll see you." I pulled on the strings of Colt's University of North Carolina sweatshirt.

"Yeah," he said.

The truth was, neither of us came home at Christmas that year. Sam and I ate Christmas dinner at Huevos Rancheros.

I didn't come home because that was after I'd flown to North Carolina to profess my love to Colt Atwood. I was terrified he'd bring home the woman I'd watched him having sex with.

I'd lied to my parents and told them I was taking an intersession course. I thought my father knew I wasn't. I thought my mom knew I needed space.

And the whole town grieved for the Morgans and the Atwoods while I hid away under the fog of freshman year.

I dreamed about that night for the next four years. I dreamed we'd made love in a car, against the walls of my dorm room, inside a restroom stall. And with each dream, they'd become more vivid, more real.

I'd wake up in the night, breathing hard and aching. I didn't want to live like that anymore. I couldn't. And I couldn't wait for Colt anymore.

That was when I made the decision to forget about him.

The dreams went away with his memory.

34

Grandpa Isn't Doing Well

February 2020

"Hello?"

"Hi, Scarlet. It's your grandmother." Erla's voice tries to steady itself.

"Grandma? How are you?" Scarlet's voice brings comfort to Erla. A comfort she hasn't felt in a long time.

Erla's rehearsed this conversation a million times in her head. Trying not to cause worry, but instead concern. "I called your mother and left a message. That was two days ago, and I haven't heard back."

Erla doesn't ask what her daughter does or doesn't do. It's her life and her business.

"Grandpa isn't doing so well, I'm afraid, Scarlet. Um …" Erla covers her lips. This is the part that she rehearsed that she hasn't been able to get through without tears. "He doesn't have much time left, and I think it's best you come to say your good-byes."

The line remains silent.

"Scarlet?"

"What?"

"Are you all right?"

"I'll book a flight today. I'll be there tomorrow. Can you pick me up at the airport in Arcata?"

Scarlet doesn't know that Erla can't drive those distances anymore, but she can't bear to tell her with the worry she has on her mind right now.

"Of course, dear," Erla says, thinking she'll call Laurel to help her out.

"I love you, Grandma."

"I love you too, Scarlet. I will see you tomorrow."

Erla waits for Scarlet to hang up, just as she used to do with Devon. She sought solace in being able to be the last to hang up, for fear that Devon or Scarlet might have one last thought and wouldn't be able to tell Erla if she hung up first.

The line goes dead, and Erla hangs up.

Now, Don is confined to the bed they once shared. Erla sleeps in the spare room. She doesn't sleep most nights, listening for Don, knowing full well that the in-home health care provider, Stewart, is there to meet his needs. But it's the time they have left that scares her the most.

Most nights, Erla sits in the rocking chair by his bed and watches him sleep, remembering an easier time and not so easy time. The birth of their daughter, their granddaughter, Scarlet's father—who they don't talk about. Don is a great father and wonderful grandfather.

"Erla?" Don says and then coughs. Lies on his side because that seems to be the most comfortable position. His bottom lip shakes, and that's not from emotion; it's from the deadly disease that is taking his whole life away.

Erla sits at his bedside. "Yes, my love."

"Devon. Did you tell her? Do you think she needs to know?"

"No, dear. No. She only needs to know that she is loved." Erla tries to alleviate her husband's worry.

Perhaps it is Erla's own fear of what her daughter would think of her because she hasn't ever told Devon the truth.

Life is complicated. The things people do to protect their children. No, Devon doesn't need to know the truth. Because the truth, at this point, might hurt too much.

Erla thinks better of it. "Do you want Devon to know the truth?"

Don's quiet. "No."

Erla places her hand on top of her husband's shaking hand. "Then, it's settled."

Don can't move his hand to acknowledge her hand, but he's learned to with his eyes. "You will always be the light of my life, Erla."

Erla smiles, trying to hide her breaking heart. "I know, dear. I know. Get some sleep, hmm?"

And she watches his eyes until they slowly close. She's contemplated what Don said about not wanting to suffer. To be put to sleep with medication. But today is not the day. Not with Scarlet coming home.

Maybe tomorrow.

There are the bad days when it would be easier if Don died, so he could be through the suffering and on the other side. But there are good days, too, that make the bad days worth it.

"Thank you for driving me up to Arcata, Anna. I know how much Laurel has going with the ranch," Erla says, staring out at the fog that lies like fingers between redwood trees.

"It's no problem, Erla. It was a slow day at the clinic, and Kimber can handle things for an hour or two."

If I could just drive these longer distances, it would be easier on everyone, she thinks to herself.

Erla reflects to a time when she'd drive to Arcata to pick up Devon from theater practice and not bat an eyelash. Too, with gas prices these days, she really tries to keep her driving limited to Dillon Creek and Fortuna.

"When's the last time Scarlet came home? I'm sure it will be good to see her," Anna asks as they merge onto US Route 101.

"I don't remember. It's been some time. I know she's been busy with work." Erla hesitates at first but realizes it's Anna. "Scarlet and Hank got a divorce." She is certain that was a big factor as to why she hasn't come home. She is also certain that there's been talk about why Devon hasn't come home.

"Have you heard from Colt?" It slips out of her mouth quicker than she can catch it. It isn't Erla's curiosity. It's how Anna wears heartbreak.

God Almighty, she's never seen Anna cry but maybe once when Clyda had a heart attack at Portuguese Hall. Little Anna ripped out of there and ran down to First Christian Church. Pastor Mike found her praying her little heart out. No, this is different.

"I'm sorry, Anna. I shouldn't have asked such a personal question."

"No, Erla, it's fine. Maybe it's good that I talk about it because I don't normally." Anna sighs and stares out the windshield. "Have you ever felt so heartbroken to let someone go, knowing it's the right decision, only because they need to fix themselves?"

Oh, yes. Erla does know that feeling. "Feels like your heart won't ever mend." Erla looks out the passenger window of her Cadillac. Her eyes move to Anna, who's nodding her head, biting her lip, most likely fighting tears. "Time is such a gift, Anna, and I didn't realize it until Devon was raised and more so now that Don is so sick. And love. Sometimes, we just don't have enough time with the people we love. Sometimes, we have to take the risk of heartbreak, take the chance, if we know it's the real deal." Erla rubs her hands together. "Are you chilly? Damn groundhog didn't see his shadow, and it's colder than a well digger's hind end." Erla turns on the heat. Sits back in her seat. "I heard once that true love, the kind that we all wish for, doesn't come around twice—and if it does, well, you'd better hold on to it the second time around."

Anna looks at Erla and then back to the road. "I've heard that before but not the second part."

Erla remembers Toby Lemon's words from all those years ago and says them once more in her head to spend just a few more moments with them. "Don't wait, Anna. Time is such an important commodity that we just don't treasure enough. And when we have time to look back on it and realize it, it's far too late."

Scarlet looks even more beautiful than Erla remembered. Though Erla will be the first to admit that her memory isn't what it used to be. She didn't think it was possible that Scarlet could get any more beautiful, but she has. Don has always called her a spitting image of Erla, but Erla has never seen it. Maybe when Erla was in her twenty-somethings. But Scarlet looks exquisite, standing there with her waist-length strawberry-blonde hair and her crystal-blue eyes.

It's when Devon walks up behind her granddaughter that Erla almost faints.

"Erla? Are you all right?" Anna touches her elbow, most likely noticing she went light-headed at the sight of her daughter.

"Grandma." Scarlet runs to her grandmother and throws her arms around her. She whispers into her ear, "I've missed you so much."

Erla's eyes fill with tears as she reaches around her granddaughter's little waist and says, "Oh, my sweet Scarlet. How I've missed you so." She takes in her granddaughter's expensive scent, not the one she used to have as a child—a cross between fresh earth and sweat. No, now, she smells like a deep, dark rose.

Erla and Scarlet finally release.

"Devon." Anna extends her hand. "It's good to see you."

"You as well, Anna."

Erla's gaze meets Devon, and Erla doesn't resist the urge to throw her arms around her daughter. She pulls her in and squeezes tight.

I never want to let go, she thinks to herself.

Erla's eyes fill with tears once again. Devon eventually puts both arms around her mother. But Devon smells different. It's a mix between mouthwash and sunflowers. Nevertheless, her daughter is home, and Erla has her arms around her. And just for a moment, everything is right with the world. Everything.

"Come on. Let's go home," Erla says, reluctant to let go of her daughter again, for fear that she'll run.

Erla touches her cheek with the palm of her hand. Devon looks into her mother's eyes only for a moment before she looks at Scarlet.

"Let's go see your father," Erla says.

And then Devon says, "Are you sure he's my father, Mom?"

Oh no. Oh no. Something has gone terribly wrong.

"Help me, please." Mabe jumps awake. She's breathing hard, and her heart is pounding. Fear runs through her veins like lightning.

Mabe had a dream about the boys on Waddington again.

She'd only had two beers—or was it four or five? She can't quite remember. But she wants to forget everything from that horrible night seven and a half years ago.

Mabe sits up from her chair in the late afternoon. It would be easier to push things down with beer, purchase something, anything, than feel this awfulness in her gut, in her heart.

She saw three people in Willy's Jeep turn onto State Route 211 and then onto Waddington. She stayed a safe distance behind.

And then Mabe heard the wreck, the tires squealing against the pavement. Heard the Jeep slam into the tree.

Heard the screams.

The Jeep had hit the only tree on Waddington, and the lights cast a bright white hue over the tall grass of summer. Dead Man's Curve.

Fear stirs in Mabe's bones as she remembers it.

I should pull over, she thought. *I should*, she remembers thinking.

But the police would need to be called; she was certain. She'd been drinking. What would they think of Mabe Muldoon? Her car was there; they'd know. And the whole town of Dillon Creek would know that Mabe had been drinking and driving. Even if it was four beers. For an old lady of her stature, four beers would surely put her over the legal limit.

Against Mabe's better judgment, she parked and stared out the windshield of her 1989 Buick LeSabre into the open field.

Mabe carefully got out of her car. At her age, even over seven years ago, falling could put her in the hospital for months. With her headlights as her guide, she walked the edge of the field behind Willy's Jeep.

"Is anyone there?" she said. She listened.

"Help … help me," a voice called out. A scared, broken voice that only she could hear.

The sirens of town started to blow.

Mabe's insides shook.

She should stay and help.

No, no. She'd get caught drinking. She'd likely get charged with driving while intoxicated. Her insurance would change. *It'll be expensive*, she thought.

But she couldn't leave this person to die, could she?

She could pretend she hadn't seen anything. Heard anything. She could leave now and pretend that this never happened.

Mabe hesitated when the voice from the tall grass of summer said once more, "Help me, please."

Mabe couldn't catch her breath as her heart pounded.

The sirens drew closer.

A light in the farmhouse not far from the scene turned on.

Mabe had to leave. "I'll go home and call for help, okay?" she said to the tall grass.

But there was no answer.

Mabe knew the decision she made wasn't the right one, but she got back in her car and drove home.

35

The Finals

Colt

June 2020

Coach Hindley from the other team takes a full time-out. What stands between our team and the NBA championship is the next seven seconds. We're up by two, and if Leroy Finnell hits the three, which I know the Grizzlies are banking on, it'll be all over.

Dr. Broze leans in the huddle. "How's the tendon?"

I nod as sweat drips from my face. "Fine. Feels good." It is tight, but it still feels connected.

"Slow the clock when we get the ball, kill time, be strong. Let them foul you," Coach Dickerson says.

We stand and put our hands in the middle.

Coach Dickerson says, "One, two, three!"

"Wolves!"

It's the Grizzlies' ball.

I take my spot in the middle of the key.

Paul West brings down the ball.

The clock ticks slowly.

The shot clock has already been disabled.

West calls a play, and the three opposing players move to the opposite side of the floor.

West passes to Finnell, and Finnell sets up for the shot. I keep Roarke Drummond on my back and make him fight for his position on the floor.

But Finnell, who's being guarded by Gary Lucas—who won Best Defensive Player of the Year last year—has Finnell guarded.

Finnell passes to Lee Duggard, who's in the corner behind the three-point line, and just after the ball leaves Duggard's hands for the three-point shot, the buzzer sounds.

I fight Drummond for position.

The ball is in the air.

And life just hangs in limbo.

Anna crosses my mind.

If this shot is made, the Grizzlies will win, and it will be okay. Life will go back to normal. If this shot is missed … well then, that'll be good, too.

But if something happens to Anna, then nothing at all will be right. Nothing at all.

The ball hits the rim.

Bounces once.

Bounces twice.

The entire arena is silent.

Twenty thousand fans grow eerily still.

Bounces three times.

And falls.

Out.

The entire area goes crazy.

It's a frenzy as confetti in our team colors falls. My teammates grab me and jump on me, and I'm just trying to figure out what just happened.

"We just won the title, baby!" Finnell slaps my shoulders.

It's chaos.

A reporter approaches me right after the game. "Colt, you just came off an Achilles tendon tear. Most players don't come back from an injury like that. You not only came back, but you also averaged forty-two points a game. Now, I'd ask you how you feel, but I assume your response will be something to do with Anna Cain." She laughs but waits for my answer.

My excitement dies off almost immediately at the mention of her name. I wish with everything I have that she could be here in the moment with me, but I don't say that. Instead, I say, "I'm just glad we pulled out the win," as my heart sinks.

After the trophy and Most Valuable Player presentation, I'm headed to the locker room with a team of security.

"Hey, Atwood. You were ten for twelve from the line. Everyone knows that free throws win games. If you'd made those last two shots, you'd have won the game by four."

I look to my left to find where the voice is coming from, and I realize it's coming from a bullhorn.

Up in the stands is the love of my life with a bullhorn.

"I'm sorry," she says.

And I drop my head with a big smile. Fight back the emotion. I look up at her again, scared she'll leave.

"Larry over in security wouldn't let me onto the floor. Larry, shame on you." Anna pulls the bullhorn away from her mouth.

But I'm already climbing on top of the seats to get to her.

The arena, still full with people, grows silent.

I hear the loud whispers, "Is that her?"

I reach Anna and set the bullhorn down. I take her in my arms, telling myself that this isn't a dream. That she's here. And that she waited for me.

"You came," I whisper.

She rolls her eyes. Her hands on my chest, she says, "I couldn't miss the championship game when you sent courtside tickets, Atwood."

I kiss her with everything I have inside me. All the guilt, all the hurt, all the sadness, the love, the want, the passion. I kiss her with the lips of a different man. I'm not the same Colt Atwood.

I'm healing. I say healing because we don't just stop healing. We're always on the mend, especially with a wound like losing a brother.

But Anna is here, in my arms and against my lips, and everything is just as it should be.

"Colt Atwood"—she pulls away, her eyes hooded—"from the day I could define love, I knew you and I were meant to be. I tried to fight it. Tried to push it all away because I was too scared of what we'd lose together. But I've realized—thanks to Erla and several other smart people in Dillon Creek—that I can't wait," she whispers with tears in her eyes. "A wise man once told me, 'True love, the kind that we all wish for, doesn't come around twice.'"

"Oh my God, Anna." I take her hand and put it on my heart. "I want you to know that it isn't money or basketball or things that do this to my heart. It's you. It's always been you."

"I know," she says. "I know."

And then she kisses me for who the real Colt Atwood is, not the Colt Atwood that the world sees.

We stop when we hear clapping. We look down at the sea of people below us. Beside us and all around us.

"Oh my goodness," Anna says as she sees our picture on the Jumbotron.

Reporters are clapping. Everyone is clapping, including my teammates.

I look back at Anna, just to make sure she's okay with all this. "Are you all right?" I ask and brush the blonde hair from her eyes.

"As long as we're together, I'll always be okay. Might be a shift in how I do things, but I will be okay, Colt."

She's naked in my bed. Something I've dreamed about for a painfully long time. The satin sheets make her pale skin stand out like milky white sheets.

I'm careful when I ease on top of her. Her nipples are hard, and her lips are parted, waiting for my mouth.

"I love you, Annie." I push the hair back from her face.

"Mr. Atwood, you feel very excited to see me."

"You have no idea." I kiss her open mouth, and she welcomes me with a soft moan.

I trail kisses down her neck, her chest, her breasts, her stomach, and then reach the spot I'm looking for.

Her legs fall to the sides as her hands run through my hair.

A soft cry escapes her lips as I take my tongue and gently push against her folds to get to her sweet spot.

I reach up and toy with one of her nipples and find her knot with my tongue.

"Now, you can be as loud as you'd like, Anna, and no one will hear you."

She quietly calls out as her hands tighten against my head. She moves them to the pillows above her head as I watch her from where I'm at.

I push harder with my tongue.

"Oh my goodness, Colt."

"Come here," she says.

I slide up her body and make sure she can feel my hardness against her.

She takes my face in her hands and kisses me. "Make love to me, Colt. Make love to me until our limbs become soft and limber. Make love to me until the sun comes up and sets again."

I slide inside her and close my eyes. I rest my forehead on her chest. "It feels too good, Anna. You feel too good." I meet her eyes.

I stop pushing only for a minute, just to calm myself.

She pushes me to my back and slides down my body, and she takes me in her mouth.

"Oh my God." I put one hand behind my head and the other on the back of her head, making sure her hair doesn't fall in her face because I need to see what she's doing to me.

I get lost in her, and when she comes up for air, I pull her up to my mouth. Roll on top of her and push inside her again.

We both sigh together.

Our bodies move with precision and need.

We make love in the quiet moments of who we were. And who we want to become.

We climax together and collapse against the sheets, struggling to breathe. I make sure my hands can touch her skin, just so I know she's close.

She pushes herself to the crook of my arm. "From now until forever, Colt, I want you to make love to me and only me."

"You have me."

"I'll be right back."

She shimmies out from my grip and walks to her overnight bag she packed. Grabs something and comes back to bed.

"I won't let you go again, Colt Atwood. I love you more than I did yesterday, and I want to spend my nights in your arms and my days in your thoughts. I knew I couldn't heal your broken heart that morning I found you in room two at The Gingerbread Mansion. I knew that time would heal us both and that we might not ever be the same. But as time ticked on, I knew we'd spend our lifetime making mistakes. Sometimes big ones, sometimes small ones." She pauses and kisses my chest. "The biggest mistake I would have made is not taking a risk—the risk of losing our friendship, the single most important thing in my life. I am willing to put all of my eggs in one basket because it comes down to this. Love is love, and time is limited. I'd rather spend the rest of my days basking in what real love feels like than live a lifetime of regrets or playing it safe."

Anna pulls a black box from underneath the sheet. She opens the box.

But it isn't what I think it is.

"What is this?" I sit up against the headboard, moving her closer to me, touching her, knowing I can now love her openly and not hide behind anything anymore.

Inside the box is a little picture of us from when we were about seven or so and a handwritten note in Anna's seven-year-old handwriting.

> *I, Anna Elizabeth Cain, do solemnly swear to love Colt Andrew Atwood for as long as we both shall live. Amen.*

The date reads July 12.

"Anna," I say breathlessly. This is the day Conroy and Tripp died but years before they passed. I take the picture and the note in my hands. "Where did you find this?"

"I kept it in the bottom drawer of my jewelry box." She smiles up at me.

"The unicorn one?"

"That's the one."

"So, you knew I was the one for you at seven years old?"

"I did. Tried to deny it for a long time, but I always knew."

I set the picture and the note in the black box and put it on the nightstand. "Come here." Pulling her on top of me, I rest my hands against her buttocks and let her know that I'm ready again.

One of the most intimate acts we can do in this world is show our vulnerability with someone we love and lose control.

She's sitting on top of me, all of her, and I stare deeply into her eyes, praying that she'll never have to live a day without me again because I'd rather endure the heartbreak of loss than her having to do it. I reach up and cup her breasts as she slowly rocks on top of me, her eyes narrowed in on mine. She smiles in pleasure, and I know this feels good to her. God knows it feels good to me.

We make love again.

This is where I want to be for the rest of my life.

36

The Little Black Box

Anna
July 2020

S am took everything well the day I left for the final game. I think he knew that it had always been Colt, too, just like the rest of Dillon Creek. I guess I just needed to find it in my own way.

"But if he ever fucking hurts you, let me know," he said.

Sam Houston rarely used the F-word, so when he said it, I knew he meant business.

I'm at work, and Colt is at our house, fixing a gutter. Bones enjoys Colt being home, so he spends his days at home or at the ranch with Colt and Tupac. But Bones lets me know I'm his number one by sleeping on my side of the bed, cuddling next to me on the couch, and always checking in with his subtle glances. I think Colt needs to prove himself to Bones, too.

Our house. It still sounds surreal. Our plan is to live in Dillon Creek in the off-season, and then during the season, he'll commute back and forth from San Francisco to home, which is a four-and-a-half-hour car ride but only a half hour in the private jet that Colt keeps at Rohnerville Airport in Belle's Hollow.

I took a hiatus from social media, as my Facebook and Instagram pages blew up with friend requests, follow requests, and messages. The thing is, I don't want any part of being famous. I just want Colt Atwood; with that comes a price, and I understand that.

It's funny. Colt and I spent years running from a small town that held our past together like a brick wall; we were just too scared to face it. And when we finally did, we realized it was the one thing we'd wanted all along—to find peace within ourselves.

It doesn't fix the fact that Conroy and Tripp died, and it doesn't fix the fact that our town is still fractured by its tragedy.

Nobody in Dillon Creek bothers Colt because he's the same Atwood boy who spent his summer days running up and down Main Street, chasing a girl named Anna Cain.

"Well, hello there, Mr. Atwood."

"Kimber, for the ninth time, it's Colt."

I smile.

"I know. I just like to call you that."

I stand and walk out front.

"Hey," I say.

His eyes light up, and Bones and Tupac come running to me.

Colt follows, kissing me on the mouth. "Hey, I need to borrow you for a second."

Kimber gives Colt some sort of sign, and Colt smiles.

"Got it covered," Kimber says. "See you."

"What?" I say, looking between Kimber and Colt.

"Come along, my lady." Colt gives my elbow a tug as Bones and Tupac follow us out the front door.

"This," he says, "is a top-secret place, so I'm going to need to blindfold you." Colt takes out a bandana from his back pocket.

I love how this man makes all the money in the world and still wears Wranglers and carries a bandana in his back pocket.

"Okay, what are you up to?"

Colt ties the blindfold on and takes me by the hand but not before kissing it first. "Do you trust me, Annie?"

"Always."

"All right, boys, onward," he says to Bones and Tupac, and we begin our journey.

At first, it's cement and then grass and then uphill, and then it's really steep.

We reach some sort of summit, and Colt takes my waist in his hands, pulls me to his front, and slips off the blindfold.

We're at the top of the Dillon Creek Cemetery where he's laid out a blanket and a picnic basket.

"Thought I'd take you on a lunch date," Colt says and lets go of me.

We both sit.

"Well, I'd say, it's perfect timing because I'm starving."

Colt unpacks the picnic basket and hands me a sandwich. "Turkey. Mayo only. No mustard."

I smile as I take it and bite into it.

Colt does the same.

And we stare down at our little town of Dillon Creek.

"I love it up here. The air just seems fresher, and my thoughts become clearer," I say.

"Bones!" he calls. "Come."

Bones thrashes back to us, Tupac in tow, though not as fast as Tupac used to be. Since the surgery, he's been doing pretty well though.

Bones sits at my feet, and I notice a black box tied to his collar.

My heart stops, and I turn to Colt. "What is that?"

"I think you handed me that same black box last month. Just thought I'd give it back."

Carefully and slowly, I reach up and untie the box from Bones's collar.

Colt reaches over and takes the box from me. He gets down on one knee and says, "We've been best friends most of our lives. And I promise to always be your friend first, but second, I want to be your husband. I want to wake up with you in the mornings and go to bed with you at night. I want to hold you when the world gets tough and love you when it's not. You are the better half of me, and there's never been a doubt in my mind that you are the one. Annie, will you marry me?"

My hands begin to shake. I cover my mouth and nod.

Colt opens the box and slips the ring on my finger.

I start to cry as I crawl into Colt's lap, just like a little girl would, and I make a decision that no matter what happens in life, love is always first.

I reach up and take Colt's cheeks in my hands. I kiss his forehead, his nose, and then his lips as tears stream down my face. "It's about time, Atwood. It's about time."

37

Toby Lemon and Other Things

Don Franklin Brockmeyer
October 1, 1943 to July 4, 2020

Erla is putting on her earrings in the mirror and isn't sure when she got so gray, but she knows the color of grief and heartache aren't her colors.

Devon walks in and sits down on the toilet seat lid.

It's eerie here for her without Don. And although it's a tough situation with Devon right now, she'd rather have her here, filling the empty void of Don, than be alone in a house where loneliness sits and waits.

"Does Toby Lemon know he's my father?" Her eyes are red, most likely from the tears and the alcohol that no one sees her drink.

Erla notices that she never hears her daughter slur her words. The scent of alcohol is the only thing Erla can detect from her daughter.

She wishes Don were here to help explain. To help Erla clean up the mess. She wishes she had told their daughter sooner. But everything in hindsight is always twenty-twenty, right?

"Yes," Erla whispers.

Devon's mouth drops open. "How could you do this to me?"

Erla doesn't have the stamina or the right frame of mind to talk about this right now, but she must. "I didn't do it to you, Devon. I did it to protect you."

"Protect me? From what?"

Erla puts her hand on the counter to steady herself. She knows she needs to eat but hasn't had the appetite.

"At the very least, you could have told me that Don wasn't my father so that I didn't have to find out through other avenues. Like, paperwork in the attic. For Christ's sake, Mom."

"You're right." Erla is tired, and she isn't up for yet another argument.

Scarlet pokes her head in. "Mom, lay off. Grandma just lost her husband, your father, the only father you have ever known, so I suggest you get your shit together and get ready for the service."

Scarlet has always been a breath of fresh air, Erla thinks to herself, placing her hand on her granddaughter's shoulder.

She's tough as nails, and she will do anything to protect the ones she loves.

"Scarlet, this isn't between you and me. It's between your grandmother and me."

Scarlet crosses her arms. "I think you've gotten your point across."

"Why'd you hold it in all these years, Devon? Why wait all this time, and then, finally, when your father is on his deathbed do you confront us with this?" Erla says, surprised by her own words.

Devon doesn't answer. She just stands and leaves the bathroom. "I've got to get ready."

"Devon Yvonne Brockmeyer. You stop right there." Erla is suddenly overcome with anger.

Devon stops. Turns. Faces her mother.

"The truth is, it mattered but not enough. We gave you the best home, and we made the best decisions we could. And I never will regret having your father raise you as his own. The only regret I have is not telling you sooner. So, if you want to be mad at me, fine. Be mad. And if you don't want to speak to me, then don't. But God Almighty, stop making me pay for trying to protect you." Erla's voice is shaky when she finishes.

"Come on, Grandma." Scarlet takes Erla by the shoulders and leads her out of the bathroom.

The service was nice. The whole town of Dillon Creek shut down for their Don. Erla knows he would be fit to be tied in heaven, knowing the good folks of Dillon Creek were losing business and money on his behalf.

Devon didn't show up to her father's service after she left the bathroom this morning, and that had to be okay. Scarlet stepped in, as did Laurel, Clyda, Pearl, Mabe, and Delveen.

They made the day bearable.

When it is all said and done, Erla takes off her quarter-inch heels and sits in Don's chair, watching the hummingbird seek its nectar.

"Oh, Don." She twists the tissue in her hand.

When Dr. Cain came over that morning to administer the drug that would put Don to sleep so that he'd never wake up, Erla told Don she couldn't go through with it.

Don, at this point, could barely talk. He shook and shimmied and couldn't gather his thoughts. When he muttered the clear word of, "Please," she couldn't refuse him the dignity.

Erla had made Scarlet and Devon aware of Don's wishes and their plan when Don became miserable and incapacitated. So, when Scarlet and Devon and Erla were there, Dr. Cain put their sweet Don to sleep.

And what happened to his body was a miracle to witness. He stopped shaking. It relaxed, and he smiled. Erla hadn't seen Don's smile in a long time. His big, beautiful smile overtook his face, and eventually, he stopped breathing. Then, his heart—the thing that beat for Erla, Devon, and Scarlet—no longer pumped. Erla wept for the lifetime they'd spent together, for the love they'd shared. Erla wept for Scarlet and Devon, hoping that, one day, they'd find the kind of love that she and Don had.

When Erla had told Toby she was pregnant but told him she'd fallen in love with Don, Toby Lemon had said, "True love, the kind that we all wish for, doesn't come around twice."

Erla knew he was talking about his Jenny. What Erla and Toby had had was a night when the moon was full and the wine ran high. But what Toby and Jenny, and Erla and Don had was something so much more.

Erla watches the hummingbird and reflects on her beautiful life. Her rich life full of goodness and beauty, heartbreak and love. Her marriage to Don was so much more than fifty-four years of love; it was fifty-four years of promise and hope and faith.

While Erla's heart aches for the time being, she knows it will mend differently, and although she wants the heartache to stop, she knows she has to be there for Devon and Scarlet until the good Lord decides to bring her home.

As one marriage comes to a close, an end, she thinks to herself, *another one will start a love affair that will last just as long as Don and mine.*

38

After the Wedding

Anna and Colt Atwood

Colt and Anna Atwood were married at The Atwood Ranch on July 12, 2020.

The reception is coming to a close, and James asks his daughter, Anna, outside for a minute. They walk out of the fence that separates the pasture from the cement and face the pond.

They stand there in the moment, breathing it in.

Finally, James says, "I know you don't agree with what I did, Anna, but know that I did it because it was the humane thing to do. And I know I'm the reason you didn't become a doctor."

"Dad, it wasn't Don's time, and you know it. I not only don't agree with what you did in your professional life, but I also don't agree with what you've been doing for years even though Mom lets you get away with it."

James's lips form a thin line. "She told you?"

Anna laughs. "No, Dad, Mom didn't have to tell me. It's been quite evident—at least to Adam and me—that what you are doing isn't right."

James places his forearms on the fence and leans in. He allows the crickets to lure him to a place of calm and serenity, grateful that his daughter and son know. "What about Amelia? Does she know?"

Anna shakes her head. "I don't know, Dad." She looks off into the distance.

"I'm doing what I think is right. I've stayed."

"And Mom has stayed because she loves you."

This hits James.

"Let her go, Dad."

A lump forms in James's throat.

"Look, I have to get back to the guests, but I hope you understand two things. One, you took an oath when you became a doctor. To protect human life, not end it. And two, let her go, so she can find a man who loves her the way a man is supposed to love a woman—not the way a dad is supposed to love his family."

Anna goes to leave, but James places a hand on his daughter's. Tears form in his eyes.

"For what it's worth"—James tries to compose himself—"I'm sorry. For everything."

Anna nods.

Some fathers are superheroes to their children. And some fathers are just ordinary people, trying to do what's right.

While life has no guarantees, no predictability, the one thing that is always constant is love. No matter how much time we have, love deepens, no matter the consequences.

Epilogue

Don looks down from atop the Dillon Creek Cemetery and watches his wife battle the demons of their past. Watches helplessly from the hill and knows now that they did exactly what they had to do for their family.

"She'll be all right, Don," Conroy says, putting a hand on Don's shoulder.

"Just wish I could help her." Don realizes his body is back, healthy and no shakes.

Conroy Atwood shakes his head. Strait, his dog, at his feet. "That's not what life is all about up here. She'll get through it. She'll look back on this, and although it'll hurt, she'll know she's stronger for it." Conroy takes his hand from Don's shoulder. "Besides, she'll be here soon enough."

Don nods. "So, how does this thing work? This whole heaven business."

"A day at a time, Don. A day at a time."

Tripp Morgan, John and Francine Muldoon, Borges Atwood, and Joe Crane come forward and stand with Conroy and Don, looking down at their quiet little town.

The End

Acknowledgments

When I set out to write this series, I knew I wanted these particular books to be local to my area. I wanted to capture the beauty of my home, my people of Humboldt County. I want my readers to know what a sweet little slice of heaven we have here in Northern California—from our beaches to the tallest trees in the world. Alas, the Dillon Creek Series was born.

First, I'd like to thank Ashley Bolton from Ashley Bolton Photography for her incredible images for each book cover. You have an absolute gift of storytelling through images. You took such care with each photo session, each edit, and the outcome blew me away. What started as a professional relationship quickly turned to a lifelong friendship. I'm grateful for you.

Hang Le, my cover designer—You took Ashley's photographs and added your incredible magic of creating book covers that made my eyes leak when I first saw them. You have a way of taking what I have in my head and putting it into a beautiful picture that encapsulates my stories. I adore you.

At The Bluff is a local ranch and wedding venue in my area, and I messaged Merit Brodt one day and asked if she'd be willing to let Ashley and me come out and take some photos for my upcoming book series. She gladly obliged. I can't thank you enough, Merit, for allowing us to do that. I hope you can look back at these covers and be proud.

To my cover models, Holden Palmer and Taryn DeMille—Thank you for your time, faith, and patience in this process. You both are just as beautiful on the inside as you are on the outside, and it was so great to work with both of you.

Jovana Shirley, my editor and formatter—You are extremely great at what you do. You take my books and make the words find their place. I'm so honored we get to work together.

Julie Deaton, my proofreader—Thank you for putting the finishing touches on my books, and your attention to detail blows my mind. I'm so thankful you're in my corner.

Jessica Estep, my publicist, the other half of my brain—You are a dream. I don't know what I'd do without you.

Book bloggers—You promote our books for fun and for free. We can't do what we do without you. Know that all your hard work doesn't go unnoticed. Thank you for taking the time with mine.

My readers—Oh goodness. Thank you for embarking on this journey with me. Thank you for believing in me. It's because of you that I get to do what I love day in and day out.

The Bailey Bunch, my reader group—Together, we are strong. Thank you for being in my corner.

Brandon, Teyler, and Kate—You are the greatest gift of all. Thank you for being my soft place to land.

A Note to the Reader

THANK YOU FOR READING *TAKING ANNA*.

If you enjoyed the book, please consider leaving an honest review on the website where you purchased the book. By leaving a review, it makes the book more visible to more readers. The more reviews, the better promotional opportunities for the author.

Get the latest information on book releases, sales, and more.

Sign up for J. Lynn Bailey's newsletter at http://bit.ly/2VVmqna to get sneak peeks, early excerpts, and free books.

Have you joined my reading group The Bailey Bunch at http://bit.ly/2EscfjT? Join for behind-the-scenes book information, giveaways, and top-secret book information. Learn about the inner workings of my writing process and my crazy ideas.

Connect with J. Lynn online:

www.facebook.com/AuthorJLynnBailey

www.instagram.com/jlynnbaileybooks

https://twitter.com/authorJLynn

www.jlynnbaileybooks.com

About the Author

J. Lynn Bailey is an award-winning and best-selling author who has loved to write since she learned to read, around the second grade. She earned a bachelor's degree and master's degree from Humboldt State University.

When she isn't running her children to their next sporting event, watching *North Woods Law*, or on the hunt for her next Laffy Taffy joke, you can probably find her holed up in her writing room, feverishly working on her next book. She lives in Northern California with her family.

OTHER BOOKS BY J. LYNN BAILEY

THE GRANITE HARBOR SERIES

Peony Red
Violet Ugly
Magnolia Road
Lilies on Main

THE DILLON CREEK SERIES

Taking Anna
Saving Tess
Leaving Scarlet
Loving Camilla

STAND-ALONES

Standing Sideways
The Light We See
Black Five